# RABBIT IN THE MOON

# RABBIT IN THE MOON

## FIONA MOORE

EPIC
PUBLISHING

Epic Publishing

Mighty, LLC.

370 Castle Shannon Blvd., 10366

Pittsburgh, PA 15234

www.epic-publishing.com

First Printing: 2024

Epic Publishing is an imprint of Mighty, LLC.

The Epic Publishing name and logo is a trademark of Mighty, LLC.

ISBN (trade paperback) 978-1-7346486-7-6

*To B. Jane Moore*

"It was all right up until the bunny girls,
and then it just got weird."
– Overheard at a screening of *Apocalypse Now*

# CHAPTER ONE: RABBIT SEASON

KEN USAGI, CROUCHED at the prow of the low flat boat in the mangrove swamps of upstate New York, saw it first. A flicker of something off-white between the twilight trees, not a bird, not one of the horrible oatmeal-coloured giant squirrels (they'd had to shoot another last night and it had fallen into the camp chirping and twitching; nobody had dared even suggest that they should do the sensible thing and skin it and cook it). An enemy sniper? Despite his lack of field experience, Ken knew better. He crouched lower, willing it to show itself. He knew he should feel afraid, yet the comforting familiarity of the swamps, evoking early childhood memories of riding the poling boats through the tropical Toronto causeways, kept the adrenaline from coursing.

The adrenaline had been coursing the night he ran all the way out to the tundra, the sound of his Gore-Tex trouser legs squeaking against each other as they scissored over snowy hills, thick tread boots crunching the Nunavut late-winter snow. He had come out there before, mostly to escape the bigger children who always seemed to find him, saying *swamp-boy, refugee*, and other things he couldn't repeat to his worn-looking parents, but he had never run so hard as when he had that *thing* after him.

———————

"Storm coming," Al said idly to Ken, his right hand on the outboard in the stern, keeping the boat on course as he cradled a pistol with his left.

Captain Manders slowly turned his leathery face, with the remains of a slightly fey handsomeness, and slit his pale eyes meaningfully at the Black youth. Al raised an eyebrow at the rebuke.

"Come on, sir, if there were Reds in this neck of the woods we'd know by now," the young man protested. "Just trying to make conversation."

"Trouble can come from anywhere," Manders retorted. Again, Ken wondered at the peculiar accent. The Seaboard States, with their dwindling population, battling their neighbours on one front and the environment on the other, were more than happy to accept volunteers, mercenaries really, from Texas, Westcoast, or even Europe, but it was unusual to see one in charge of native-born Seaboarders.

"Ah, you're seeing Reds under the bed again, sir," Al replied. Then again, perhaps Al wasn't a native-born Seaboarder himself. He sounded like one to Ken but come to think of it, he'd never told Ken exactly where he was from.

"Mind the tiller, private," Manders said with finality,

and Al quieted down with a slight pout on his post-adolescent face.

That day he had gone out to the snow-heaps at the edge of the town, where the industrial-scale hydroponic agrotech plantations loomed, to be alone, hating the Inuit children with their funny language he could never learn. He missed the hot swamps of his hometown, the threadbare stuffed rabbit he'd lost in the rush out of the South, sinking beneath the waves in the wake of the overcrowded commandeered ferryboat, *never mind, Kennie, you're a big boy now*, brooding, conjuring up armies from the South, from the fierce Red States that kept threatening war with the Seaboard or Westcoast, drawing up battle plans with pebbles and discarded bottle bits. Something bigger than him, bigger than the Inuit boys, bigger even than the teachers who kept telling him it was up to him to stop complaining and fit in.

Looking up, he froze. He saw a rabbit, white for winter, hopping along urgently. Behind it was a raven, hopping in front of it was another raven. They were driving it on, herding it, chasing it with their wings every time it tried to break away. He did not think they meant that rabbit well. Ken ran at the grouping, yelling, scattering ravens and rabbit alike, hoping the rabbit would understand later that he'd saved its life.

"Do you see something?" Manders joined Ken in the prow of the boat, moving in that silent way he had.

Ken indicated the jungle. "Not sure if it's an animal or a sniper."

"If it was a sniper, we'd know by now," Manders said. "What did it look like?"

"Just a bit of white, something following the boat through the jungle."

"Keep a lookout," Manders said. "We're due at the Detroit Front by tomorrow night, so I don't want to waste time chasing phantoms. But if it is something, I'd like to know about it."

---

Ken's parents, hearing his stammered-out story later, said it must have been old Nick Fivefingers, the local tramp, in a Hallowe'en mask. The police chief who took Ken's statement the next day put it down to a recent screening of the *Star Wars* prequels and an overactive imagination, and warned his parents gravely against too much General Grievous. But Ken knew what had chased him for three kilometres through the snow, bursting ptarmigan-like out of the drift in a flurry of black and white bones and ragged fur and feathers, bigger than a grownup, bigger than a bear, then running, running before he found himself falling, bright light and rush of stinking air and he was lying on his back in a heap of melted snow with nothing to prove to parents, police chief or, later on, worried school guidance counsellors, that it had ever been there.

---

Ken felt that animal being-watched instinct, before he even saw it again, flickering through the trees. A cold shiver started at the top of his scalp and ran down his neck (where his hair had been pulled back in a tight sweat-resistant ponytail; barbers were scarce in the swamplands, and he didn't have the courage to shave his head like Al did or hack it off raggedly like Manders).

"Did you see that, sir?" Al said, before Ken could even open his mouth.

"Yes, I did." Manders shifted position in the boat, adjusting to a kind of down-on-one-knee pose. But for the accent, the semiautomatic shotgun and the combat gear, he might have been Daniel Boone, all stubbly beard and farmer's tan, scouting through the primeval wilderness of America. "Get down, Usagi, last thing we need is another inquiry into the death of an idiot journo."

Ken obeyed, but dug in his bag for his binoculars. He had to see it, to know for sure that it was what he thought it was.

---

In a way, the spirit or imaginary monster or Nick Fivefingers with too much whiskey incident had some kind of cathartic effect. Although the local children still teased him, particularly Steve Tulugaq, the police chief's son, who knew how to jimmy the lock on the filing cabinet where his father kept transcripts and statements, it didn't seem as important anymore, and his lack of caring eventually caused them to start leaving him alone. As he began working out, joined the school hockey team and got grades good enough to mark him out as someone who could be asked for revision advice, though fortunately not good enough to mark him out as an incurable nerd, he began getting on with the others. Even if, occasionally, in moments of boredom, he would doodle the creature's bony, beaky, bucktoothed face on random pieces of paper, in school, at university as he drifted through a major in English and journalism followed by an interminable internship at globeandmail.com, and out into the adult world.

---

A few minutes later, Ken saw it for certain. Just for a minute, but he recognised that bony face, that skinny frame, which could, admittedly, have passed for scrawny old Nick Fivefingers (now long-dead of exposure) albeit in a Hallowe'en mask of a kind the general store never sold.

"Got it!" he hissed.

"Thought I told you to stay down," Manders said absently, holding out a hand for the binoculars. "Hm, yes," he said. "Funny-looking thing, isn't it?"

"Will-o'-the-wisp," Al remarked.

"What?" Ken said.

"Will-o'-the-wisp," the young man repeated. "Don't you know? A kind of spirit, you see it out in the swamps. It pulls people off course, out into the treacherous parts where you drown."

"Swamp gas," Manders said dismissively.

"Isn't," Ken heard himself saying. "Al's not entirely wrong, captain."

---

"Kennie, why?" his mother asked. "You can surely aim higher than Iqaluit Online News. The salary's less than *half* what that environment zine was offering you, and you *know* there's no future in online media..."

"I want to go South," Ken had said, resisting anger at her use of the nickname. It wasn't her fault, just too many memories of what had happened when the other kids found out what his mother called him. She was right about the online media—as pads became harder to get, fewer people read the dotcoms—but job security could wait.

"Let him go," his father said. "It's just nostalgia. Misplaced memories of Toronto. When he's done making his macho gesture and found out there's nothing South but fish and Americans, he'll come back."

"What if he takes a bullet before that happens?" his mother mourned. But Ken's father was wrong. He no longer wanted to go back to Toronto; he knew it would be nothing but swamp now, and he wanted the ethereal green place of his earliest memories to remain inviolate. But something was driving him South, to the place where armies fought over the bare remains of the increasingly scarce fertile land, and away from that godforsaken place of snow half the year and dust the other half, of decaying polar ice and ravens and rabbits and diminishing marine life statistics, slightly hysterical assertions that the hydroponic systems and the much shorter winters would make Nunavut the agricultural saviour of the world, the last of humanity fading out against the surging ecosystem. He thought, *Better to be eaten by bears than nibbled away by rabbits.*

---

"You know what it is, then?" Manders asked Ken softly. They could see the strange thing flickering closer to them now.

"Sort of," Ken said. "I've seen something like it before, and other people have seen them, too." He dug into the pack at his ankles, pulled out his armoured fieldpad, and called a file up onto the screen. The pad was about thirty years old and an army reject, but still serviceable once reconditioned.

Manders took it, scanned it with practised eyes. "So, what is it doing?"

Ken had recorded so many interviews with Seaboard soldiers that once-thrilling tales of hand-to-hand combat in the eerie jungles of Illinois, stories of battles in the open desert south of Detroit with ageing kerosene-powered tanks, had lost their glamour and so, his mind drifting, he almost missed the crucial detail.

"Hang on," he said. "A weird bony thing?"

The Marine paused, frowned. "Fuck it, I knew you wouldn't believe me."

"No, no, I do," Ken said hastily. "Tell me what you saw."

"Well," the Marine continued, brows beetling further into her scarred face, "it was the strangest thing. Skinny, like a skeleton, only not quite, you know? Like a famine kid, but huge, seven feet tall in this funny mask, kind of beaky, and this outfit like feathery rags. Don't know where it came from, one minute we're shooting at each other over a rise, and the next minute it's standing in the middle of the firing."

"What happened then?"

"Well, we kept shooting, obviously," the Marine said. "And this creature, this thing, just raised its arms and— blam. Next thing I knew the two grunts beside me were crispy fried, and same with the Reds on the other side, once I got a look at them. Don't know what saved me, maybe it was 'cause I was sunk behind the ridge, reloading. The thing was gone, and there's no proof it was ever there. Captain says it's PTSD, and you know, I kind of wonder if he's right."

Ken watched the movements of the creature. He found himself remembering the rabbit, desperate, driven along by the ravens. Unable to understand, to see the bigger picture. The birds now hopping in front, guiding it, now flapping behind it in a burst of wings, chasing it, carefully keeping it in line.

"It's either following us or—"

"Or?" Manders looked up from the fieldpad.

"—it's herding us."

---

The man outside Ken's studio apartment was polite, probably sixty-something, with thinning short hair and a pleasant smile over a sharp black suit. He introduced himself as Hase, an officer in the Seaboard Intelligence Corps, glancing briefly at the spare white walls with their studentish collection of 1970s movie posters, the Swedish knockoff flatpack furniture, the half-packed rucksack and bedroll.

"I understand you've been asking a lot of soldiers questions about some... thing they see on the battlefield," he said.

"Yes," Ken said. "It's my job. This is my press pass." Hiding the memory of stories the other war correspondents told, of people who asked the wrong questions disappearing, maybe turning up later in conveniently untraceable pieces in the war zone. He'd had his share of spat insults, demands to know when Nunavut would stop pretending to be neutral and recognise the Red menace for what it was, barely polite refusals to his requests for an embedded post, all par for the course for any of the foreigners in Seaboard territory. He told himself this visit was no different, just more official intimidation. Hoped he looked brave.

Hase sat down heavily. "Maybe twenty-five years ago, I wouldn't be here, telling you this," he said, without the slightest humour in his voice, "but the war's changed a lot of things. I don't work for the FBI anymore, hell, there *is* no FBI anymore—" Ken began to speak, but Hase gestured impatiently, "—the Reds may *call* their intelligence corps the FBI, but it's sure as hell not the one *I* knew, and the Seaboarders aren't quite that deluded—so the information I have from back then is mine to keep or give away as I see fit." He activated his pad, showed Ken the files. Ken noted with slight envy that the pad was a relatively new Korean import.

"Bunnygirl.rtf?"

"It's what some of the soldiers call it, the Bunny Girl. Or them. Could be there's more than one; if there's only one, it sure moves around. I first heard about it from soldiers coming back from war zones. This bony scavenger-bird thing, appearing in the middle of skirmishes, or ghosting along with patrols. Some of 'em think it's Death. They got songs about it."

"And you?"

"Whatever it is, it's not too bright. That's why they call it the Bunny Girl; it seems to just dumbly follow the troops around, like some gal who doesn't know better. But it's pretty deadly if you get it on the wrong day, and not in the way you expect."

---

"Can you get me closer to it?" Ken asked Al.

Al glanced at Manders for affirmation, and the captain looked at Ken. "You got an idea, Usagi, I'd like you to run it past me."

"It's just..." Ken struggled for the right words, awkward under the military glare. "I think we should call its bluff," he said. "If it's herding us, then the last thing to do is let it."

Manders nodded at Al. "Take us into shore, private," he said.

"But what is it, really?" Ken asked.

"I wish I knew," Hase said. He transferred the file to Ken's fieldpad. "I don't know if it's alien, or some weapon built by the people who were here before us—no, I don't subscribe to all that Great American Empire shit, but they did know how to make things we don't—or what. I don't believe in the supernatural, but who knows, maybe I'm wrong. Whatever. We just think it might be important." He looked Ken in the eye. "You're starting out to the Detroit Front tomorrow, aren't you?"

Ken nodded. His first embedded post. "I'll be meeting a two-man patrol boat at the marina and riding up with them along the Great Lakes. Get some stories from close to the front lines."

Hase sighed. "Yes, that's what you say, but I know you're really going out there looking for that thing. I know you've seen it before."

Ken couldn't resist. "You ever see it yourself?"

Hase nodded slowly. "Once," he said. "Out near O'Hare, around the start of this war. Ran into a militia patrol. My driver was killed; I only got away because it went for the militiamen." He handed Ken a data dot. "This is an app. Download it onto your pad, and when you find it, activate it. There's a lot of money riding on finding those things, learning where they're from, and tracking them to the source."

"Supposing I say no?"

Hase smiled. "You know how your request for embedding finally came through? Well, there's a condition." He held up another data dot. "This here is another app. Do this thing for us and you've got SIC-mandated carte blanche anywhere you can find Seaboarders or their allies. Don't, and you're going to be back in Iqaluit covering the techno-agricultural beat within the month."

Ken nodded. At least things made more sense now.

---

The boat bumped the shore. Ken leaped out, surprising even himself with the speed of his movements, chasing the flickering creature through the trees. He heard a crashing sound behind him: Manders and Al, or perhaps just Manders, following. He flung himself at the creature, tangling himself in the ragged, reeking fabric, and brought it down.

---

"Kenichi Usagi," the young soldier said, looking at Ken's press pass. "What sort of a name is *that*?"

"I don't know," Ken said. "It's Japanese, and I don't speak it." Semi-truth; his father, driven by memories of his own childhood, had enrolled young Ken in Saturday-morning language classes, but they'd been mercifully abandoned along with Toronto, and he saw no reason to translate his name for the kid. "Does it matter?"

"Not much," said the youth. "I'm Private First Class Benjamin. Benjamin Bunny."

Ken stared. "You're kidding."

"Ignore him," said a tired voice behind them, cracked with a sharp accent. A worn, leather-skinned man with faded captain's bars on his collar and an ugly harelip scar on his face slung a bedroll into the boat. "His name's Al Benjamin, and the only thing remotely rabbit-like about him is his wearisome drive to leave as many offspring behind as he can. Now, Usagi, I don't take passengers and it's a three-day trip under the best of conditions, so journo or no, you alternate between watch and tiller along with us."

"Yes, sir." Stowing his fieldpad in his camera pack, Ken followed.

---

"What the fuck—" Manders, crashing to a halt behind him, instinctively swung his gun to ready position.

Ken looked back, his arms spread where he'd pulled the furs open on the struggling creature. It looked different up close; hard to tell, now, if it was more like a rabbit or like a bird. "I know," he said. "It's some kind of robot thing. Or cyborg."

"That's insane. Not even the Taiwanese have managed to build—"

"Not the Taiwanese, I don't think," Ken said. "There were theories that it was the old Americans, before the split, or aliens, and I wasn't too sure, but look, it's human-made, and it's recent, and it's got a purpose." He showed Manders the odd seed-pod cases under its forearms. "I think they're some sort of projectile firing thing. And around its body; hooks for, I don't know, grenades perhaps?"

"A kind of mobile armaments platform," Manders mused, lowering the gun. "That thing in the middle—some kind of power core?"

"I guess," Ken said. "I don't think it's got any actual weapons left, or it'd have used them on me. I think it's just following its programming."

"Its programming being?"

"That's the question," Ken said. Drawn North for some reason, looking for something or someone. The one driving the rabbit on, the other leading the rabbit forward. Something bigger, bigger than him, bigger than his boss, the government, the war even. Something that had been driving him on, even when he didn't realise it. And then he remembered, remembered how, after meeting the thing in the snowdrifts, he'd stopped running from the bullies, started his slow trajectory South. He knew he had to stop being the rabbit now, start being the raven. Stop running away, start chasing. Find what the *something* was. Take control.

Ken reached out, grabbed the apparent power source, pulled and twisted. Manders gasped slightly as he did, half-reaching out as if to prevent him. Ken dug through the flimsy plastic and membranes like a butcher, cutting or ripping out anything that looked like it could store data, contain a programme. Then he stood, pushed the metal, bone and fur thing into the swamp. It fell with a splash, then sank gracefully out of sight, in the water, so much like the waterways of his earliest childhood. His stuffed rabbit falling, falling into the water from the ferryboat, *never mind, Kennie, you're a big boy now*. Al watched straight-faced.

Ken straightened, looked at Manders. "I've got to go South," he said, surprising himself with the sound of conviction in his own voice. "Way South. Mexico, maybe, or further. That's where these things are from, that's where this one was headed." Where the ravens were driving the rabbit. He thought of the app, wondered when he dared activate it. "I need to find out what they are and why they're here." For Hase, but also for himself. To find out who was capable of building something like the Bunny Girl. To stop running away, start chasing. To find out if, somewhere down South, there was hope. Or death. Either way, child-hood's end.

Manders looked in the water for a while, until the last white trace vanished. "Come on, then," the old soldier said, straightening up and shouldering his gun. "We've got another three hours before it'll be time to make camp, and then on to Detroit."

# CHAPTER TWO: FOUR HUNDRED RABBITS

THE MAN WAS STOUT, puffy, and balding, clad in a quilted waterproof suit from an expensive fashionable tailor. He clambered awkwardly over the sandbagged defenses which walled the makeshift camp off from the rising river waters, the long braid which compensated for his receding hairline hanging bedraggled in the rain. "Excuse me?" he said. "I was told I could find a biotechnician here?"

Totchli looked up with annoyance from his scroll. Swiping it closed—he'd have to finish the stock-take on the latest delivery of emergency ration packs later—he thrust it into his belt and peered at the man from under his round straw hat, through his thick black fringe of hair, vaguely remembering that he ought to get it cut sometime, and the dismal ongoing rain. He nodded shortly. "I'm the biotechnician. My name's Totchli." He tried not to be impolite, but also to make it as clear as possible to the man that they had flooded-out refugees to evacuate—*as if it isn't stupidly obvious*, he thought.

Around them, the business of the temporary camp went

on; two soldiers, oddly young and fragile-looking despite their padded battle gear and impressive biceps, humped the bags full of ration packs up from what had once been the town marina, cursing and complaining loudly as they splashed through the ankle-deep water from the temporarily erected pontoon dock. A group of children appeared to be engaged in a game, gathering different sorts of rocks and placing them, with much intense discussion, in little heaps on a square marked out in rope lines on the wet earth. Totchli, though, recognised this as work, preparing the ground for a new instahouse to shelter more refugees. Soon the children would be relocated to somewhere drier, where their parents could count the cost of lost homes, businesses, livestock, and consider whether to salvage what was left or to make a fresh start; now, even their play was co-opted to the survival effort. Behind him, Totchli could hear the rattling of ceramic pots and plates beginning in the instahouse officially designated as the camp's kitchen and dining area, and the familiar sharp smell of cooking. *Beans again*, some part of him noted with resignation. Somewhere a baby cried, on and on, a thin drone like a plague mosquito.

The man grinned at Totchli, looked him up and down. Totchli knew he was hardly impressive. Not unfit or undernourished, but short, and thin despite many hours of effort with weights and high-protein diets. He was clad in a more practical but less stylish version of the man's own quilted suit, with high, ugly, chicle boots. The man's scrutiny also brought him to full awareness of the fact that he hadn't bathed in five days—something easier to ignore when dealing with the refugees and flood relief personnel, who were all in a similar state—and was in desperate need of a sauna and haircut. "Totchli, eh? Should have known I'd find you in the drink," he said, with overfamiliar bonhomie.

"What vision did you see in your namequest, four hundred rabbits?"

Totchli suppressed a further surge of irritation. The word *totchli* meant "rabbit", and the most common symbolic connection with the name was the Four Hundred Rabbits, perpetually inebriated gods of drunkenness. He'd lost track of the number of times he'd heard that joke or similar, particularly in the months he'd been working with the flood relief service. He also didn't particularly want to discuss his namequest. For some, worldquesting during the ritual of adulthood was a transformative experience, a time of spiritual awakening where one truly came to know oneself though an inner journey. For Totchli, it had been nothing but disappointment; he had emerged from his trance after twenty-four hours with a tragically banal narrative, an unromantic spirit animal, and a new name that altogether too many people found funny.

"No," he said shortly, "only one." He saw the man go pale at the remark. The One Rabbit was the symbol associated with famine, and environmental disaster. Probably not something he wanted to hear invoked, given the circumstances.

Totchli felt an initial burst of satisfaction, then worry that he had once again gone too far. *Problem with you, Totchli, you're too blunt*, as his boss at Calixtlahula Biotechnical Temple told him regularly, usually as preamble to a short admonitory lecture about being polite to the right people as the keystone of a career in the sciences. Considering that he was well-dressed, well-fed and clean, the man was probably another bureaucrat from the Ministry of Disaster Relief. They came less frequently these days, now that the crisis had sunk into an everyday routine and was no longer an opportunity for politicians to show off their generosity, but they still came—or else someone from the Ministry of Taxation, come to check up on the corvee labour detail. Either way, insulting him could do Totchli more harm than good.

"I'm sorry. Just give me a minute here," Totchli hurriedly said to the man. Nearby, Cuetzpalin, who had been studiously fixing a portable turbine and pretending to ignore the conversation, caught Totchli's eye, stepped forward, wiping her greasy hands on her leggings, and indicated that she would take over with the emergency ration packs. Totchli mumbled his thanks, then touched his scroll to the one hanging from Cuetzi's belt. A chime indicated that the data had transferred, and Cuetzi, with a practiced gesture, unholstered her scroll and flicked the display open, ghostly numbers floating in the air above the cylindrical handle of the device.

Totchli took the newcomer's elbow, a gesture of placation, and led him over to the dining instahouse, where a steaming ceramic urn guarded by a taciturn, blunt-jawed old man offered a bitter lukewarm fluid purporting to be chocolate. "What's this all about, in any case? I mean, why talk to me in particular?"

The stout man waved his hand, with its ostentatious gold data-ring, over Totchli's scroll handle. Responding to the ring's signal, the scroll sprang to life, displaying a wall of bureaucratic text. "Corvee," he explained. "You've been requisitioned."

Now Totchli was really annoyed. "I'm already *on* corvee," he told the man shortly, not caring this time if he was too blunt. "That's why I'm out here counting sandbags and raising instahouses, instead of in the biotech temple splicing genes." He hoped there hadn't been a mistake. Corvee labour was a pain in the ass, but it did mean a substantial tax reduction, and he didn't want to get into a protracted battle with the taxman over money owed. Outside the instahouse, the children had downed tools and were squaring off over some arcane matter of child politics, their high voices rising in a passionate dispute.

"You've been re-requisitioned," the man—the taxman, apparently—insisted, pointing to the relevant clauses in the document on the scroll. "Don't look angry, it's for something you might like better."

Totchli peered. "Colonisation project?" he asked.

The man grinned. "Yes. Get packing, I'm supposed to ferry you back to Axox' this evening."

———

Totchli generally found Axoxoctic too large, too noisy and too crowded, glaring spare architecture of mostly yellow brick and plain black instagrowth, infested with boring, fat and self-important merchants moaning about what the weather was doing to the shipping trade, where it wasn't infested with students lounging about the temple yards in quilted vests with beakers of chocolate, peering around to make sure their friends could see how sophisticated they were. He hated the tall buildings, the uncannily organic architecture of the more recent instagrown buildings, the sense of over-precise organisation and the lack of greenery anywhere other than officially maintained gardens and parks. Given a choice, he preferred small cities, or at the very least the ancient ones like Mexicociti, out in the suburbs of Axoxoctic, with its mellow crumbling ruins and ancient tunnels. At the same time, he couldn't entirely suppress a surge of excitement, and nostalgia for his own recently completed studies at the Biotechnical Temple there. Besides, after three weeks on the labour detail, he was looking forward to seeing something that wasn't water, trees or canvas.

Off the boat after an interminable and sleepless journey, he strode quickly through the narrow grid of city lanes, the normal harsh brightness of an Axoxoctic dawn softened to a greyish dullness by eight relentless weeks of rain. As Totchli walked, he found himself noticing small details here and there: a bright green streak of algae under a drain spout, a poster for a new videoplay flapping wetly against a wall with a sound like a sea lion's flipper, gods gazing down resignedly from a faded banner over a small urban temple, advertising next week's partial eclipse ceremony. Likely to be rained out, Totchli reflected, picturing a few determined elderly worshippers in oilskins, and whichever under-priest had drawn the black bean, stoically casting their straw sacrificial effigies into a spluttering bonfire. The determined faces of early-morning chocolate drinkers peering out from the crowded insides of cafes; a wedge of repair workers moving swiftly on some errand, to fix a burst pipe or collapsed roof perhaps, their leader focused and professional, the rest shambling behind with an air of resigned confusion suggesting recently requisitioned corvee labourers. While Axox' had not been as badly affected by the weather as the upcountry towns, Totchli reflected, there was the same sense of a world in flux, swept along by the rising water.

At last, the Biotechnical Temple loomed suddenly up out of the cityscape, a broad, terraced and flat-roofed building thick with greenery and, even at the early hour, blazing with electric light. Relieved, Totchli threaded his way through the temple gardens, feet finding the old paths, recent memories rushing back coloured with fresh nostalgia.

Finally he presented himself at the temple doors, only to be whisked off with his wet gear and worn camping pack to a suite of clean rooms painted a subtle blue—visitors, obviously, getting much better treatment than students—and encouraged to wash, visit the steam room, rest, avail himself of the copious print and film library if he liked, and to please be ready to meet Ocelotl in the refectory at noon.

Ocelotl proved to be a short, middle-aged male-berdache with a practical haircut and understated jewelry, and a slightly-too-ready smile, clearly someone who had mastered the art of being polite to the right people. "You're Totchli?" he said, deploying the smile at the younger man.

"Yes, and of course I know who you are." Totchli smiled back, cautiously, to cover his startled reaction. The man had seemingly appeared out of nowhere. "I saw your interview on my scroll last week."

Ocelotl grinned widely, taking a seat at Totchli's table and waving away a server. The woman rolled her eyes at them and bustled off to tend to a small group of students at the other end of the near-deserted, low-ceilinged room. "Oh, yes, the one about improving the electronics in vision-quest facilities. The interviewer was far too kind. Do please carry on eating, I'm sure you've had a long journey."

"I've been working in the Eastern flood area for four weeks," Totchli said, gratefully resuming his meal. It was a tremendous relief to eat something with actual meat and fresh vegetables in it, rather than the usual tasteless beans and reconstituted onions-and-peppers. "Believe me, this is the first edible food I've had in that time."

Ocelotl nodded. "Things must be bad out there, if you think our food's remotely edible."

Totchli smiled, slightly artificially, wondering why Temple technicians always joked about the inedibility of the food, and always seemed to think this was an original observation. "Could I ask an obvious question?"

"Depends on how obvious," Ocelotl replied, evenly.

Totchli lowered his voice slightly. "I was told this was to do with my being seconded to the colonisation programme. That's not exactly your field, so, uh"—he trailed off a bit—"why are you in charge?" Ocelotl was well-known for his research into vision-quests: the technology of the vision-tanks, the process, and the interpretation of the resultant journeys after the questors came out of their trances. Important as these were, particularly for coming-of-age ceremonies and for people seeking spiritual advice and guidance, Totchli didn't really see what they had to do with colonisation.

"It's a convoluted connection," Ocelotl admitted, leaning back in the cheap wooden refectory chair and examining his fingernails, a brief moment of seeming vulnerability before he was back again, all brightness and teeth. "The short version, though, is that I've also got something of a name as an administrator, too, so I'm a safe pair of hands. I expect you wonder what you're doing here," he said, abruptly focused on Totchli again.

Totchli nodded. Not that he wasn't grateful, but there were any number of junior biotechnicians in the province, and most of them had better credentials than him. He had drifted into the job unenthusiastically, following his parents in the family profession, the pressure to do so all the greater after his sister announced she was going to become an actor and headed determinedly off to Texcocociti to pursue an artistic career. He continued to work, competently at least, as a lab assistant on a project aimed at splicing maize genes to make the plants more flood resistant. The job was interesting enough and paid well, leaving him free to pursue his interests. He spent most of his evenings reading classical literature and occasionally cultivating something vaguely resembling a social life mainly revolving around the Temple's reading club and the small-but-adequate local sports center located near the compound where he was renting two rooms and a bathhouse from one of the Temple administrators. His parents had almost, but not quite, given up hinting that he could have a better career if he'd apply himself more. And then the floods came.

Now, it seemed as if everyone was focused on surviving year to year, shoring upriver barriers and reconstructing houses. When he'd last spoken with his father—the emergency camp had a radio, and labourers were allowed one hour a week each to use it—the conversation had revolved mainly about how his parents were planning to sell the family home and move into one of the new instahouses on reinforced piles, that were allegedly guaranteed to be earthquake-proof and flood-proof, of how things were going for Totchli at the drowned-out village, how his sister had accepted a teaching job in the South. Unspoken, the fact that the South was still relatively free of flooding, if not of forest fires.

"This is your first time doing corvee labour, isn't it?" Ocelotl asked.

Totchli nodded, trying not to seem annoyed at the reminder. He'd been a little excited when the requisition came, glad of the change of scene, and hoping that it would mean adventure, saving the vulnerable and protecting civilisation. It had rapidly turned out to be nothing but dull, if necessary, work. If it wasn't heaving sandbags about and finding billets for refugees, it was sitting in an office drafting databases and processing financial claims, all under the direction of government workers and soldiers with far more experience. Between his undistinguished scientific career and his equally dull corvee work, now in its third week, about the only thing he could think of which might qualify him for a colonisation venture was that he had a well-documented knowledge of ancient literature, having won a prize at school for an essay on military fiction in classical civilisation as well as his activities with the Biotechnical Temple's reading group, and a related interest in amateur archaeology, spending every free weekend during his studies wandering the ruins at the center of Mexicociti, and volunteering for up-country expeditions during, and occasionally outside, the school vacations, to the point where his dissertation supervisor had threatened to cut him off if he spent one more day with a trowel in hand.

But Ocelotl was continuing. "The situation..." Ocelotl lowered his voice, dropped his smile. "I'm speaking in confidence here."

Totchli nodded again, feeling awkward. He realised he was holding his spoon tightly in one hand, and lowered it gently to his plate, hoping he didn't look too nervous.

"You know the idea behind the colonisation project, of course," Ocelotl said. This in itself was hardly a secret. Some politicians had been arguing for decades that, given dwindling resources, the possibility of exploring the unpopulated wastelands to the North, where the ancient Americans had lived, should be at least considered. The media were likewise inclined to feature various plans for colonisation as news features on slow days, or run inexpensive documentaries and videoplays speculating on the outcomes of such a venture. "And that we finally sent an expedition North at the start of the year?" This was less well known, but Totchli nodded, remembering a small item coming up in his scroll feed. He'd earmarked it, mainly because he was curious as to whether it would be near any archaeological sites, but forgotten about it since then.

"I'd assumed it was going well, since there hadn't been any reports...?"

Ocelotl looked grimmer. "Afraid not."

"Oh."

"There haven't been any reports at *all*," Ocelotl said. "Communication once a week for the first few weeks, then strange, scattered broadcasts, then for the last fortnight nothing at all. You can understand our concern."

"Yes."

There was a pause. "Indeed," Ocelotl said. He took a deep breath. "You were Cipactli's student?"

"One of them." Cipactli had been the dissertation supervisor who had threatened to expel him, so Totchli couldn't imagine that she'd recommended him in any way. Totchli remembered her as a thin, beaky, reptilian sort of woman, inclined to taciturn silences followed by rather spectacular outbursts of temper. "We weren't the most compatible of research teams."

Ocelotl's smile returned, faintly ironic. "She said a few things about you, and admittedly not all of them were complimentary, but one thing she did say was that you were very good at keeping confidentiality." His voice lowered again. "What we need is someone who can go out to the colonisation site, find out what went wrong, and either report back or"—he spread his hands—"take care of matters on the ground, if necessary. Can you?"

Totchli felt afraid, but nodded.

"Good man!" Ocelotl was back to hail-fellow-well-met mode. The server reappeared, unasked, carrying two cups of chocolate, which she set down in front of them and then, with a small scowl, bustled off again. Ocelotl took his cup and leaned back, rubbing his thumb on the handle as if it were a priceless beaker rather than cheap brown institution-ware. "Cipactli said something else about you, which helped your name come forward," he remarked. "She said she thinks you're bored."

"Bored?" Totchli now felt like he was on trial.

Ocelotl looked him square in the eye. "That's not a bad thing," he said. "If you're not bored, then you're working at or over your level of competence. Or interest, perhaps. She said you were a good student, but she got the impression your heart wasn't really in biotechnical studies. That you'd rather be somewhere else." When Totchli hesitated, Ocelotl added, "It's all right. You're not a student, this isn't an exam. It's just that, if she was right, then a trip like this might help you figure out why you're bored, and what would make it better."

Totchli's face must have given him away, because Ocelotl nodded, seemingly satisfied. "I'm a quest techni-cian. You do it for long enough, you begin to spot the signs of someone who needs a journey. You were called up for corvee, of course, but I noticed you volunteered for the flood-hit areas. To me, that suggests either a survivalist, a masochist, or someone looking for adventure. You're more likely to find it going North looking for missing colonists than you are hunting sandbags."

Totchli nodded. Ocelotl had touched a nerve, it was true; he found it hard to argue with this assessment of his situation, despite his misgivings about Ocelotl's suggestions.

A bell sounded, indicating the start of a new hour. Around them, Totchli noted, tables were filling up, and the room was gradually warming with the cheerful noise of debate and discussion and the scent of hot roast capybara. Ocelotl waved to a pretty woman in a red dress walking away from the refectory, carrying a bowl. "Hey, Mazatl! Come join us, I'd like you to meet someone."

The woman quirked an eyebrow, came over. "Mazatl, Totchli." Ocelotl gestured vaguely by way of introduction. "Maz is a medical doctor, doing research here at the temple in vision-quests, but seconded to the colonisation project part-time. She'll be the one making sure you've got all your injections and aren't about to go prophetic on us," Ocelotl said, then, to Mazatl, "Totchli here has volunteered to go upcountry, for the colony project."

Mazatl smiled, Totchli fancied a bit flirtatiously. "So you did find somebody suitable," she said to Ocelotl, then, looking Totchli squarely in the eye, "Brave fellow."

"Buy you some palm-wine later and tell you all about how brave I am?" Totchli suggested, smiling back. Mazatl's lips quirked ironically, and she shook her head a fraction.

"Wait till *after* I've stuck you full of medicine thorns, see how keen on it you are then."

Totchli opened his mouth to reply, but Ocelotl leaned in, smiling paternally. "Plenty of time for that later. For now, Totchli, we're planning on having you start the day after tomorrow, there's a boat going upriver. We'll make sure you're equipped with the latest gear, Maz will make sure you don't catch the mosquito plague, and I'll provide you with a report on everything we know about the situation."

"Sure you still want to go?" Mazatl said.

"Of course he is." Ocelotl scowled at her.

"Course I am." To cover his nervousness, Totchli took a sip of chocolate, wondering just what the hell he had talked himself into. "More exciting than counting sandbags."

# CHAPTER THREE: DESERT FOX

**THE GENERAL TURNED AND SMILED.** For no good reason, Ken found himself thinking of larvae: white, glistening, silent.

"Kenichi Usagi. Ken," he said, brandishing his press pass upward a little desperately while trying to keep his balance on the unsteady aluminum dock. A small knot of NCOs with clipboards, responding to an unseen signal from the general like deer to the scent of a wolf, silently and quickly moved out of her orbit. "War correspondent, with Iqaluit Online News."

The general nodded. Ken had an impression of short blonde hair, muscular body, plain uniform, not much different to the ordinary troops' but tailored and pressed. "Then you're the biotech expert." She moved off. Ken glanced helplessly back at the soldiers who had escorted him out from Albany-New-York to the Detroit Front; Al was studiously tending to the baggage, his pudgy face pursed as he heaved rucksacks out of their boat with unhurried ease, but Captain Manders gave him a small, fluid nod to indicate he should follow the general.

"I don't know that expert is really the word, uh, ma'am," Ken said. *Mistake?* he wondered. He remembered his old boss at globeandmail.com: *Problem with you, Ken, you're not assertive enough.* "I'm—I've had some experience—"

"SIC called ahead. They said you're an expert, and that makes you the expert." The general was striding off, clearly expecting Ken to follow her. Ken was also aware that Manders was keeping within earshot, stealthily, and tried not to think of how ridiculous the whole thing must look: the tall, muscular general, pursued by a skinny, pale young man with an unkempt black ponytail, and a lean, seam-faced warrior in a worn-out uniform unhurriedly bringing up the rear.

Ken started, awkwardly, to try and explain the misunderstanding. How he'd had an accidental encounter with a Bunny Girl, one of the strange cyborg creatures which were turning up on the battlefields where the Seaboard States and the Red States fought it out over increasingly scarce water and land reserves. An encounter which, unlike most of the people in that position, he'd actually survived. How he'd been approached by a member of the Seaboard Intelligence Corps and tasked with finding out what the cyborgs were and who was sending them. And how he'd been under the impression that the fact that the Bunny Girls were more than just a rumor spread by exhausted and traumatised soldiers was a closely guarded secret, even in intelligence circles. "I'm certainly not any kind of expert—"

But the general wasn't listening. She paced mightily away from the gleaming-new loading dock, heading with practiced steps towards a grey concrete-and-rust hulk. Beyond the river, the sparse vegetation gave way to the chilly sand of the desert. As they approached the building, Ken realised, first, that it had once been a factory of some kind, and second, that it was now the local Seaboard Army headquarters. Deprived of its original function, it looked like a desert fortress, a castle keep. A compound of small grey concrete buildings, ringed around by a larger, rectangular structure forming a squared-off U-shape: Three sides of a square, with the fourth wall being visibly of recent construction, sandbags and quick-set fauxcrete. Soldiers dressed in loose but warm khaki desert camouflage, heads wrapped in fringed scarves against the bright sunlight, trotted briskly about the compound in pairs and trios. Ken was surprised by how clean and well-turned-out they were, in contrast to the more relaxed, even scruffy, attitude adopted by the military in Albany-New-York and Deecee. He had expected things to get more and more informal the further into the war zone he was.

The general headed towards part of the building which formed the outer wall of the compound, ducked a rusty spar with an unconscious grace, emerged into a dark, musty and nearly windowless stairwell, then turned and ran lightly up a set of newly installed aluminum steps leading to the top of the building. "We've modernised the place a little," she said. The roof was covered with asphalt and was clearly in extensive use; walls had been erected around the outside, about which sentries patrolled rhythmically, like the denizens of a medieval castle under siege. One corner of the U had been repurposed as a helicopter landing pad, yellow circles marked out in spray paint; Ken wondered if it ever saw much use, given the sparing use of air vehicles by the fuel-hungry Seaboarders.

The general had turned in the opposite direction and was hurrying towards the other corner of the U-shape, facing south. A small cluster of meteorological instruments faced southwest; she glanced disinterestedly at a couple of analogue monitors before going to the railing and standing, looking out at the sand dunes.

"Out there," she intoned, gesturing at the grey desert landscape, still cold despite the sunshine, "the battle zone. A couple of miles from here, the enemy."

"Is this safe?" Ken blurted out clumsily.

"For now," the general said. She paused to reset the scene. "The enemy," she repeated, "or, perhaps I should say, the enem*ies*." She paused again. Ken said nothing, aware that Manders had silently joined them. "We're not just fighting the Red States," the general said. "We're fighting the weather, too. Lose more to the sandstorms than bullets, and would you believe we get malaria mosquitoes coming off the river a couple times a year? And in third place, after the weather and the Reds, is the biotech. The fucking animals."

"Animals?" Ken thought of the Bunny Girl. It was animal-like, with its bony, beaky face and ragged, emaciated frame, but too humanoid to call it an actual animal. *Like a skinny drunk in a Hallowe'en skull mask.*

"Show you," the general said. She turned from the railing, a little cupped windvane moving slightly at her passing, and headed back down the staircase, strode through the busy compound and ducked into another of the factory buildings, through what had probably once been a loading area, and into what had evidently been a kitchen. Most of the original equipment was long gone, but a long counter and sink ran along the outside wall, and a boarded-up serving window graced another wall. The room was evidently now serving as a morgue, from the trolleys and stashed equipment, though most of the trolleys were empty at the moment. At the back of the room was a large specimen refrigerator, a clockwork generator rattling noisily away beside it. The general pulled the fridge open, removed a large tray covered by one of the ubiquitous khaki scarves. She placed it on a trolley, pulled back the scarf.

On the tray was the partially dissected corpse of a fox, oversized ears, sand-coloured fur. Wrapped around its head and jaw was a black, smooth, apparently plastic, organic-looking structure, which extended down its back, covered its ribcage and then disappeared into the animal's body. The dissected portions showed thin black plastic tendrils, like the cilia of lungs, thrust purposefully into organs, nerve tissue.

"What is it...?" Ken asked.

"Biotech," the general said, as if this was self-evident. "We get this a lot. Little animals. Foxes, coyotes, sometimes bobcats, even lizards. Got a fridgeful. Patel! *Patel!*" The last was bellowed, and for a moment Ken thought she had gone mad, but then a small brown woman in khaki, a medic's badge on her shoulder, peered round the door questioningly.

"General Volpone, ma'am?" the woman said.

"Patel, good to see you. This is Usagi, the biotech expert out of Deecee. Bring the Fed boy up to speed, would you?" She stepped back, joining Manders, who was lurking quietly near the sink.

The woman looked at Ken with polite hostility. "I'm Medic First Class Sarasvati Patel." Something about her manner told him he did not get to call her Sarasvati. She was compact and muscular, hair cropped into an efficient cap, but with a slight softness about her frame which suggested she ran to plump if she neglected her physical activity. "So you're the biotech expert?"

"No, I'm really not." Ken didn't try to hide the nervousness in his voice. If he read the situation correctly, Patel must be the one behind the careful dissection and curation of the animal corpses. "You're the authority on this, I'm just a journalist, I, er, met some of the biotech once. And, um, this is Manders," he added awkwardly. The soldier nodded, then moved forward to join them, as if invoked.

Patel visibly relaxed, and Ken discovered he'd been holding his breath. She raised an eyebrow, unsmiling but less hostile. "Typical Deecee, the first person they can find is automatically the expert."

Ken felt relieved. "I certainly wouldn't call myself a cyberneticist..."

Patel nodded. "I *am* a cyberneticist, actually," she said. "Of a sort. Working in prosthetics. Then the war came, and they started calling up the reservists. Sent me out here. I was expecting to spend my tour of duty dodging bullets and bandaging limbs, but then these started showing up. Naturally I'm interested. Something to while away the evenings, so to speak." As if realising she'd been complaining, she cast a quick guilty glance at the general, whose expression had not changed. She inclined her head briefly, as if to tell the medic to go on.

"How did they start showing up?" Ken asked.

Patel opened the fridge, removed a few more trays and placed them on the trolley, uncovering them to show other small animals with biotech attachments. "First one got shot by a patrol. Accidentally. They heard a noise, thought it was a Red, and then when they saw what was on the body, they brought it back with them." She unveiled a slightly-worse-for-wear coyote corpse. "This is it. That fox you were looking at, there was a family of them. One of the cooks had made friends with them, was feeding them scraps, then one day one of them turns up looking like that. Scared him." Another was a much larger black plastic rig, no animal attached. "This one was a deer—"

"Hold on. A *deer*?" Ken frowned.

Patel looked down her nose. "It's a mixed biome here. Fifty years ago, this area was grass, woodland, lakeland even. It may be desert now, but some of the former inhabitants haven't got the message."

"Sorry," Ken said, thinking of Nunavut and the Arctic animals persisting even in the warmer climate. "Anyway, tell me about the deer."

"One of the artillery had been secretly potting game to supplement the ration. He was spooked enough by this to turn it in and confess. He got two weeks of KP, and informed that he'd get more if he didn't start hunting on a regular basis and giving the take to the cooks." Ken looked to see if this was a joke, but Patel's expression hadn't changed. "That's the largest one, and we haven't seen any others that size since. They've all got stories. But you get the idea. First none, then a few of them, then more and more. Steady increase. Now we get a couple of sightings a week, weather permitting."

"And they're dangerous?" Ken asked.

Patel rolled her eyes. "They're *bombs*," she said. "They blow up. We don't know how to tell when They can go around for weeks at a time being perfectly harmless. But then they head straight towards the nearest group, and bang." She spread her hands in a gesture of dispersal. "My best guess is, they're some sort of weapon gone rogue. They don't seem to favor one side or the other, but any grouping of more than four soldiers, or some kinds of large vehicles, and they just home in on them." Part of Ken was appalled. The other, more analytical, part dryly remembered the stories of the Bunny Girl's reported attraction to troops, pyrotechnic tendencies, his own encounter, *it was there, towering over me, then it raised its arms and was gone in a flash of light,* and filed it away.

"So, then!" The general strode forward, smiled broadly. "What we want to know is, can you hack these things so they attack Reds, and only Reds?"

---

"I think it's a completely unethical idea," Ken said. He, Manders and Al were holding a council of war in the fortress' makeshift guest quarters, which appeared to have been an office of some kind in happier days.

"What is?" Al asked, lounging idly on one of the cots.

"All of it," Ken said. "In the first place, what sort of sick mind comes up with this idea, grafting bits onto animals and then detonating them like little organic bombs?"

Al laughed, and Ken glared at him. "Probably a better way to go than whatever happened to that poor cow you had for dinner last night," the young soldier pointed out. "There were some guys back in prehistory used to train dogs to run under tanks, and strapped bombs to them. Not a new idea at all."

"And in the second, what sort of sick mind finds out about this and immediately tries to figure out how to weaponize it against the enemy?" Ken continued.

Manders, who was sitting cross-legged on another of the folded-out cots reassembling the parts of a rifle he'd been cleaning, looked up and shrugged. "What were you expecting?" he said in his cracked-reed voice. "Volpone's a general. Her job is to keep her troops safe and do as much damage to the enemy as possible."

"I'm a journalist, I'm supposed to be neutral."

"You're embedded with Seaboarders," Manders pointed out. "Not Reds. If the Reds attack us, they'll kill you same as Al and me. You can't possibly be neutral."

"*I'm* neutral," Al said. Manders gave him an irritated look.

"Not caring's not the same as neutral, private," he replied, almost affectionately. "Anyway, our job's done, yours and mine. We brought the one-man ethical committee to the Detroit Front, now we just await further orders."

Al looked at Ken, sideways and up. "What are *you* going to do?"

Ken grimaced. "What I said I would," he answered. "I'll study the biotech, see if I can figure out what it is. See if there's any way I can get it out of the war zone without hurting anybody."

"Yeah, good luck with that." Manders half-smiled. He shrugged, stood, put the rifle carefully in the corner of the room, buttoned his jacket and went off in the general direction of the canteen.

---

"So, remind me again why we're doing this," Al grumbled, pulling his uniform jacket closer around him and glowering at the sunset as if the fall of night had personally offended him. They were waiting by the compound's motor pool, a small collection of SUVs, motorbikes and other vehicles, including what looked like reconditioned cars and tractors, located a small way outside the main compound, in what seemed to be a surviving section of the factory's parking lot. The troops had cordoned it off with fencing and barbed wire, and commandeered the parking attendant's office.

"I want to observe them," Ken said. "What Patel said,

about them approaching groups, but also vehicles. It might be important, so I want to see what they do."

"Can't you take Manders?" Al asked.

"Rather not," Ken said curtly. He was concerned about the way the old soldier had been shadowing him, listening to his conversations with Patel but not really offering opinions.

Al tried a different tack. "Or at least, go in the daytime? The others here say the Reds tend to attack at night if they're going to."

"Patel said the biotech animals are most active around twilight, and said she'd take us to a couple of places where there are bigger than average concentrations. She also said we'd be sticking fairly close to the compound, and that any Reds who evaded the patrols would be visible for miles."

"Huh," Al said.

"She knows the territory better than we do," Ken insisted. "Oh, here she is," he added, as a dark, compact shape approached the pair, coming round the corner of the office.

"Medic Patel," she said, extending her hand to Al.

"Private First Class Alistair Benjamin," Al replied. "You can call me Al." Ken raised an eyebrow.

"We're lucky," Patel observed as she took down a clipboard, signed something, then led them to a small open Jeep. "Reds are still quiet, and the storm that's been forecast has held off. We might have to get back quickly." She drove them a few kilometers north, into the desert, before stopping and settling down behind a dune. She handed round pairs of night-vision binoculars.

"You've got *these*?" Al looked at his in amazement.

"They're very expensive and almost irreparable, so be careful," Patel warned. "General Volpone had to pull some strings in Deecee for them." Ken wondered what they used them for, then decided he was probably better off not knowing.

After about fifteen minutes of watching, they sighted their first animal, a fox with the tell-tale black, smooth protrusion on the back of its neck.

"Follow it?" Ken asked.

Patel shook her head. "Biotech is fresh. Look at the skin around the implant, it's raw and red. It's just going to wander around, act like a fox. It's only when the implant's taken that they do different things."

The fox trotted northwest over a couple of dunes, disappearing into the gloom.

A little later they saw a pair of coyotes. One implanted, one not.

"Interesting that the other one's still with it," Ken said. "You'd think they'd avoid anything that unusual."

"Another one going west," Al said, as Ken made a note on his fieldpad. "About ten degrees north of true."

"And another," Al said. "You noticed yet, Usagi, they've all got things in their mouths."

"What?" Ken surged up, raised his binoculars. "You're right. That one's got a rock, that one's got a stick. That one there's got another rock. What's that one got?"

"A tailpipe." Patel sounded amazed. "We've been noticing little metal things going missing lately. We'd been blaming birds—crows, or ravens. But look at that one." A fox, carrying what was unmistakably an aluminum canteen fork. "Probably stole it from the compound. Well."

After a few hours of observation, they had logged nineteen more animals in various stages of implantation, most of them heading in the same direction, all of them carrying small objects. Rocks, or plant matter, or pieces of metal.

"Let's go," Patel said. "I want to know why they're doing that."

Al shrugged. "OK."

"On foot," Ken said, "and carefully. Don't approach any of them. We don't want to get blown up." Patel gave him a look—*what are we, stupid?*—but struck out on the trail of the animals.

After about a half-hour of walking, the desert gave way to a small oasis of brushland and conifers.

"Maybe they were just looking for water?" Al said.

"Then why not go to the river near the fort?" Ken asked.

"Frightened off by the people?" Al shrugged, but didn't pursue the thought.

"It doesn't explain why they're carrying things, either," Ken said.

"Oh, my God." Patel, who was taking point, stopped short. "Look."

In a small clearing of trees was a structure, about the size of a small house or a prefab. It was black, seemingly plastic, with twisted spires extending from the top. Ken found himself remembering an educational toy given to him as a child, for growing coloured crystals out of a super-saturated solution; the result had formed similar delicate points, fairy-tale castles, before eventually collapsing into slurry.

As they watched, a marmot with a large, black, smooth cover almost obscuring its head and an egg-sized piece of granite in its mouth waddled forward through the brush.

"Down!" Patel shouted, flinging herself to the ground. Ken and Al followed suit, right before the creature exploded.

A minute later, Ken was keenly aware that he was lying across Al's legs, with Patel's elbow in his ribs. He pulled himself up to a crouch, looked at the explosion site with a weird sense of detachment.

"Look at that." He pulled out his fieldpad with numb fingers, swiped it on, thumbed the video app, began filming.

Among the red and grey bits of animal—hard to recognize as anything once living—the plastic cilia were moving, like worms. They were seeking out the ground, burrowing into the soil, then latching onto the black structure and growing onto it. A bobcat, one in an earlier stage of implantation, trotted in, placed a piece of broken glass gently on the ground, trotted out. As they watched, some of the cilia latched on to the glass. Black substance flowed over it, absorbed it, pulled it into the structure.

"They're building," Patel breathed. "Bringing in raw materials, then detonating to release the system that turns them into the structure."

Ken laid down the fieldpad. He didn't know if it was a delayed reaction to the marmot's explosion, or the weird, grotesque sight of the moving cilia, but he felt sick and faint.

Patel, though, was energised. "We'll have to come back tomorrow night. Bring more equipment, better cameras. This could be the most important discovery of the last ten years."

---

"So, our hypothesis," Ken said to the general, "after several nights of observation, is that the pods aren't a weapon, but a construction system." He flicked through photos, footage clips, of the grove. "They latch on to an animal host, grow to maturity, then induce the host to head out to this structure and detonate. The biotech material then forms part of the castle-like structure."

"Interesting," the general said. "So why run towards troops?"

"We're still not sure," Patel said. "Our best theory has to do with the animals mistaking groups of humans for the structure—perhaps a similar size, perhaps a similar heat signature. We managed to borrow some thermos-sensing equipment from the scouts." Again, Ken had wondered how the scouts had acquired the equipment, but didn't think he was likely to get an honest reply, if he got any at all. "And here's the report." She handed it over. "The structure is warm, about the same as human blood heat. So. We're not sure if some of the biotech is faulty, or if they're all just programmed to go for something about the right size and temperature."

"What's the structure for?" the general asked.

"We're also not sure about that," Ken said, pulling up another file of pictures. "But it looks like some sort of habitation, or headquarters. See, there's an opening at the front and you can just see that it's hollow, there's multiple rooms. There's a couple of other small lumps that have been growing—they might be subsidiary structures."

The general frowned, her mouth quirking as if she'd heard something she didn't like. "Well, no way the Reds are behind *this*," she said. "They haven't got the technical capability or the money to buy it."

Manders, who had been silently perusing the printed reports, frowned. "Another group?" he mused. The idea seemed to intrigue him, though he didn't elaborate on why. Ken wondered who he might be thinking of. There were rumours about secretive separatist groups in Mexico and further south, but communications were scarce where they existed at all.

The general turned to Ken. "Can you send these files to

my pad?" She pointed her fieldpad at his, sent him the address.

"Certainly," Ken said, fingers working over the pad in reply.

"One other thing," Patel added, almost coyly. "These are reports from some of our other outposts on the fringes of the United Prairies, and one from a scout troop, and here's another from a civilian supply caravan headed to Westcoast. It looks like there's been at least five sightings of similar structures to the Southwest of here. Mostly around the Cascades and the Rockies, though there might have been one in the Sierra Nevada." Ken nodded. Thus far, his hypothesis that the origin of the biotech was in the South was supported. "My guess is, it likes mountains—though I haven't heard of any sightings in Appalachia, or the Northern section of the Rockies." This was still the subject of intellectual debate between Ken and Patel. She thought it favored certain terrains and soil types, Ken's theory had to do with altitude.

The general winced further, nodded. "Leave it to me," she said.

Manders turned to Ken. "You going out there again?" he asked.

"Tonight," Ken said. "Why?"

"Because..." Manders looked a little embarrassed. "I'd like to see it."

---

The structures were definitely larger now and shone slightly in the moonlight. Manders spent a few minutes gazing at the biotech castles, face its usual neutral mask.

When he spoke, however, there was a warm undertone

to his voice that Ken had never heard before. "Pretty, isn't it?"

Ken nodded.

"When I was a boy," Manders continued, "I always wanted to find something like this. That's part of why I went to South Africa, then came here." He paused a bit longer. "But there was never anything new to discover. Everything had already been found. Any new things were down to climate change, or degeneration. Something like this, though... gives you hope. Maybe there really *is* something new out there. Something that isn't the same old man versus man, man versus nature."

Ken stayed silent, hoping he would go on. He had never heard Manders talk for so long, or even admit anything about his background before. But the old soldier just watched for a few minutes more, then shrugged and headed back to the Jeep. "Time we got back, before they close the gates," he said.

---

Coming out of the brightly lit motor pool office, Ken, night-blinded, ran into the general.

"I-I'm sorry, I—" he stammered, frightened.

She smiled slightly, picked up her fieldpad. "Don't worry, Usagi, no harm done. You're out late."

"I was out at the biotech site," Ken said. "Gathering more data." He realised he'd forgotten to say *ma'am*, but she didn't seem to care.

The general nodded grimly, as if she'd just been reminded of a problem. "Yeah," she said. She fingered the fieldpad, and Ken saw the Pentagon encryption notice on the document on the front.

"Everything all right?" he surprised himself by asking.

The general nodded again. "Question, Usagi," she said, indicating with a shrug for him to walk with her back to the compound. "What drives you on?"

Ken was puzzled. "Sorry, I don't understand?"

"There's something driving everyone." She fingered the fieldpad almost unconsciously, glanced at it. "What's driving you? Why come all this way, just for biotech?"

Ken remembered. Seeing the Bunny Girl bursting out of the snowbank years ago, his life as a climate refugee in Nunavut eclipsing his uncomplicated-seeming early years playing on the waterways of Toronto before the city succumbed to the rising lake. Having to go south, to the war zone, to solve the mystery, to learn if there was a meaning to it.

"It's like a compulsion," he explained. "I have to find out what it is. Where it's from."

"But it's from inside," the general said. Ken nodded. They reached the main compound, the makeshift fourth wall and its narrow entrance; two sentries crashed to attention, and the general saluted them almost off-handedly.

"They say some of us are driven by things from inside," the general said, "and some by things from outside us." This seemed to require a response, so Ken nodded again, cautiously. "But it's not true. It's like those foxes. There's things inside us, *and* outside us, pushing us on to goals, even ones we don't understand. And like for those foxes, it's hard to tell which is which." She paused outside her quarters. "Think about it, Usagi. And goodnight."

Ken was propped up in the sunshine in a corner of the compound near the guest quarters. He was idly watching a small knot of soldiers running through an arms drill while uploading a trio of short pieces to Iqaluit Online News (a human-interest article about life on the Detroit Front, an interview with the general and another with Patel, none of them making the slightest reference to biotech), while idly taking a few notes on his fieldpad.

*More structures discovered to the Southwest,* he wrote. *Correlate with Bunny Girl sightings? Any connection?* Then he wrote, *Legends of California, South of West-coast—the huge biotech facilities of the so-called Great American Empire. The Mexican Traditionalist Movement. King Solomon's Mines?* Then, finally, and underlining it, *Colonisation?*

Then the explosions started.

"Reds!" shouted Al, his smooth-shaved head popping out of the guest quarters like a rabbit's.

"Don't be stupid, private." Manders appeared just as quickly around the corner, making Ken wonder if he hadn't been observing him again. "It's coming from the Northwest; the Reds are to the Southeast."

"Northwest..." Ken found himself running towards the motor pool, the two soldiers in pursuit. He encountered Patel on the way, cut off her babbled urgent explanation with an equally urgent nod. All four sprang into the nearest Jeep, ignored an outraged squawk of protest from the motor pool office, and drove off towards the grove, the wind whipping up around the vehicle.

They saw the smoke long before they reached the burning oasis. The general was standing and watching at a safe distance. Off to one side, a biotechnical fox hurled itself into the flames. Heat-seeking, or looking for something the right size.

"What the hell?" Ken was too incensed to remember his military protocol.

The general turned. "I know it's pretty," she said, slightly condescending. "But it's a threat. An unknown, and one that can, and does, kill my men. Not having it around here, understand?"

"It's..." Manders emerged to his right. "...understandable, Usagi."

"It's crazy," Ken exclaimed.

"And you, Patel." The general rounded on her. "I know you're a scientist, but I need you to be a medic. Keeping my kids alive, understand? Not obsessing about foxes in party hats. Orders come through."

She paused, for maximum dramatic effect, raising her voice so that the other soldiers could hear. "Big push next week. Can't say anything else, but it means no more side projects. Need everyone focused. Military priorities have changed."

"There's bigger things than this war!" Ken found himself yelling, to his surprise. "This could kill us all, or save us all, and you're worried about military priorities?"

The general silenced him with a freezing look. Ken cringed under her gaze. "Military priorities," she said quietly, "*will* kill us or save us. We are living in the here and now, Usagi."

"Storm!" One of the demolition crew came running, as the wind began to get fiercer.

"Back to base!" The general forgot Ken, leaped into her SUV, briefly cursing at her driver as he struggled to get the vehicle moving.

"We'd better go." Patel pulled on Ken's arm. "A Jeep can be buried in one of these, in minutes."

---

Ken left a note for Patel, thanking her for everything she'd done and asking her, if she still felt like it, to send him any further data she could find on the biotech. Something told him she wouldn't, though. Hefting his pack, he walked to the motor pool with his authorisation to select, apparently, any vehicle meeting a certain set of size and type criteria.

Despite the early hour, the camp was busy. The orders the general had mentioned were generating a flurry of covert movements, hushed conversations that ceased when-ever Ken passed, groups huddled over weapons and vehicles doing strange and complicated things. There was a light in the general's quarters, figures against the curtains. The makeshift morgue, in the kitchen, was dark. He'd hoped for a nod, or a look of recognition at least, from the sentries—some kind of goodbye—but of course, they were far too well trained.

"Going, Usagi?" He turned to see Manders and Al, also carrying rucksacks and bedrolls.

"Our orders came through," Manders said. He held up a piece of greyish paper. "Something about you having carte blanche from the SIC, and about us accompanying you wherever your mission takes you." He paused for effect. "Mission. That's what it said. Something you're not telling us, Usagi? Biotech expert man?"

Ken sighed. "Sort of. Remember how I told you, back in New York, that I had to go South, find the source of the biotech?" He briefly outlined his history with the Bunny Girl (omitting some of the less flattering details) and his encounter with the SIC, concluding: "So, because I met the Bunny Girl a couple of times, they want me to try and find out where they came from."

"Why?" Al asked.

"Probably like General Volpone—so they can weaponize them," Manders said.

"Probably," Ken agreed. "But this, the desert castles... maybe they're not weapons, or not all weapons. Maybe some of it is stuff we can use to rebuild, out East, drain the swamps, balance the climate. We don't know until we find it." He lifted his pack. "I've got to go West, and South. West first, because the area to the South is a war zone, and I don't feel like explaining this to the Reds. The Prairies at least are neutral."

Manders nodded. "West it is then," he said.

Al pointed. "Look at that."

Ken followed with his eyes, gasped involuntarily. On a dune over the motor pool, there it was, unmistakably a Bunny Girl. Famine-child rags overlying a metal frame, bony, beaky skull-face on top. Maybe it had fabric, or flesh, covering it once, but now it was like the ghost of a man-raven, some kind of fantastical creature.

It stood watching, then raised its arms and vanished in an incandescent burst of light.

"It's a sign," Al said. "There *is* a connection. All the biotech."

"I told you," Ken insisted. "It's all the same, it's coming from the southwest. Maybe it's humans, maybe it's... I don't know, not human. But there's something out there that's more important than the war. More important than my job, than our jobs."

Manders shrugged, apparently unmoved by the sight. He unhooked the motor-pool authorisation clipboard, scribbled on it for a minute, then led them to a large, sand-scoured but impeccably maintained SUV.

"This one should do. It ought to be stocked enough for a couple of days, and we can resupply in the United Prairies." He opened the driver's door, got in, gestured for the others to follow.

"Isn't this one the general's vehicle?" Al asked as he took the back seat and spread his bulky frame out over it.

Manders cracked a smile. "Only unofficially," he said.

"I get to drive it next," Al said.

"Have you even got a license?" Manders asked skeptically.

"Course I do!" Al was indignant. "And I was driving for years before I got one. So don't you worry."

Ken took the passenger seat. "One question. Is your first name really Alistair?"

Manders turned to Al incredulously. "Alistair? Is that what you told him?"

Al smiled broadly. "Sometimes it is."

The car moved out into the pre-dawn desert landscape.

# CHAPTER FOUR: THE TWISTER

THE BOAT WAS flat and sturdy, with a canopy over the rear covering the rattling, rusty electric engine and providing shelter from any oncoming rain. Ozomatli, or Oz as she preferred to be called, was at the very front of the boat, looking over the edge at the passing fields and forests, clearly enjoying the feel of the sun on her strong brown back. Coyotl, her superior officer, was bolt upright at the rear, steering with her sole remaining arm, a slight frown on her taciturn, ugly face, like one of the squat sandstone figures that framed the doors of the temples. Itzcuintli and Tototl (who were, apparently, Itch and Tot most of the time) were in between, but rather closer to Oz than to Coyotl, and creeping closer all the time. They were attempting to play some kind of electronic gambling game with their scrolls, which was undoubtedly against regulations, but Totchli had already gathered that Coyotl's attitude to these was fairly selective.

Totchli was also in the back of the boat, propped up against several large bags of new-smelling camping equipment, ignoring the occasional muted cheers and invective from the young warriors in the front of the vessel, going through the notes on his scroll and trying not to reflect sourly on the fact that his life at present seemed to involve nothing but water, boats and trees. Further dampening his mood was the state of affairs with Mazatl, or rather the lack thereof. They'd had the drink of palm wine he'd suggested, followed by dinner together and a brief clinch in the gardens of the Biotechnical Temple, but she'd seemed quiet and detached, as if she was simply putting up with the relationship for the sake of some other, unknown purpose, and Totchli was uncertain whether he should pursue things any further. She hadn't come to see him off, either.

He pushed Mazatl out of his mind, focused on the passing coastline. The boat was two days out from Axoxoctic, heading for the coast, driving hard all day and overnighting at military facilities. It had been a crowded and slow journey at the start, the river network thick and churned with boats heading in and out of the city, noisy with horns and invective between the pilots and navigators. Before long, however, traffic had thinned to the occasional barge and long-distance liner, becoming livelier around a town or large farm, then thinning out again. As they drifted Northwest to the edge of the inhabited world, the boats had become cruder, older and rarer, the inhabitants shabbier and more taciturn; today, it had been several hours since they had last passed a vessel of any size at all.

The warrior corps had recently established a permanent base, Outpost One, on the borders of civilisation, with a view to conducting research into survival under extreme conditions, which apparently included sending out, and supporting, expeditions to the North. It was there, according to Ocelotl, that Totchli was intended to go first, before striking out for the colony. As a reward to himself, and to pass the time on the journey, Totchli had purchased a couple of new translations of classical novels and a scroll-based interactive story, but he had reluctantly decided that he should put in a little work time and read, instead, the documents that he'd been provided with before leaving the Biotechnical Temple.

The first set of documents on his scroll related to the colonisation project, its aims and justification, and, finally, some preliminary surveys. A small exploratory expedition had made a number of forays North—quite some distance, Totchli noted—and mapped out potential sites for an experimental camp. The team had recommended siting the colony further North and East, but the selection committee had vetoed this due to fear of contamination from ancient sites, which were rumoured to carry disease and other mysterious dangers. Totchli read the survey results with a particular degree of interest. His reading of classical literature had fueled an interest in ancient civilisations. On one of the archaeological digs, he'd once found a copper coin with almost indecipherable writing and the faint outline of a man with a rather pointed chin, which the dig supervisor had told him was an artefact of the Northern civilisation, and more evidence for contact with them in earlier times. This report, although not a specialised one, contained a number of pictures and maps of ruined cities and the possible sites of ancient historical events. He noted that the colonisation site which had been selected was near the ruins of Tihuana, and he wondered if the great city still looked anything like it had in classical times, the days of the great writers and filmmakers. He pictured the gleaming buildings of ancient movies, then, in his mind, imagined them turned into crumbling stone and concrete like at the historic centre of Mexicociti; reflected that if the colony succeeded, there might be archaeological expeditions in time, excavations and ground-soundings. Perhaps there might be time for a side trip this time... he shook his head and focused back on the document. He read the rationale behind the choice of site: close to the seacoast for ease of shipping, near natural sources of fresh water. A forest with what the scout reports suggested was rather abundant edible flora and fauna. Low radiation levels. Natural mineral deposits suitable for growing instahouses.

The next set of documents related specifically to the colony in question, and its possible troubles. Two preliminary forays were detailed: one by mechanical scouts, armed with seeders, the other by humans. The personnel setup was outlined. Twenty-five people, all four genders, everyone over eighteen, a mix of scientists and warriors: the latter mainly from the reconstruction, logistic and maintenance corps, like the warriors Totchli was sharing his boat with, the former heavy on people with athletic or survivalist hobbies. Medical reports that Totchli barely understood, other than that everyone seemed to be reasonably healthy. He noticed Mazatl's seal at the bottom of some of them and paged hastily along. Rigorous psychological testing... Totchli tried to page into the file and discovered the test results had been redacted. *What was the point of including that link then, Ocelotl?* he thought peevishly, and continued on through the unredacted sections. The leader was a warrior, Axotl, a mid-ranked career man better known for administration skills than for distinction in battle. The second-in-command, a male-berdache research biologist in his forties and former bolas-throwing champion named Meztli. There were maps of the site: a fairly flat, wooded area, fruit trees and vines mostly, near a river, reports of available game and wild forage. There were lists of cultivated plants, equipment, seeds for starting instahouses, and biotech equipment for taming, and using, animals. Next came inventories of equipment for sculpting instagrowth buildings, establishing control centres and technical points, all using projected available resources.

Then the colonists were sent out, and Totchli paged impatiently through the fairly banal initial exchanges. A testing platform set up, a crucial item required, messages sent to family or loved ones back home. Then a period of more detailed communication. Pictures and chemical samples of fruits and flowers, and new species of animals. Someone found out her husband back in Tepexpan was having an affair, and, after a flurry of notes back and forth, was persuaded to stay, however unhappily, with the project. A heated exchange over what to name a kind of big predator someone had managed to get pictures of. It looked like a jaguar, but about three times the size, and with its spots extended out into long stripes, like the rings of trees.

As time passed, however, the personal messages became fewer and terser, and the reports likewise more perfunctory. No problems ever noted, at least not serious ones. He noticed that after a while, Axotl stopped signing off on reports, leaving it to Meztli or one of the other senior officers. The last few messages were peculiar ones. Seemingly from Meztli, they were mainly cryptic quotes from literature or possibly poems made up on the spot. Some of them sounded familiar, but Totchli couldn't quite place them. *I watched a snail crawl along the edge of a straight razor. That's my dream; that's my nightmare. Crawling, slithering, along the edge of a straight razor... and surviving.*

Totchli shivered, looked up, took some reassurance in watching the young warriors at play, the two boys having abandoned their game and joined Oz at the prow of the boat. All three had stripped to loincloths and boots in the late-afternoon heat; Oz trailed her hands in the water, then rolled over onto her back, showing off her high, small golden breasts and her compact, muscular arms with artless grace. The warriors' voices were cheery, mildly edged with flirtation. It made Totchli think of Mazatl, and his mood abruptly soured.

Coyotl caught his eye, shook her head with a quick, brief smile. She had close-cropped, curly hair almost the same brown shade as her skin, and her stocky, muscular, square frame strained against the light-yellow linen tunic she wore as she shifted position. The left arm of the tunic was cut off and sewn shut where her stump ended, a few inches from her shoulder. Totchli guessed her to be about forty-five or fifty, from the lines on her face. "We'll be arriving soon," she said. "Been to Outpost One before, Rabbit Boy?"

Totchli shook his head, shut off his scroll. "First time." The nickname was another thing irritating him. Coyotl had applied it to him to distinguish him from Tot, who apparently had the corner on that particular sobriquet. The young warriors were respectful enough not to use it directly to his face, but that was about all.

Coyotl nodded. "Thought so. I mean, I'm sure I'd've seen you out there before if it wasn't," she went on, hastily. "Not that you look like a greenhorn or anything." Totchli smiled slightly to indicate that he hadn't taken offence, and she went on, "I've been up there quite a few times this past ten months or so. I draw a lot of courier duty. Don't need two arms for that," she said, glancing at her stump. "Just gotta be tough, and not easily bored." She shrugged. "They usually want something shipped from civilisation upcountry, and sometimes people taking back before their time's due. Boss up there is Zorrah, you know Zorrah?"

"By reputation," Totchli admitted. She was in the top rank of the warrior corps, and so was occasionally to be seen on news feeds, usually expounding bluntly on the need to take action before the weather got any worse.

"She's tough, and they need that up at Outpost One," said Coyotl. "It's pretty isolated out there; furthest edge of the Empire, middle of a desert plain, looking up at the North. Nearest farm's a half-day away by fast boat. Other side of the desert's the sea. Sometimes, faced with all that, people will go a little squirrelly." She shrugged. "Not always the ones you expect, either."

"I think that might have happened to the colony," Totchli ventured, indicating the scroll.

Coyotl raised a brown eyebrow. "Could be," she said. "They vetted them more carefully than usual, though, looked for people with a track record in spending months out in the bush. Met a few of them before they headed out. Didn't seem like the sort to bug out after a couple months in the woods. My guess is the environment got them—that or the biotech malfunctioned, and the animals turned on them. You see some funny things out here, sometimes."

Totchli looked out at the rapidly thinning greenery. They had stopped at the farm Coyotl had mentioned several hours previously, buying disks of bread and rounds of cheese to eat from the farmer, a pleasant enough woman who obviously knew Coyotl and her crew well enough to engage in a long and involved session of banter about people whose identities were a complete mystery to Totchli, who ate his food in an unnoticed and slightly embarrassed silence. Now, after almost two days' journey out of the civilised world, the land was rough, rocky and flat, and the waterway was also beginning to look less maintained, more natural. They'd had to extend a canal off the main water transportation network between the cities and the farms, just to get to Outpost One, according to Coyotl. She'd told him that it had taken months to get it approved, and even longer to get it dug. Luckily, a few scouts had already gone up and seeded the land with instagrowth, so the buildings had begun growing during the process of approval, and it had just been a matter of making them properly habitable once the canal was navigable. If the colony did eventually prove successful, Totchli supposed, someone would start digging a canal system out there. As it was, the boat would have to follow a nearby small river out to the ocean—Totchli was really not looking forward to it—and then go up along the seacoast, then they'd have to find someplace to safely moor the boat and go the rest of the way on foot. They could have taken a glider, but they were expensive and limited in how much they could carry, and Totchli, for one, was much happier relying on boats.

The young warriors, by some unspoken signal or recognised landmark, began preparing to land, putting on their light, padded summer gear and locating their equipment, still keeping up the same stream of annoyingly cheerful banter.

Coyotl nodded to the shoreline. "There's Outpost One," she said. Totchli could see it, silhouetted against the horizon: a low, flat, rectangular building of black instagrowth, with a few narrow windows and a reinforced door which, at present, was open to the elements. From there, a path extended down to a small instagrown jetty. Totchli had never seen one like it and supposed it must have been custom grown. Totchli could make out smaller instagrowth buildings scattered nearby. A few warriors of all sexes were strolling around the area, attending to duties without too much haste or worry. Somebody sighted the boat and hailed it. Coyotl hailed back, and after a brief shouted consultation a runner was dispatched. He came back with a few senior-looking warriors, just in time to meet the craft at the jetty.

A middle-aged pale-haired woman who appeared to be the leader of the group, from her bearing and the decoration of her clothing, stepped forward, spoke a brief greeting to Coyotl, and held out an unceremonious hand to Totchli. "You must be Totchli, the biotechnician? Good. I'm Zorrah, the local commander. I'm in charge of Outpost One. They radioed ahead to let me know you were coming." After a brief round of barked-out introductions to the rest of her team—Totchli did not manage to catch a single name—she strode off, leaving Coyotl and her warriors to secure the boat and unship the baggage. Coyotl indicated to Totchli with a small nod that he should follow Zorrah. Feeling foolish, he trotted after her, trying to keep up.

"You'll stay here for a couple of days in Outpost One— we call it the Bunker, by the way, don't ask why—while we brief you with what little *we* have on the colony," she was saying as he caught up with her, apparently not noticing that he had fallen behind. Tall and square, she had a long stride that Totchli struggled to match; her thick, straight hair, dyed a sandy gold, swung against her collar, a small touch of fashion in an otherwise functional appearance. "Not that we've got much more than Ocelotl probably gave you, but it's at least fresher. And out here, you get some idea of what they're up against. Facilities here probably aren't what you're used to back in Axox', but we've got good labs if you need some space for testing, and the guest quarters are clean, even if they're not palatial."

"Don't worry, I've spent the past few weeks working on

flood relief. After folding cots and new instahouses, any place is great," Totchli said, then felt a stab of regret. *Too blunt again*, he thought, *or too ingratiating. Or maybe she's going to think I'm insulting her guest quarters—they're probably new, too—or maybe she thinks I'm a snob about instahouses—well, it's true, I don't like them, they're ugly and they smell like eggs and they're always either too hot or too cold—but I should at least be polite...*

But the warrior was striding on, not reacting. "I'm not based in Axox', either, I'm up at the Temple in Calixtlahuaca—" he began, then shut up. No sense devaluing himself further in her eyes. "I take it I'm not going North alone?" he began again. Nothing he said seemed to be remotely intelligent, or even appropriate.

Zorrah, however, didn't seem to have noticed anything wrong. "No," she said. "We're detailing you a boat party. The one you came up with should be adequate, d'you think? We can put together another if you like, but it's just as easy to reassign them to you."

"Yes, fine," Totchli said, not entirely relishing the prospect of yet more electronic games and flirtation, but at least he'd got to know Coyotl and her detachment, and he wasn't sure he wanted to start again with strangers.

Zorrah continued without acknowledgement. "Obviously you can't take more supplies than you can carry, but that should be more than adequate. We don't know what, if any, facilities are left at the colony, of course, but the Temple said you were pretty used to roughing it. Can you live off the land?"

"If I have to," Totchli said. He'd had the usual training in hunting and preparing game, though he resolved quietly to let the warriors do as much of that as he could.

"Good fellow. Here we are," Zorrah said as they neared

the low, flat black structure. "The Bunker here's our main administrative area. Radio-relays in case you need to send a message home, plus a mindlink chamber for brain-controlled equipment. Living quarters are behind it—" She gestured, and Totchli noticed three smaller instagrowth buildings, flat and broad like the Bunker. "Lefthand one's for visitors, Coyotl will make sure your things get stowed there. You'll have your own room, but she and her kids'll be down the hall. Each building's got its own steam-bath, you'll be able to use it any time you like. Cookhouse is back and to the West, you can't see it from here, but you can follow the smell at dinnertime. I'll see you get meal tokens. Next meal starts at sundown. Meantime, I thought I'd give you a tour of the perimeter, show you what we're doing." She paused at the Bunker door, looked back down towards the canal. Totchli followed her gaze, looked out at the broad, yellow, rocky wasteland.

Despite the clear dark blue sky, Totchli shivered. He was used to the lush environment of the South, where it was sometimes difficult to separate where forest ended and town began, and concentrated populations, often to the point of annoyance, one of the many things that sent him fleeing out to the isolation of the archaeological digs and the cryptic languages of the dead. Much as he hated crowds, he found that, out here on the plain, he felt unnaturally exposed, small, and strangely alone.

"Gets to you, doesn't it?" Zorrah said, apparently reading his mind. "You get used to it, but yeah, it's strange the first time you see it. But we've got to get people habituated to new environments. Not just people. Part of what we're doing here, well, I say 'we' but it's the scientists more than my lot, is field testing cultivars to see if we can develop things that'll grow in the North."

"Like what?" Totchli asked, interested and feeling more in his area of expertise. Zorrah looked slightly surprised, so he explained: "Back in Calixtlahuaca, I was working on a project developing flood-resistant maize strains. I just wondered if similar..."

Zorrah nodded, smiling a little. "Good. Yes. Let's do the bureaucracy later. For now, I'll show you the fields. It's the usual maize-beans-squash principle, of course, but working on hardier stock, able to get more nutrients from the soil, need less sun." She launched off at an angle, headed towards what Totchli now suddenly realised was a large, cultivated area to the northeast of the Bunker. A few modified scouts teetered mechanically along the rows, followed by dark human figures, stooping occasionally to tend a plant or record an observation on a scroll. Another machine kept up a constant monotonous spray of water moving along the field.

"Could be fairly generally useful," Totchli said, following her.

"Is," Zorrah replied, her tone friendly and conversational, but emphatic. "Developed for general use, but obviously we've got a special interest in it, what with the colony. Colonisation's the only way forward now. Civilisation's getting smaller, people hungrier, valleys are harder to cultivate. We lose more forest every year, you know how it is."

"And the obvious place to go is North," Totchli said. They passed a barren area where a couple of warriors were covering a square of instahouse seeds with rocks; Totchli could see another instahouse half-grown behind them, its delicate spires reaching like feathery stalactites up towards the sky. "Too many people to the South, well, too many people we've got peace treaties with, anyway. North's uninhabited. Well, obviously some of it's uninhabita*ble*, but it's a big North, I can't see how *all* of it can be."

Zorrah frowned, her slight moment of relaxation fading. "Obvious," she said. She slowed her strides. "Yes, it is really." Her tone made it plain she didn't think it was a good idea.

"Where else?" Totchli asked. "Europe? How would we get there? We don't have the boats for it, and for all we know there could still be people there. Can't go colonising some place where there's already people, it wouldn't be fair."

Zorrah frowned again, almost sadly. "Forget I said anything," she said, speeding up again. "I'm jumpy. Let's just put it down to this current business, whatever happened to those people who went North."

"No, I'm interested," Totchli went on, feeling strangely reckless. "Where should we go, if not the North?"

Zorrah thought for a while, then opened her mouth to reply. Before she could speak, the air was split by a loud whistle which seemed to come from Zorrah's waist. Totchli jumped, but Zorrah, apparently unstartled, clutched reflexively at her side, and Totchli realised it was the radio on her scrollcase making the noise. "Mirror!" she swore, then, by way of explanation, said, "Emergency warning. Go!" as she wheeled on her sharp bootheels and took off towards the Bunker.

Totchli followed, unable to match her speed. Behind him, in the fields, he heard shouts, the ratcheting and clanking of machines being switched off and immobilised. Totchli dodged as a small phalanx of scouts flashed past on spindly mechanical legs, expressionless skull-faces gleaming whitely as they made for a small black outbuilding that was apparently the machine-shed. Totchli wondered who was running them, then remembered that Zorrah had mentioned a mindlink chamber, and, in any case, they probably had a survival routine programmed in.

Others, humans, were rushing towards the Bunker, from fields, projects, maintenance areas. "Twister!" shouted one warrior to Totchli, making an urgent whirling gesture with one hand.

Totchli pulled up short, gasping for breath despite the hours he put in at the sports centre, turned to look back at the fields, and saw what looked like water going down the drain, but in the sky. Yellowish clouds had come in from out of nowhere, overpainting the blue, and far away he could see something living, a spiral whirling around and around in a dark line, thin at the bottom and thick at the top, like a root, drawn on the parchment of the sky.

"What is—" But he was cut off as something short, brown and bearlike descended on him, grabbing him physically and hauling him into the Bunker entrance. Belatedly, he realised it was Coyotl. The momentum flung them both forward and there was a brief panicked tussle of limbs on the bare black instagrowth of the Bunker floor.

"You all right?" Coyotl asked, helping him up and holding him critically at arm's length, looking him up and down as if making sure he had all his body parts.

The thick metal doors clanged closed as a last couple of warriors lunged through, dragging a third who had the faintly bewildered look of someone who'd just been forced out of a mindlink. Far to the front, Zorrah was disappearing into the deepest recesses of the Bunker, shouting orders as the personnel swung into well-practiced emergency routines.

"Yes," Totchli managed. "I'm all right. What *is* that thing?"

"Twister," she said, sitting down on the bench near the entrance. Totchli did likewise, to get out of the way of the sudden onrush of shouting Bunker personnel. "You never seen one before?"

"No," Totchli confessed. "Never even heard of it."

"Huh." Coyotl shrugged. "You *are* a city boy, aren't you? They get them around here, a lot. It's a storm where the winds come together, make a kind of funnel, or spout. Sucks things—people, animals, houses—up into itself. One reason the base looks like this." She gestured. The Bunker was much the same inside as out: thick, bare instagrowth walls, small windows, close and square, warrened with corridors. "Saw one once, a few years back, when they'd just started the place. They're getting more frequent, they say."

"Shouldn't you be...?" Totchli asked, gesturing to the other warriors rushing about.

Coyotl shook her head. "I'm just the courier. Best thing you and I can do is just stay out of people's way." She paused a little. Her stump twitched, involuntarily. "Didn't get a chance to see if the kids got in. Hope they're all right."

Outside the small window, the dark funnel was coming closer and closer, almost upon them now. Totchli could hear the noise of the wind, louder than any natural sound he'd ever heard. He resisted the urge to crouch down like a child and whimper, hands over his head.

Coyotl nodded, a sympathetic look on her pug face. "Scary," she said. "You never completely get used to it." Absently, she reached her good arm out and stroked Totchli's back as if reassuring a child, seemingly as much to comfort herself as him. "So, we're going North with you, then?" She spoke in an almost artificially conversational tone. "Looking forward to it. I was bringing supplies up to Outpost One for the colony for months and months, never seen the place. Been South—*way* down South—when I was a young woman, but never been further North than the Bunker here. The kids, now, they've never been down South, even. Be good to show them the world's bigger than just Axox'. Hey"—again she sounded like a mother, talking to a child—"be brave, fellow, we're likely to see stranger stuff than a twister when we go up North."

After what seemed a far longer time than it should, the wind passed. Another alarm sounded, and the warriors began to move about at slower speeds, smiling, chatting with relief. A few were wandering about with scrolls in hand, taking a roll call.

"There you are, ma'am!" Tot and Itch shouldered forward, grabbing and hugging Coyotl. Totchli saw their expressions mirrored on Coyotl as she returned the gesture.

"We were worried that—" Itch began.

"Weather's afraid of *me*, kids," Coyotl grinned. "Take more than a bit of wind to finish me off." She pulled back, looked at their faces. "What's wrong?"

There was a long pause.

"Oh." Coyotl said. "You're sure?"

Itch and Tot both nodded silently. "She was at the boat. Too far out," Tot said.

"Mirror," Coyotl said, quietly, like an invocation, a prayer, not a swear-word. Perhaps, Totchli thought, it was.

"Maybe she'll be back in a day or two?" Itch ventured. "Some of the ones here, they say people disappear in the twisters, then they get found later?"

"*One* guy," Tot said, "had this story about a *boat* that got picked up by a twister, *and* its cargo, and do you know, they found the whole thing a day's journey into the desert, just lying there..." He trailed off awkwardly, looked up at the ceiling, then the floor. "*Could* be true," he muttered defensively.

Coyotl grimaced. "Maybe," she said, with what was obviously false reassurance. "But if not, we'll have to go without her when we leave for the North." She shook her head and spoke, apparently to Totchli. "Strange sort of war we're in, but it sure leaves casualties, same as the regular kind."

Totchli found he couldn't look at her.

# CHAPTER FIVE: WILD HORSES

A FADED PLACARD on the side of the United Prairies government waystation proclaimed, in cheery old-fashioned letters, The Only Way is UP! As the SUV approached the building, Ken felt a rush of nostalgic cynicism; he vaguely recognised the logo, a product of an era when the governments of North America more generally had time and money for sloganeering. Beyond the waystation, he could see the outlines of small buildings in the distance, dust-coloured against the dust, and the silver gleam of something that was either a silo or a refinery tower, Ken couldn't exactly tell which. Nearby, a slightly darker herd of animals wandered, seemingly unattended, across the plain. Cattle? Horses? Hard to tell.

Manders, who was driving, pulled up at the front, applying the handbrake with a sharp ratcheting noise.

"This it?" Al asked from the rear seat, where he had been curled up without a seatbelt for the past few hours. The teenager's ability, and desire, to sleep under any circumstances never failed to impress Ken.

"This it, private," Manders echoed. A moment later, a

tall White man with a neat beard, face tanned and seamed like Manders' own, clad in jeans and plaid shirt with a skew-whiff brown badge to indicate his government affiliation, strode out of the building and leaned on one of the porch awning's supports, waiting for them to leave the vehicle.

"Usagi, you want to take point on this one?"

Ken understood. As a civilian, and a citizen of Nunavut, he was best placed to allay any suspicions about their presence. He stepped out of the SUV first, keeping his hands visible, and smiled as he walked towards the man. He could hear the other two doing likewise: Manders, slowly and without making any threatening movements; Al, loosely and with an air of complete unconcern.

"Hello!" Ken said, feeling nervous. "Is this the UP waystation?"

The man didn't crack a smile. "One of 'em, yep." His eyes traveled beyond Ken, to the other two, narrowed slightly at the sight of the Seaboard States Army uniforms, narrowed a little further (or perhaps Ken imagined it) at the colour of Al's skin.

"I'm Kenichi Usagi," Ken continued, holding out his press pass. "Journalist, from Iqaluit."

The man took it, looked at it. "*You* may be," he said. "What you doing with a couple of Seaboarders?" Now he did smile slightly, as he jerked his head South. "The war's *that* way."

Ken nodded. "I'm the official Embedded Journalist with these two. A trade caravan on the way to Oregon, out in Westcoast, has gone dark, last reported position in the Cascades," he explained. "They've been sent to find out what happened." It was a less suspicious story than the truth: that they were seeking the source of the biotech, the builders of the peculiar cyborg creatures who would turn up unexpectedly in the combat zones and ignite in an incandescent all-consuming blaze, the black glittering castles in the woods, the boundary between urban myth and reality. Since Patel's research had found a number of the black castles in the mountain ranges to the West, the Cascades seemed the most likely site to aim for, and since, according to Manders and Al, small parties of soldiers were occasionally sent out to investigate when trade caravans disappeared, it was a fairly plausible cover story.

"We'd've gone cross-country," Al interjected, "only the war got in the way. So we had to come North." Manders gave the young man a narrow-eyed look, but didn't say anything.

The government man seemed a little more relaxed at the reply. The trade caravans between the Seaboard States and the countries of Westcoast and Beecee usually travelled through the neutral UP rather than risk a perilous trip through Red State territory, so it made sense that a rescue operation would follow the same route. "We haven't had a caravan through here in a few weeks," he said.

"I expect they kept South. Things hadn't heated up around the ex-Michigan area when they were going by," Ken said, grateful that Manders had taken the trouble to research normal caravan activity before they left Detroit, and had taken the trouble to drill the other two on the minutiae of such operations in case of queries.

This seemed to satisfy the man. He turned his attention to the soldiers. "And you two are?"

"Captain Henry Manders. Seaboard States Expeditionary Force." The ice having been broken, Manders shouldered forward and took charge.

"I'm a little man from another place—" Al began.

"He's Private First Class Al Benjamin," Manders said with what Ken was beginning to realise was familiar weariness. "Don't mind him."

The man looked at Al speculatively. "Don't see too many—" Apparently rethinking what he was about to say, he cut it off.

"I'm sure you don't," Al said firmly, a thin eyebrow raised challengingly.

To save his embarrassment, the man turned to Manders. "You don't sound like a Seaboarder," he said.

The old soldier nodded. "I'm from England originally."

Ken felt a thrill of shock go through him. This was the first time since the Detroit Front, and only the second time since they'd begun traveling together, that Manders had directly acknowledged his foreign origins. And actually coming out and saying that he was from Europe. At least a month's travel by boat, with the constant risk of Red State and Newfie pirates (and the occasional Seaboard privateer, though the Seaboarders wouldn't admit to it), and almost unaffordable.

"Long way," the man said, echoing Ken's thoughts.

"Came over some time ago," Manders said, in a tone indicating that there weren't going to be stories. "Not so many pirates then."

The man seemed to remember his manners. "Hackney," he said, extending his hand. "Willard Hackney. What do you need?"

Manders took out his battered green fieldpad, called up a list of items they were running low on. "We need fuel and provisions. You still take American government credit?"

Hackney nodded. "We take Seaboard scrip," he said, a barely noticeable subtextual insult. Both Seaboarders and Red States referred to themselves as the United States of

America, heirs of the old American Empire. Somehow Ken couldn't see either Manders or Al rising to it, though. He wondered if he'd wound up with such a pair of insubordinate and informal types by coincidence, or whether the SIC had some kind of agenda at work. "UP government's got an agreement with yours, that we feed and fuel your people up here, so long as they pay their bills."

"They've got the same agreement with the Red States, too," Al remarked to Ken sotto voce. "Better hope there aren't a few of *them* out behind the barn."

But Hackney was continuing. "Food I can get you straight away," he said. "Fuel you're going to have to wait a couple days, till the tanker from the refinery comes through. I can put you up, though," he said, gesturing to the upper story of the house. "Bunkroom's plain, but clean, and better than a tent."

"Cost four times as much though," Al annotated. "UP's make their money selling what they've got to the rest of us for twice what they'd pay themselves."

Manders heard the whispering and shot a brief admonitory glance at Al, who smiled at him. He stepped back to Ken. "What do you think, Usagi?" he asked. Ken was a civilian, but he was the nominal authority on the mystery biotech, meaning that Manders had apparently decided to give him final say on decisions. Some of them, anyway.

"Might not be a bad thing," Ken said. "Patel's map didn't show any of the castles around here, but it's on the trail. So, if there's any biotech in the area, one of the locals might have a couple of stories we could follow up. I can ask questions—gathering material for an article, all that." Inwardly he was hoping Manders would agree; he was tired of sleeping in the tent or the back of the SUV, of eating food out of packages, and, he thought, maybe I'll get a chance to wash.

Manders turned back to Hackney. "Okay, we'll take a look at the bunkroom," he said.

---

The airlock of the Sir John Franklin Memorial Biodome burst open, and Ken was confronted by a strange apparition, clad in shorts and a T-shirt despite the cool Arctic spring weather, with stubbly beard and stringy hair, and brandishing the remains of a stalk of supercorn. The T-shirt, Ken noted distractedly, was a grey which had faded down from green, and had once, apparently, been graced with a picture of a horse. "Oh, you must be the journo," the apparition said, apparently not noticing Ken's startled reaction. He transferred the stalk to his left hand, extended his right. "I'm Joe Qimmirjuaq. Doctor Joe Qimmirjuaq, but call me Joe. Nicetameecha."

Ken shook the proffered hand, introduced himself.

"I'm guessing you weren't born around here," Qimmirjuaq said, gesturing Ken into the airlock.

"I'm from Toronto, as was," Ken said.

"Refugee from the flooding, then?"

"I was just a kid at the time," Ken said shortly. On the short drive out from Iqaluit to the Biodome, he'd seen no less than four SWAMPIES GO HOME slogans daubed on building walls. "I've lived up North since I was eleven." And, apart from a few years attending university in Whitehorse, all of it in Nunavut, he reflected.

"Hey well. So, you want the ten-dollar tour, I expect?" The airlock eased closed behind Qimmirjuaq with a sigh, as he led the way into the steamy green interior of the

Biodome. "Biggest agrotech facility on the continent, bread-basket of North America, new technology's gonna feed the world?"

Ken nodded. "That's about right." He thumbed the recorder on his pad into action, steeled himself for the usual parade of statistics, demonstrations of new genetic variants, bombastic and optimistic stories celebrating Nunavut's Agrotech Revolution.

---

Hackney turned out to be a better source of local information than first appearances would suggest. The purpose of the UP's government waystations was, it seemed, to provide food, supplies and lodging to the inspectors, judges, repair personnel, and any other public employees traveling across the vast territory. In addition, they had a wireless link with the central government in Prince Albert, a connection which Hackney shared with anyone who couldn't afford a pad or a box of their own. "Lot of folks out here can't. And the government's got better satellite hard-ware than the companies do," Hackney added, as he helped Manders, Ken and Al find and shift packages of food and bottles of water from the big storeroom. "Need it, in case of emergency calls. Course, we don't tell the locals directly, but everyone knows. And as the satellites drop, and fewer and fewer companies can afford to replace them, well, corporate coverage gets less and less..." He gestured expres-sively. "People using their pads and boxes less and less. But they still need to keep connected."

"What do people do around here instead?" Ken asked. He was taking mental notes on the setup, some part of him thinking that there might be an article in the waystation system, perhaps even a chapter of a book. The ground floor of the building had a large storeroom in the back, with the middle area divided into a living area for Hackney, with a kitchen and a bedroom. Then there was a narrow room at the front which seemed to serve as a waiting area, meeting area and occasional dining-room, with a small office off to the side, tucked in front of the stairwell, containing the computer box, a filing cabinet, some books, a ludicrous amount of flimsy grey paper covering almost every available surface, and a framed poster advertising an exhibition of Sioux art at a museum in Regina. The whole interior was painted in shades of yellow and brown that had been popular for government institutions ten or fifteen years previously; Ken wondered how Hackney could stand the unrelieved drab colours, but he didn't seem too bothered.

Hackney checked the use-by date on the side of a crate of ready meals. "For fun? Getting drunk, mostly." He was deadpan, so Ken couldn't tell if he was joking. "For work? Bit of cattle ranching, bit of mining," he said. "Used to be good farming territory when I came out here, around twenty years back. Dust bowl, now. It's better off than some places—least we still got the mine, and them new breeds of cattle from the South, seems like they can live off any bit of scrub. But yeah, some years folks go hungry."

"No agrotech facilities?" Ken asked. He had spent a while working on the Nunavut agrotech beat when he'd been an intern with globeandmail.com, between graduating from university and landing his current contract with Iqaluit Online News.

Hackney snorted. "What do you think this place is, Nunavut?" he said. "The companies are all busy investing in the no-longer-frozen North. They say there'll be some sort of trickle-down effect once they've got the technology cheap enough, but I say that'll be never."

"You couldn't buy a biodome, set it up here?"

There was a slight edge to Hackney's voice. "Even if the community could afford it, the soil's worked out," he said. "Arctic agriculture works because the soil's okay, and even then you know they have to do things to the plants."

"What do you do for food?" Ken asked.

"We mostly import it," Hackney said, the edge in his voice sharpening, "from the Yukon. And Nunavut."

Ken changed tack, decided to pursue the rogue biotech angle. "I've been working on a story about modern myths and legends," he said. "Ghost stories, strange animals, weird castles and cities in the middle of nowhere, things like that. Like the Bunny Girl?"

Hackney nodded at the name, and Ken felt encouraged. So, the stories had traveled this far. He thought of the collection of chips and the remains of a motherboard from the biotech device which were stashed deep in his backpack. "Ever hear anything like that from the ranchers?"

Al, who had just come in from the front room where they were assembling the supplies, snorted. "Attack of the fifty-foot chinchilla," he said. Taking out a packet of cigarettes, he headed for the back door.

Hackney smiled a little. "Can't say I have," he said with what struck Ken as a carefully noncommittal tone, or perhaps he imagined it. "Why not go into town tonight, have a drink at Louanne's? Maybe you could ask a few of them yourself. Might want to tell you their stories." Again, Ken wasn't sure if there was an edge to the offer.

As he was about to accept, he heard Al exclaim from outside. "Quick, guys! Look at this!"

Ken was out the door in seconds, Hackney behind him.

Bursting out the storeroom door onto the back porch, Ken caught a glimpse of hooves, manes, a sudden snort and a flicker of wild eye as two brown-and-black horses, seemingly inches from the back step, took fright and ran.

"Aw, you scared them," Al pouted. "We used to have wild raccoons and deer coming up to the houses back in Boston. Never seen a wild *horse* do that before."

"Sorry," Ken said.

"Don't be," Hackney said. "They're a nuisance. Always hanging around the back, hoping for handouts. You'll get plenty sick of them before you leave here."

———————

Qimmirjuaq paused, mid-statistic, to rush at one of the sugarcane stands and screech. Ken was taken aback, until he saw three little brown forms bolt out of the stand and disappear through an almost invisible crack in the dome wall.

"That's another one I'll have to patch," Qimmirjuaq scowled, examining it. "Damn rabbits. Half-tame, not enough fear of humans. When they're not chewing through the film, they're hanging around the office, hoping for handouts. I'm bloody sick of them."

"I'd've thought a biodome would be rabbit-proof?"

"Don't underestimate rabbits," Qimmirjuaq said, moving on to the next agricultural wonder. "Buggers'll find a way to get to you, no matter how secure you make the place."

———————

"You sure about going into town, sir?" Al asked later, when they were alone in the bunk room, spare and plain as promised. It took up half of the upstairs area, with the back half consisting of more storerooms, though, Ken reflected, the same rooms could have served as bedrooms or offices in more populous days. "Bet it'll be boring as hell," Al went on. The young man lounged on an iron-framed bed, watching the others prepare. Ken had managed a much needed, if cold, shower and a shave, and was now braiding his long black hair behind him, feeling much more relaxed.

"I think it's a good idea, private," Manders replied. He had his worn and faded uniform jacket up on a coathanger and was efficiently brushing the dust out of it. "Since we're here, may as well find out if the biotech has penetrated this far North. Remember the Detroit Front? Some of it, at least, likes dry areas."

"But you saw how he was looking at me," Al complained. "And he's supposed to be one of the civilised ones. You can bet they're all a bunch of dumb fucking racists."

"These aren't the Red States, private," Manders said.

"No, but some of them are pretty close," Al said. "Geographically, I mean."

"He didn't give *me* any trouble," Ken said.

"He prolly thinks you're an Inuit," Al countered.

Manders stopped brushing, frowned. "That's a good point. This far South, Inuit aren't likely to be common, or particularly well liked for that matter—no offense, Usagi."

"None taken." Ken, having spent most of his sojourn in Deecee being given an earful by angry Seaboarders raging about the "damn smug Eskimoes," had become resigned to the fact that most Southerners couldn't tell a Japanese-Torontonian from an Inuit.

"So, why the treatment for Benjamin, and not Usagi?" Manders gave a few last vigorous swipes at his jacket, examined it critically and put it on. "I've decided, private. You're coming with us, and that's an order. Consider it a scientific experiment."

---

"Shouldn't the rabbits be white, this time of year?" Ken asked as they moved on slowly through the sugarcane stands.

Qimmirjuaq shrugged. "Every year, they take longer and longer to go white," he said. "Adapting to the climate. These days, the brown ones can hide themselves in the biodomes, while the white ones end up standing out a bit too much against the gravel." He thought a bit. "Got a guy in the mammalian research division says some of them don't go white at all anymore."

---

Louanne's was apparently the only place in town which sold alcohol. Indeed, its only competition as a venue for entertainment was a faded doughnut shop proclaiming itself to be Tim Horton's (presumably a local affiliate that kept on going after the chain collapsed) and a church of no stated denomination. It was a Thursday night, and the town was fairly quiet. Near the bar, Ken could see a group of boys clustered around a Jeep with its hood up.

As they got closer, Ken realised they were younger than he thought. Eleven, maybe twelve at a stretch. One of them sighted the strangers, made an unheard remark. Half a dozen heads shot up like meerkats, staring at the trio with Hackney, then the group sprang as one into the Jeep, and drove off. The driver, Ken noted distractedly, looked about

ten. Al's smile tightened in an I-told-you-so way. "Redneck
country," he murmured softly.

Louanne apparently had spent a lot of money on redec-
orations about fifteen years previously, but hadn't done
much since. The walls were white, with framed stills (and
one preciously curated LCD slideshow) of various local
sports teams and memorable feats, which seemed mostly to
involve men standing next to the carcasses of ungulates of
varying sizes. The carpet was red, industrial, but mended
repeatedly since such things became harder and harder to
find. An ancient sticker in the window, behind a curtain
which had once matched the carpet, offered free wifi, and
another, almost as old, proclaimed that the establishment
accepted contactless payment. Ken vaguely remembered
similar signs from his earliest childhood.

The bar was about half full of men, and a reasonable
minority of women, dressed much like Hackney. Most looked
curiously, though without overt hostility, at the strangers, and
a few, true to expectations, gave Al a slightly harder look.

"Whatever their problem is, private, it's not your skin,"
Manders muttered a few minutes later, jerking his head to
the group of off-shift miners congregating at the bar. Ken
noted that there were, indeed, a small number of them with
skins as dark as, if not darker than, Al's. The Black miners
were giving Al the same curious glances as the White ones.

"What the hell is it, then?" Al groused.

Hackney seemed to become more cheerful, greeting a
small party of people occupying a table at the bay window,
and offering to buy a round. "This is Keith," he said, introducing another brown and wrinkled White man to Ken.
"He's a rancher, and his wife Kara, she's a computer operator at the mine."

"And this is Josh," Kara, a plump dark-haired White woman in a navy tank-top, said, hugging a skinny pale teenager in a black shirt, who looked embarrassed. "He's helping his daddy on the ranch."

His daddy gave her a sharp look. "He's in grade ten," he said, and Ken sensed a longstanding argument in the background. "Homeschool. He'll enroll at the Online University of Regina when he's passed his SATs."

"Of course," Kara said.

"So you're an Embedded Journalist?" Josh asked, clearly trying to sound more bored with the idea than he was. "What's that mean?"

Ken nodded. "It's a long tradition in the Seaboard military. I work for Iqaluit News Online. I follow these two around, write reports on what they do, and if it's an interesting enough story, people buy it."

"What if they're not doing anything interesting?"

"Josh!" exclaimed his mother.

Ken smiled. "It's a good question. When there's nothing to report, we work on insight features. At the moment I'm writing up one about legends on the battlefield," he said, feeling a little pleased with the segue. "Stories about the ghosts that soldiers see, rabbit women or coyotes with strange heads."

"The owwwls," Al drawled, raising his pint of lager, "are not what they seeeeem."

"Can't say we have many stories like that around here," Keith said.

"There's the injuns," Josh said and was shushed by his mother.

"Injuns?" Ken frowned. He remembered the word vaguely from his comparative historical literature classes. A pejorative for Southern Natives. "You mean Cree? Anishn-abe?" He remembered the poster. "Sioux?"

"Just a local story," Keith said. "Ghosts, seeking revenge for ancient genocides. But I wouldn't say anyone's seen them." Josh looked like he wanted to say something, but kept quiet. Ken wondered if he could manage to get the boy on his own sometime. "Just if something goes wrong, or missing, we say it was the injuns. You know."

"Sort of like how the soldiers blame things on gremlins? Or talk about the Bunny Girl?" Ken was slightly pleased at how he had managed to work that in there.

"So! tell us the latest war stories," Kara put in, changing the subject a little too eagerly. "Willard said you were out on the Detroit Front. What are things actually like there? The latest zines are saying Volpone pushed the Reds back another two miles, but we're never sure what's true or not, and in any case, it always takes the zines a while to get here from the big towns."

"Websites are saying—" Keith began.

"Websites never tell the truth," Kara said. "They're either government-controlled, or they're conspiracy theorists. Zines are the way to go."

"I bet you've been a lot of interesting places," Josh went on, ignoring his parents.

"Not really," Ken said. It was true; since leaving Nunavut, he'd spent a few months hanging around Deecee, then went West through the swampland to Detroit, before going North again. "I haven't been in the field long."

"Any place is interesting," Josh said, "if it's different to where you started."

---

"And then you got the southern ones," Qimmirjuaq said. "Came up here when the Great Lakes flooded, same as the people." A slight glance at Ken, perhaps to see if the analogy was reading. "They don't go white at all. But they interbreed with the local rabbits, changing the gene pool."

———————

Late that night, Ken was awakened by something. He kept still, then heard it again. The sound of metal clattering, footsteps or maybe hooves. Voices.

He opened his eyes. Al was sprawled across one bed, snoring; the other was empty. Manders, in undershirt and shorts, was standing to one side of the window, flattened against the front wall, a pistol in his hand. Ken found himself wondering distractedly where it had come from. At his last check their arms complement had consisted of two rifles, both locked in a gun-safe downstairs. The old soldier was motionless, staring down to the front of the waystation. He noticed Ken, gestured for silence.

Ken crept to the window, as quietly as possible, looked out. Saw two riders on horseback, skinny young people in rags, long hair fluttering in the moonlight. A blond boy, a black-haired girl. They had knocked over a compost bin, and were laughing as the horses picked through the recent garbage for food.

"Hey!" Another voice. Hackney, a tattered flannel bathrobe over his sleeping clothes, wielding a rifle. "Out of there!" He shook the gun threateningly, but didn't point it at them.

The riders jeered, but as he stepped forward, they quickly kneed their horses away, galloped off across the country.

"Injuns?" Ken whispered. "They're not biotech..." But then again, the riders hadn't seemed quite human. Something about them was wild, animalistic. If there was something like the biotech implants that had fastened on to the animals near the Detroit Front, only one that affected humans, made *them* act strangely... they *did* seem to have a strange affinity with those horses...

"I'd like to know more," Manders replied. "We'll ask about it in the morning."

---

Ken nodded. "Like biology class," he said. "The animals adapt biologically, the humans adapt culturally." He gestured to the biodome.

Unexpectedly, Qimmirjuaq scoffed at this. "That's the line you'll be taking in your feature, right? The rabbits change their colour, the humans build agrotech facilities?"

Ken was taken aback enough not to dissemble. "Uh, yeah," he said.

"Well, that'll play all right in Iqualuit," Qimmirjuaq said. "That's the sort of message they want to hear."

"Do you have another one?" Ken asked, stung.

"Actually," Qimmirjuaq said, "since you mention it, yeah."

---

But Hackney wouldn't be drawn. "Just some local youngsters, making trouble," he said, before insisting that he had to check the messages on the box, and disappearing into his office.

Manders frowned across the table where the trio were having breakfast. "How old are you, private?" he asked.

"Nineteen, last birthday," Al replied. "Drafted at eighteen, right at the end of my freshman year at Cornell. Got two more years in the service, if I survive 'em."

Manders nodded. "Notice something odd about Louanne's last night?"

Ken followed his lead. "Josh," he said.

"The only teenager there, was Josh," Manders agreed. "And we haven't seen any in or around town, apart from the pair last night. Under-twelves, yes. Over-twenties, yes. Nobody in between. No wonder they were looking at you, private. You're not the wrong colour for these parts, you're the wrong *age*."

"D'you reckon?" Al said, mopping up a reconstituted egg yolk with his second helping of canned bread.

"Maybe they just don't drink?" Ken said. "What's legal age around here?"

"Who cares?" Manders said. "Apart from Josh, not one teenager. Not in the bar, and not hanging around outside the bar, or the garage, or the mediatheque. Or driving up and down the streets. That normal in Nunavut? That teenagers all hide away indoors like Red State women?" Ken shook his head, remembering hockey games, snowmobile and quad-bike races, school dances. "Something's up here," Manders concluded with a grim set of his mouth.

"I doubt the tanker will be here today," Ken said. "Why don't we test that hypothesis? Go on a recce of town, calculate a few average ages, ask some questions."

Al looked sceptical. "What do you think it is?" he said. "Some sort of plague? Something in the water?"

"Well," Ken said, "it could be implants, like the animals back in Detroit. Smaller ones, harder to see. Or it could be something else, affecting their behaviour. We know the Americans, back in the day, had engineered viruses, they say they even had custom-made diseases. If they could do it, our mystery biotech-makers could."

Al shook his head. "Biotech," he said firmly, "ain't magic. And these guys ain't wizards." But he went into town with them anyway.

———————

"They don't like to hear this," Qimmirjuaq said, clearly also indicating, and I bet you don't either. "Fact is, all of this agrotech stuff, it's just a stopgap. Oh, sure, I've heard it all about the agrarian revolution, better living, all that—can't say I should really complain, either, since agrotech is paying my bills right now. And it might keep us going in some reasonably civilised form, with diminishing returns, for the next fifty years or so." He flicked derisively at a bamboo stalk.

———————

Ken was outside the local vehicle repair shop, in the sunshine and dust, making a note on his fieldpad about the lack of apprentices, when someone called his name. He turned, and it was Josh.

"Dad sent me to pick up the Landrover," he said, jingling keys. "What are you doing?"

"Nothing much." Ken stowed his fieldpad. "Just passing the time. Might write something about how the people live around here."

"You mean people in Nunavut would want to read about *that*?" Josh scoffed.

"You'd be surprised," Ken said. "Like what you said last night, about how any place is interesting if it's different to where you start. I mean, what you have here, it's nothing like Nunavut." He gestured. "Low population density. Grasslands." He thought a bit. "Horses."

"Huh. *I* can't wait to get out of it," Josh said.

Ken sympathised. "Where would you go, if you could?"

"Oh, I don't know," Josh said.

Ken was suddenly aware of the sound of hoofbeats, somewhere nearby, and then that Josh was no longer looking at him. Ken followed his gaze, saw a group of young riders on horseback, tattered clothes, flying greasy hair, at the end of the road. He locked eyes with one of them, skinny, blond, mounted on a brown horse with a white, black-spotted rump. Possibly the boy he'd seen last night. The eyes were foreign, disdainful and uncomprehending. Inhuman. Like the eyes of a wild hare.

One of the riders fixed on something, shouted. His horse whirled, as if in telepathic communion with him, and sped off, the others in pursuit.

"I don't know," Josh repeated. "Just... out of here."

Ken dug into his pocket, found the chips and motherboard he'd recovered from the destroyed Bunny Girl in the swamp. He showed them to Josh. "Ever seen anything like these?"

Josh looked at them, uninterested. "No, that's not what I mean," he said.

"Or animals with bionic implants?" Ken struggled to describe the ones at the Detroit Front. "Like black plastic, growing out of their spines and skulls?"

Now Josh was looking at him as if he was crazy. "What?"

"Just some biotech," Ken said. "We saw some at the

Detroit Front. Was wondering if anything like that had ever been seen in the Prairies."

Josh shook his head. "Yeah, I know it's not very high-tech around here. But that sort of thing's not what I'm looking for. And East's not where I want to go. Or North. Or Westcoast."

"Then where?"

Josh sighed. "You wouldn't understand."

———

"So, what then?" Ken asked.

"If the species is going to survive, we're going to have to change. Physically, perhaps. Like the rabbits. We can't go on pretending that we can keep on living like we did. Look at computer equipment; it's getting scarcer and scarcer, the harder it gets to ship from Asia—and nobody here's taking up the slack of making the stuff, and no surprise. There's still a few programmers and repair-people in the big cities, yeah, but less and less each year, and almost none when you get out into the rural areas. People can get on just fine without it. And what about the satellites?" He whirled, jabbed startlingly at Ken's pad. "Nobody's put any up for years. Nobody can. Every couple of years we lose another, and, sooner or later, there'll be no more communication."

"So, we're going to revert to the primitive or something?"

"Maybe so," Qimmirjuaq said. "There's a rumour that something like it happened in the South—south of California, I mean—before things went dark out there. The Mexican Traditionalists had some kind of manifesto..." He shook his head, as if distracted. "Primitive's the wrong word, though. Think about it, for a hundred and fifty thousand years, maybe, humanity was a low-population-density, hunting and gathering operation. Maybe a bit of domestication, they think, but no big-scale agrotech. Some places, too, it's not that long ago. My ancestors, maybe a couple of hundred years." He thought a bit. "I think we might be about to revert, if you like, back to normal."

————————————

The gas tanker turned up that evening, driven by two sunburned women in matching UPetroco-logo bandannas, and refueled the waystation's tanks. Manders bought several extra jerrycans for the back of the SUV, while Al traded one of his cigarettes for a small bag of marijuana from the auxiliary driver.

"Don't get too much real tobacco these days," she said cheerfully as she pocketed it. "Enjoy the sinsemil', it's not Beecee's finest but it's getting there."

"Stay for dinner?" Hackney asked.

The driver shook her grizzled head. "Got to make the UPetroco checkpoint before midnight," she said. Extracting the auxiliary driver from conversation with Al—to their mutual disappointment—she hurried them back to the tanker and drove off.

"We'll have to go tomorrow," Manders said quietly to Ken.

"I still don't know what's—" Manders nodded firmly, cutting him off.

"I know, but we can't leave it any longer without looking suspicious. Maybe we'll just have to leave it a mystery."

"We'll go into town again," Ken said. "There's no teenagers in town, there's a lot of them on the hills. And I think... something's happened to them." He told them briefly about the ones he'd seen. "We should at least try to find out what it is."

"Mind you," Qimmirjuaq said, "it'll be a pretty rough transition on the individual level. Personally, I like my heated house and my box and my GM coffee, and that I've lived past forty with no serious diseases. But if it's a difference between individual comfort and species survival, the winning throw usually goes to the species." He paused a bit. "I'm getting too grim, aren't I? Come on, the next section's just through that airlock—I'll show you that coffee plantation, and you can try some of the output." He smiled, placating.

Ken followed, with a glance back at the small party of brown rabbits, crouching outside the facility, waiting till the humans passed to creep back inside.

As they were packing the SUV and preparing to go out to Louanne's, there was a frantic knocking on the door. Upstairs, Ken heard Hackney open it, then Keith's urgent voice. "Need to use your box," he was saying. "It's Josh, he's missing."

"You can call out if you like," Hackney said. "But I think we both—"

"I know," Keith cut him off. "But I'm hoping maybe he's run off to the big city, he always talked about..." He stopped. Ken, halfway down the stairs, hesitated in turn.

Al burst into the room. "They're outside," he said in a strained voice.

Hackney, Keith and Ken followed him out. There were a dozen riders out front, surrounding the SUV. Manders, his back to the vehicle and hands raised like a fighter, surveyed them continuously, expression calm but eyes ticking from one to the other. He'd dropped a box of MREs, brown packs spilled out around his feet.

At the sound of the door, one of them looked back. Skinny, black T-shirt. Ken recognised Josh. A slight flicker crossed the blank face, and he nodded to the others. The horses turned and rode away.

Keith rushed after them, futilely, swearing. "That's my son, you hear me? My son!" he shouted. Ken felt ashamed to see the man like this.

Then Keith turned, glared at Ken, Al and Manders. "*You* did this," he said. "He was all right till you got here." With a noise that was like a sob, he jumped into his Landrover and drove away.

Hackney was watching the riders go. "That's my kid out there," he said. "The blond-haired one, on the Appaloosa. Takes after his mother. Local girl, met her when I first came out here to work. When he left, she... couldn't take it."

"I'm sorry," Ken said awkwardly.

"We thought at first it was just cussedness," Hackney carried on, not meeting Ken's eyes. "Kids being kids. Then, maybe, some kind of disease. Like as if the Red States or the Seaboarders had poisoned the water. We get radioactive dust up from Wisconsin sometimes, you know. Another reason there's not so many kids around here. But they didn't seem like crazy people."

"So what is it?" Ken asked.

Hackney sighed. "I understand some of it. Look around you," he said. "How much longer do you reckon we have? Farming's ended, ranching's on the way out. Mine's still working, but only so long as Nunavut's there to buy the potash. Some say in fifty years, those of us left, we'll all be living like those kids. That we'll have to." He nodded. "But I don't understand why they want it *now*. The way they live, half of them'll be dead at forty, and the other half'll be worn out by then. Mexico"—he snorted derisively—"Mexico's gone dark, and no wonder. They've had schooling, they know that. Why choose to live that way? I don't get it, I really don't."

Ken shook his head, felt his eyes prickling unexpectedly with tears. "We're going in the morning," he said.

"I know," Hackney said. Then, "It's not your fault he left. It would have happened sooner or later. Keith's just..."

Ken shook his head. "We're all of us in the same situation. I understand." Maybe, he thought, if we can find the source of the biotech, it might make a difference. Or it might make no difference at all. Like Qimmirjuaq said.

He watched the silhouettes of the riders in the distance. Once he thought he could identify Josh, but before long, he realised he couldn't tell them apart at all. Just a party of rapid, brown creatures, circling the town, waiting.

# CHAPTER SIX: THE SCOUT

TOTCHLI, crouched at the prow of the low flat boat along the coastline of the North, saw it first. A flicker of something off-white between the sunlit trees, not a bird, not a deer or a giant squirrel (some abstract and detached part of him wished it was; there was good meat on those things, and Tot was a surprisingly decent hand with a bolt-shooter). Flowing. A jaguar? Despite his lack of Northern experience, Totchli knew better. He crouched lower, willing it to show itself. He knew he should feel a sense of familiarity—memories of family trips taken along the canals out to the seacoast, then down to resorts and beaches in the South, or of expeditions setting out to ancient field sites—but the twisted fruit trees of the alien Northern landscape kept the adrenaline coursing.

"Storm coming," Itch said idly to Totchli, his hand on the tiller. Coyotl slowly turned her ugly face, leathery with sun exposure, and slit her dark eyes meaningfully at the youth. Itch raised an eyebrow at the rebuke.

"Come on, ma'am, if there was any danger in this neck of the woods we'd know by now," the young man protested. "Just trying to make conversation."

"Mind the tiller, Itzcuintli," Coyotl said with finality, and Itch settled down, a slight pout on his post-adolescent face. There was a low snicker from Tot, pretending to sleep on top of the baggage.

"Do you see something?" Coyotl joined Totchli in the prow of the boat, moving in that silent way she had.

Totchli indicated the jungle. "Not sure if it's an animal or a human."

"If it was one of ours, we should know by now," Coyotl said. "What did it look like?"

"Just a bit of white, something following the boat through the jungle."

"Keep a lookout," Coyotl said. "We're due at the colony site by tomorrow night, so I don't want to waste time chasing phantoms. But if it is something, I'd like to know about it."

Totchli felt that animal-being-watched instinct before he even saw it again, flickering through the trees. A cold shiver started at the top of his scalp and ran down his neck (where his hair had been pulled back in a tight, sweat-resistant ponytail; he was a little too vain to crop his hair like the warriors).

"Did you see that, ma'am?" Itch said, before Totchli could even open his mouth.

"Yes, I did." Coyotl moved forward, drew her pistol and sighted along the shore. "Tototl, stop faking, front of the boat. Totchli, get down."

Totchli obeyed, but dug in his bag for his binoculars. He

had to see it, to know for sure that it was what he thought it was.

A few minutes later, Totchli saw it for certain. Just for a minute, but he recognised that bony face, that skinny frame, like a priest in a raven mask.

"Got it!" he hissed.

"Thought I told you to stay down," Coyotl said absently, holding out a hand for the binoculars. "Hm, yes," she said. "Funny-looking creature, isn't it?"

Totchli nodded. "Did a bit of work with them when I was a student back in Axoxoctic. Useful things." They'd used them as guides, muscle and bearers when out doing fieldwork. This one, though, looked dilapidated and ragged, as if it had been out in the rain a long time. Totchli could make out some military glyphs on its rags.

Coyotl handed him the binoculars. "Take us into shore, Itch," she said. "It's just a scout, no danger."

"Unless it's armed," Totchli reminded her.

Coyotl shook her head. "Even if it is, look at it," she said. "It's drifting. Wandering along the shore like it's lost. It's not going to discharge."

The boat bumped the shoreline. Totchli leaped out, surprising even himself with the speed of his movements, chasing the flickering cyborg through the trees. He heard a crashing sound behind him. Coyotl and Tot, or perhaps just Coyotl, following. He flung himself at the creature, tangling himself in the ragged, reeking fabric—*something's wrong, who's in charge of maintaining this scout?*—and brought it down. A small knot of hairless mice, disturbed from whatever they were doing by the sudden onslaught, let out a collective passionate shriek and bounded away, squeaking in alarm.

"What the hell?" Coyotl, crashing to a halt behind him,

stump flung out for balance, instinctively drawing a bead on the scout with her bolt-shooter.

Totchli looked back. The scout had stopped resisting, gone into quiet mode. He pushed himself up, wiped his forehead. "Look at it," he said to the old soldier. "It *was* armed, but now it's discharged everything. It's just drifting around, maybe following an old guard programme. Or perhaps"—a thought occurred to him—"it heard our motor, homed in on it. Programmed to find the nearest humans in the absence of its handler or other remote instructions."

Coyotl frowned, looking at the faded glyphs on its arms. "It's from the colony," she said. "Got to be."

"Doesn't look good, does it?" Totchli deactivated the scout, flipped it over, removed the main circuit and stowed it in his waistpouch. Someone back at the Bunker, or in Axoxoctic, would want to analyse it for data, figure out what had happened. He stood up, stretched. Looked around the glade they'd fetched up in, he saw stout trees with dark green leaves and almost luminous giant white flowers, scented like a festival. Things rustled in the bushes, kept up a kind of insect murmuring. Across the sky, the grey edges of clouds moved slowly, deliberately against the white. Somewhere in the distance, a raven cried out, once.

Something large and ragged hit him blindside, crashed him to the ground with a shout. Struggling, he realised it was a human being, a man, eyes wide, head bald, ragged, reeking of sweat, urine and unwashed clothes, grappling with him as he'd grappled with the scout. Totchli fought back desperately, helpless with panic, trying desperately to remember the few wrestling moves he'd actually been able to learn in school, *nothing works, I'm going to die*. Suddenly the filthy man stiffened, sat bolt upright, eyes wide. Then he went limp, fell onto Totchli like a stinking bear pelt.

"You all right, Totchli?" Someone shoved the unre-sisting stranger off him, and he realised it was Coyotl. She held out her hand to pull him up, then, as he leaned against a flower tree and panted for breath, she squatted, pulling a small length of cord from her belt, rolling Totchli's assailant over and tying his wrists, with a practiced one-handed effi-ciency Totchli didn't want to enquire about. "Useful martial arts trick I learned down South," she said conversationally as she worked. "Knocks a grown man out, one-handed even. But the trouble is, it doesn't last more than about five minutes." She straightened. "Tot! Itch!" she called.

Tot emerged into the clearing, followed a minute later by Itch. They scanned the grove, saw the deactivated scout, the unconscious man. Itch swore automatically.

Coyotl nodded. "Yeah," she said. "I think we might be getting an idea why the colony hasn't been returning our calls."

"You don't think he could be a native—"

"Don't be stupid, Tot," Coyotl cut the young man off, and he had the wit to look embarrassed. "One, no human beings have been reported this far North for two genera-tions. If there were natives, either the original scouts or else the colonists would have sent word back and initiated contact. Two, look at his damned *clothes*; unless the natives have accounts with tailors in Axox', I think he's likely to be one of us. Do you recognise him, Totchli?"

Totchli started. He cast his mind back to the personnel files on the scroll. "Uh. Not sure." A name came swimming up. "Might be Cuiatl? The expedition's botanist. He looked a lot cleaner in the pictures, though." She was right about the clothes, he realised. Filthy and torn as they were, he was wearing something barely recognisable as a work tunic and leg protectors, with embroidery around the edges indicating a reasonably expensive Axoxoctic clothing shop. His footwear had gone missing somewhere along the way and his feet, Totchli noted detachedly, were blistered and cut. *Not someone used to going barefoot, then.*

"Cuiatl?" Coyotl said to the man. His eyes cracked open and he looked at her, but did not respond. His face was a neutral blank under the dirt. "Huh," Coyotl said. "He's going to be one hell of a job for the vision-quest techies, when we get him back."

"Should we go on?" Totchli asked. "I mean, we've found this man—Cuiatl, or whoever he is—and the scout, both in a hell of a state, so we've got proof that the colony's gone down and some evidence of how it happened, and it could be dangerous to go any further."

"And what would we do about him if we did?" Tot asked.

Itch jabbed Tot reprovingly in the ribs. "Idiot. If *he's* alive, there could be others, needing help. We going to leave them?"

"You wanna wind up like him?" Tot retorted. "No sense more people going crazy. And what if the colonists have *all* gone the same way? You wanna wind up *dead*, Itch? I say we've done our job, take off back to the Bunker and get them to send in some scouts instead."

"Some warrior." Itch scowled.

"I may be a warrior, but I'm not a stupid warrior," Tot said. "I got into this game to save lives and get a trade, not get myself killed by some crazy biotechnician upcountry. As for you, if you're so bloodthirsty, why are you in the shitting *logistics* corps? Wouldn't the damned infantry have you?"

"Hand me your scroll, Itch," Coyotl said, ending the argument. As the young men glared silently at each other, she thumbed up a map, checked it. "Thought so. We're actually not too far from where we were going to land and walk upcountry to the colony. It should be about an hour's walk from here." She nodded, as if she'd confirmed something. "Tot, you take the boat and our friend here, go back to the Bunker, and then come back to pick us up along with any survivors. Itch, Rabbit Boy and I will go inland, see if we can find the colony."

"Uh..." Tot looked down at Cuiatl, who had apparently lapsed into unconsciousness again. "What if he wakes up?"

"We've got sedatives in the medical kit," Coyotl said. "We'll dose him before he gets on board, and you can just keep dosing him till you get him to safety." Tot still looked doubtful, so Coyotl continued, "I thought you joined up 'cause you wanted to help people, learn a trade? How the hell will you cope with a boatful of scared, panicky flood refugees if you can't handle one scruffy old guy, who probably hasn't eaten in days? Even if the worst happens, strong kid like you should be able to put him down, no problem."

Tot shrugged, but seemed a little more confident. Coyotl's lips quirked slightly. "Good man. Let's get that boat loaded."

Suddenly Cuiatl's eyes opened. He jerked upwards, scrambled, ran, hands still bound behind him, towards the water.

"Stop him!" Coyotl shouted. They crashed through the woods after the man, but it was too late; by the time they'd reached the shore Cuiatl had dived off the rock-face and was in the depths of the full tide, sweeping away with the current, out to sea. Totchli grabbed Itch in time to stop him hurling himself in after the man.

There was a shocked silence.

"Bad luck," Itch ventured after a few minutes. "Dying

and not getting buried. No prayers, no grave-goods, no sacrifices."

Tot jabbed him again, but said nothing. He was undoubtedly thinking the same thing, though he also seemed a little relieved at not having to take the man back to Outpost One on his own.

"Well," Coyotl said. "That settles a few things. New plan, boys. We'll keep the boat moored here; Tot, you make camp and guard it till we get back." Tot looked resentfully at her, and she snarled at him, "First you didn't want to take the boat back, now you do, make up your filthy, stinking mind, you rat." Tot's expression changed to something more apologetic, and Coyotl's voice softened. "It's OK, kid, I don't know what's going to happen either. But that's warrioring, understand? Keep busy, that's the secret. Build a fire, catch some fish, settle in for the duration. You'll have memorised the Survival Codex. Remind yourself. Go through the practical bits."

Tot looked at his feet, and Coyotl nodded briefly. "All right, then. The rest of you—Itch, Rabbit Boy—with me."

Now it was Itch's turn to look mutinous. "Bad luck," he said. "We shouldn't go any further. It's just asking for it. First that scout, now him..."

"And you, Itzcuintli"—Coyotl rounded on him—"aren't the one making the decisions here. Understand? It's Rabbit Boy's mission if it's anybody's, so he decides what we do and where we go. I'm the one who decides if it's worth the risk getting there. You're the crew, you don't get any say in the matter. Am I making myself clear?"

Itch looked away, nodded. Coyotl breathed out. "I understand, kid, really I do. We've all had to get past some boundaries." She touched his shoulder. "Say some prayers for the dead if it makes you feel better, for the Serpent's sake," she said, not unkindly. "His family will take care of the rites when we get back, and you're a big lad to be afraid of wandering spirits. He's not the first man I've seen die at sea with no rites, and I've never been attacked by ghouls."

She turned back to Tot. "We'll radio in every four hours, Tot. If we miss two check-ins in a row, send up a flare and get back to the Bunker, stat. No heroics."

Tot nodded. He and Itch shared a brief hug before Itch slung his pack over his back and started off through the jungle, towards the clearing where they'd found the scout, followed by Coyotl. Tot settled down in the boat, loading his bolt-shooter, looking neutrally at Totchli.

Awkwardly, Totchli found his bag and slinging it over his shoulders, hurried after the warriors, wondering what was at the end of the trail.

## CHAPTER SEVEN: BUNNY GIRLS

THE SUN WAS SETTING over the miles and miles of fields, occasional burned-out or abandoned buildings, and hills.

"At least we're getting hills now," Al observed. "Sick of all that damn prairie."

"Any closer to figuring out where the hell we are, Usagi, beyond damn fool general observations like 'somewhere in Montana, I think'?" Manders changed gear with a determined gesture, not looking away from the road.

"Trying..." Ken swiped through the various maps on his fieldpad, trying to find something that reasonably matched the terrain. He shared Al's sentiment. He had never really thought about what prairies were like until being confronted with them, and all that strange flatness, with the occasional silo or refinery tower suddenly looming up like a fairy-tale giant, had been making him strangely uncomfortable.

"At least, could you tell us if we're still in Seaboard-held territory?" Al said. "Something tells me the Reds wouldn't respect our neutrality."

"I'm pretty sure we are," Ken said, but he wasn't. According to the maps he'd downloaded at Hackney's waystation, they were, but he knew how quickly the front could change. Satellite access had been too limited and sporadic since then to provide any news.

"Someplace safe where we could stop for the night would also be good," Al added. They'd mainly been camping out in the open as the simplest option, putting up the tent when the weather got rainy. They hadn't found another town large enough to have a waystation since Hackney.

"Working on that, too," Ken said, checking another map.

Then, by the side of the road, he saw it.

———————

Bony, bucktoothed, with feathery rags hanging from its famine-child arms, or armature. Like a skeleton in a rabbit mask, indicating the road, *That way madness lies*. A ghost, resurrected from the broken remains in the New York swamps, last seen drifting over the Michigan sand dunes. "I saw you die," Ken murmured, feeling on the verge of hysterical laughter.

"What?" Al said.

"Nothing. Just—" Ken indicated. "Go left at the fork. Keep going till I tell you." He looked back. Not surprisingly, the Bunny Girl was gone.

It was back again about fifteen minutes later, ghosting ahead of the SUV. "Straight on," Ken said.

"I'm fairly sure I saw one of those Bunny Girl things just now," Manders said conversationally, still not taking his eyes from the road. "Like the ones we saw in New York and Detroit. Wouldn't be following it, would we, Usagi?"

"We would," Ken said firmly. "It's the best lead we've had all day."

"We're *supposed* to be following the trail of the biotech, after all," Al said innocently.

They drove on through the gathering darkness.

---

Finally, it appeared in front of the vehicle. Manders braked, but the thing was moving too fast, faster than Ken had ever seen. Running ahead, spindly, rags waving, fast as a car. Then it seemingly flew up, ptarmigan-style, like the one Ken had seen so many years ago, and vanished.

"The hell?" Manders said.

"Look." Al reached over the backs of the seats. "Up ahead."

The lights of a camp shone off to the side of the road; flickering firelight, lanterns, a few strange things that looked to Ken like shipping containers, or prefab houses, on wheels.

"Could be Reds," Manders observed.

"Reds, with trailers?" Al scorned. "Come *on*, sir."

Manders nodded. "Got to be some sort of civilians. Question is, are they friendly?"

"If they ain't friendly, we're armed," Al said, with the same innocent tone as before. Manders shot him another look, and Al smiled.

"We drive up slowly. I'll take point on this one; if they're hostile, they might shoot Usagi, and we need his brain," Manders said matter-of-factly, approaching the camp.

Closer to the encampment, Ken could see figures around the fire. A gigantic muscular one, small ones, normal-looking ones. A crazy part of his mind whispered that he had wandered into Middle-earth. He told it to be quiet.

Manders pulled up, got out of the vehicle, holding his hands up. "Unarmed," he said, though Ken privately doubted it. "Captain Manders, Seaboard States Expeditionary Force, on a rescue mission."

The figures turned to each other. A silent conference took place, then one stood, moved into the light of the head-lamps. "You're welcome here," it said, in a strange voice, high for a man, deep for a woman. "We are the Circus of Form. Body-mods and acrobats." The figure gestured to one of the trailers, which was painted with a garish slogan: *Polymorphia: Circus of Form, World of Wonders*. "We're heading out to the Seaboard lines, to give a show. You can stay with us tonight, travel with us if you like. I'm Lee the Androgyne."

The androgyne was tall, slender, with a figure that managed to be curvy and breastless at the same time. Bare and scrubbed face, but with a look which suggested makeup, clad in jeans and an expensive T-shirt with roses all over it, honey-coloured hair long and pulled back into a functional ponytail, but shining and sweet-scented, giving a hint of past and future glamour. Manders turned back to the SUV, nodded. Ken turned off the vehicle. He and Al emerged.

"Ken Usagi, Embedded Journalist, Iqaluit Online News."

"I'm Private Benjamin, but if I can call you Betty, you can call me Al," Al said. This time *Ken* shot him a look, but the androgyne didn't seem upset.

Lee moved back to the fire, introduced the others. "Tina, the Strong Woman." The tall mountain of muscles gestured.

Her face was like a normal-sized woman's; below that, her arms and legs bulged, her tiny waist pulsed with energy. Her skin was dark, her hair bleached a surprising platinum. "The Bonsai Girls, Marcie, Lacey, Georgie, Trish and Sally-Ann." These were the five smaller figures, who appeared to Ken to be near-identical, perfectly proportioned little women with short chestnut-brown hair and cheery, toothpaste-advert smiles. "Leopold the Human Tiger, you can call him Chris." A man whose face was half-cat, striped with tattoos, with whiskers and padded cheeks and lips; hair teased upwards, ears pointed and, when he smiled, teeth sharply pointed, too. "Lucio the Tattooed Man. Luke. He don't say much." The man in question looked up, waved. A couple of dozen earrings glinted from his bald head. He wore a thin T-shirt, the blue and red detailing on his skin visible through the fabric.

"...and you're also acrobats?" Ken asked, feeling a little wild. Trying and failing, in his mind, to discern an ethnic origin for any of them.

Chris nodded. "We do a show. Six numbers, acrobatics, performance art. It's a new take on the old traditional traveling freak show."

"Body-mods," corrected a Bonsai Girl sternly.

Chris conceded. "The new take is that we're freaks by choice, not by genetics."

"The human body should adapt to the new environment," rumbled Tina, looking at the bottle, tiny in her hand. "So says Carver."

"Carver?" Al asked.

Something tickled at Ken's memory. "Carverites," he said. "It's a religious group, isn't it?"

Tina nodded. "Sort of. More a philosophy, or a way of life. We believe that just as we can genetically and surgically correct what once were freaks, so we can, genetically and surgically, adapt to the new environment."

"Those horse-kids would *love* them," Al commented. Ken couldn't tell if he was being sarcastic or serious.

---

There had been Carverites in Toronto, when Ken was small. He remembered standing on the dock by Ryerson University, waiting for the Queen Street Ferry to come through. He was with his mother, a tense, pale, red-headed woman, who hated the way people focused on her son's dark hair and golden skin, rather than his slim frame and green eyes, and asked, *is he yours?*. She kept her face turned resolutely away from the three people with the oddly plump bluish complexions, staring eyes, and, Ken saw when one of them laughed and gestured, sharp teeth and webs between their fingers.

"Mum, who are those people?" he asked out loud.

"They're Carverites, Kennie," his mother said, pulling her beige coat more tightly around herself with her free hand.

"Why do they look so funny?" Ken persisted.

"Because they've had operations to make them look like that," his mother said.

"Could *I* have an operation to make me look like that?" Ken asked, looking down at his little, plump hands extending from his bright yellow raincoat.

"You could," his mother said, "but you won't. Because you're sensible." She sighed with relief as the ferry arrived, practically dragging him on board. The Carverites stayed on the dock, watched the boat go.

"You're welcome to stay the night, then travel with us to the lines tomorrow," Lee said, "if you don't mind chipping in."

"We've got MREs," Al said. "UP government ones. Not bad, for certain values of 'not bad'."

Lee nodded. "We'll take MREs." The atmosphere relaxed slightly, and Tina offered Al her bottle. Al took out his bag of Beecee marijuana, and the atmosphere relaxed even more, with a couple of muted cheers coming from the Bonsai Girls.

"What *are* those things?" Ken asked Al as he sat down on a low plastic bench by the campfire, gesturing at the houses on wheels.

"Trailers," Al said, surprised. "You live in them. Hook them up to a car or truck, pull them along. We had a few of them where I came from, in Massachusetts. Rich folk would use them for holidays, poor folk for houses. Guess you don't get that up North."

"No, I suppose we don't," Ken said. He tried to imagine one hooked up to a snowmobile and failed.

"Makes sense for carnies," Lacey said, sitting next to Ken. "We've got a lot of clothes and equipment to take with us on the road. And there's no way you're getting *me* in a tent." She raised a slightly lascivious eyebrow at Ken.

As Ken got older, more independent, he saw more of the Carverites in and around Toronto. Were there more, or did he just notice them? Paddling along the canals in little boats. Camping in abandoned buildings, singing weird rhythmic songs around bonfires. Going out to a restaurant

with his parents, one, crouched in an alley nearby, spoke a
calm greeting to them. "Hello," Ken said back. The man's
eyes were round and glassy, like a frog's. His mother turned
her face away.

———

"So, what are you doing out here?" Chris asked, as Al and
Lee busied themselves finding the MREs and Lucio rolled a
joint. "Rescue mission?"

Ken began to repeat the story about the lost convoy in
the Cascades. Then he realised that his audience, rather
than listening, were shaking their heads, smiling at each
other, shifting about. He trailed off lamely.

"OK, what are you *really* doing out here?" Chris asked.
"That was nicely told but, if you don't mind my saying, it's a
bullshit story if ever I heard one."

Ken looked around the fire, made a judgment call.
"We're looking for biotech," he said, ignoring the near-
imperceptible tensing of Manders' face: *Usagi, don't go
there.* "Word has it, some group out West has invented some
new biotech materials."

This time, the response was positive. "And, of course,
Deecee want it," Lacey said.

"*Course* they do," said one of the other girls, possibly
Trish. "It stands to reason. I would, too."

"Oh, *you* would," said another, and the entire quintu-
plet set went into fits of giggles. "Wouldn't use it to win the
war on the Reds, though, would you?" More laughter
ensued.

Ken was starting to feel a little lost. "What?"

"Do you know how much you have to go through, to
look like this?" the girl who was probably Trish said. "First

there's the genetic selection, then the in-utero manipulation. Then, once you're safely out, there's surgery, treatment, cosmetic surgery—identical quintuplets are, like, *non*existent—"

"We're not even actually sisters," said Lacey. "No, seriously. We were all of us deliberately born small, but only Georgie and Sally-Ann are actually biological siblings. They performed together, then, when the rest of us met up, we started having surgery to look the same." Proud smiles all around the group. "It took a lot, but once we all found each other... we knew we had to be together, whatever the cost."

"OK," Ken said.

"Anyway, if there's a way to do that which is easier, we'll take it," one of them said, Ken wasn't sure which. "If Tina's right, more and more people are going to mod themselves as the weather gets worse."

"I'm not sure it's that sort of biotech," Ken said. "What we've mostly seen so far is cyborgs, these sort of skeleton robot-things that hang around battlefields, and a system for building... castles, we call them, buildings that are about human-sized but we're not really sure what they're for... using available environmental materials." He heard Manders sigh slightly—*that's right, Usagi, tell them everything, why don't you?*—but went on. It was his mission, not Manders', and, if they were traveling people, interested in biotech, then the performers might know about other manifestations. "There might be more, but we've yet to see any that'll latch on to humans. The castles use small animals to help build themselves, and control them using these kind of pod things... but they don't seem to modify their shape."

Tina and the Bonsai Girls looked mildly disappointed. "Still," Tina said, "it's all good, all useful. Tell me more about these castles. They could be some kind of environment-safe dwelling, to protect humans in all conditions."

"Or something not-human," Lacey added dramatically. "Perhaps the alien invasion is at hand?"

"They mostly turn up in mountains, or deserts," Ken said. "We haven't seen any evidence that they protect against snow, or floods."

———

Of course, at school Ken learned other things about Carverites. *Frogmen*, the kids called them. Alleged that they were unable to breed, that they kidnapped children and turned them into other frogmen. Then, later, when people began leaving Toronto, heading North for safety, they called the frogmen crazy for staying. But Ken could understand. Would it be worth it, turning yourself into a frogman to stay where you were born, where you grew up? He liked the waterways, the ferries, the canals and the sudden floods. But he wasn't sure he'd want to cut himself off from people, change himself permanently. "We'll *all* look like that in fifty years," his father had said during an argument with his mother about whether to leave or not. Ken wondered if people could change on their own, without surgery, grow thick skins and staring eyes, if they stayed in the water long enough.

———

Lacey dug her elbow into his ribs. She had to reach up slightly to do so. "Bet you don't get many like this up in Nunavut."

"Nunavut's rich," said Chris, accepting the passing joint.

"Yeah, rich and *boring*," Probably-Trish rolled her eyes. "I bet they have church every Sunday."

"These days, most people in Nunavut follow traditional..." Ken trailed off a little, realising it wouldn't be that interesting to them. "So," he said, taking out his fieldpad, "since I'm here, would you mind providing me with an interview for Iqaluit Online?" If they could reach the camp, he thought, he could at least file a story, remind everyone that he was still out there, and taking his duties as an Embedded seriously. And, he thought, if he did, it would also tell SIC that he was out there and on the trail. Even though, the further from Deecee he got, the harder it was to remember about SIC and their interest in the biotech.

The various group members looked at each other, then at Lee, who was returning from the SUV. Lee nodded, seemingly used to the spokesperson role. "I'll tell you what you need to know."

———

Up in Nunavut, things had been different. People were rich, happy, focused on the agrotech miracle, the Inuit cultural resurgence. Body-modification became something even weirder than in Toronto, something the local kids occasionally asked the immigrants about if they were in a mood for prurient exotica. *So, Ken, is it true there used to be people in Toronto who'd get surgery to make themselves look like frogs?* Ken would occasionally succumb to the temptation to exaggerate. *Oh yes, they swim in the canals. They'd take normal children and turn them into frogmen, 'cause they've cut off their man-parts and lady-parts and can't breed.*

*They'd eat dogs if you let them stray off the leash.* All the stupid myths his mother told him never to repeat. But he liked the brief moment of exotic glamour that being able to tell the stories gave him. It kept Steve Tulugaq and the others from bothering him for a little while, and made him, for a moment, the worldly and sophisticated one, not the ragged refugee from the dead cities of the South.

———

"How about the most basic question?" Ken fell into his journalistic patter. He thumbed the fieldpad to record. "How did the Circus of Form get started?"

"It was about five years ago," Lee said. "We met through a Carverite social group in Deecee. That is, I met Tina and Luke. Chris and the Bonsai Girls joined later. There've been others, too, we're flexible in our membership. Have to be." The androgyne smiled. "But essentially, what we all have in common is: we're performance artists, we're body-mods of one sort or another, we support Carver and the idea that humans should adapt. We have the technology to do it, and that technology is there for a reason."

"And adaptations like your own..." Ken asked, wondering if he was crossing a line. "Could you explain the utility?"

Lee's eyes and smile widened, coquettish. "Not utility in the sense that some mean it," the androgyne said. "But humans need beauty, and they need art. Our modifications are artistic, to provoke thought and discussion."

"Not all of us," said Tina suddenly.

"Not initially," Lee conceded, "but you've been putting your strength to the service of art and beauty, so it counts." Tina nodded, satisfied. "Adaption is about being fit for your environment," Lee went on, "and we fit our eco-niche perfectly. We're perfect urban humans, adapted for the artistic life of the cities."

Ken nodded. "So why are you working so far from cities, coming out to the lines to perform for the Seaboard army?" he asked.

"Public service," Lee said. "We're based in Deecee, we have a lot of military and defense contacts. If we do a show for the soldiers every so often, it boosts our profile at home."

"What's your own story?" Ken asked. "As an individual."

Lee was silent for a moment. Then the words came, smoothly. "The human gender, socially, is full of many possibilities," the androgyne said. "I was a woman, when I was born. When I was older, I lived as a boy, then as a different sort of woman, then a different sort of boy. Eventually I lived as both genders, or no gender. And my body is the physical expression of that experience." A gesture along with it. "I could have remained socially an androgyne, my body gendered, but I changed myself physically, with surgery, with hormones, with makeup, to show who I am."

"Was it difficult?" Ken asked.

"It changes your life," Lee said. "In good and bad ways. I see myself as bringing change, establishing new ideas of what is normal. Some *are* changed. I chose to *be* changed. That's how it is."

There was a brief silence.

"Have to say," Al interrupted, approaching the group with a tray of heated MREs, "this place is pretty damn quiet, for some place less than a day from a Seaboard camp."

"Really?" Lacey said, accepting half an MRE.

"Yeah," Al said. "I've been a few places, you've usually

got vehicles running up and down, the sound of exercises, you know."

"Probably can't afford it," said Chris. "War's costing a bundle and not delivering."

"You know what I think the government should do," Tina said, flexing a pythonlike bicep.

Chris snorted, his whiskers flickering. "Course we do. Tell us again, Tina."

Tina looked a little hurt. "We have visitors, Chris."

"Sorry," Chris said.

"Well, *I* think we need enhanced soldiers," Tina said, addressing herself firmly to Ken and Manders. "We need to take that step. Lord knows the Reds aren't going to do it—they don't have the technology, for a start, and they're all so damn superstitious, especially about anything to do with foetuses. So we'd have the edge."

"What'd we do with them afterwards, though?" Chris said. "They can't all join the theatre, and the Olympics has rules."

"Stupid ones," Tina said.

"Yeah, but still rules."

"They'll need to adapt anyway," Tina continued, leaving it unclear whether she meant the Olympics or humanity in general. "War or no war, with the sea levels rising and the desert expanding, we'll need people who can live with that."

"Frogmen?" Ken asked.

"Yeah, that's kind of the idea," Tina said, looking a little surprised that he knew about them, but not asking.

"Have to mess with the actual genome, to make that permanent," Chris said. He accepted a plate of food from Al.

"Maybe with the biotech, we could do that?" Tina finally turned to Ken.

"I don't know," Ken said. "I don't know if it's that sort of biotech, or anything we could use on humans."

Tina shrugged, a miniature earthquake running through her brown shoulders. A vein pulsed. "If that doesn't do it, something will have to." She turned to Ken. "I could see it. Twenty, thirty years. A human society, but made up of different kinds of humans—little ones, big ones, sea-going ones, desert ones. Like how things were, back in prehistory, with the Neanderthals and the Hobbit People and all the different subspecies of human. Now, *there's* a feature for your online news. You think someplace like that would be good to live?"

Ken was taken aback, couldn't think of anything to say.

"Huh, you think?" Chris said. "Think of why there aren't any Neanderthals or Hobbit People anymore."

"The climate changed," Tina said mildly.

"Or the *Homo sapiens sapiens* killed them all," Chris said. "Unless you can find some way of genetically removing the war habit from your new species, they'll kill each other all over again. Oh, and even if you do, what happens if they fall in love with each other? Star-crossed lovers, divided by species and by plumbing?"

"Then Lee will have some good material for one of their tragic monologues," Tina retorted.

"So what *are* things like in Deecee these days?" Al asked conversationally, distributing a couple more dishes.

Chris snorted. "Deecee's fucked."

"It's not *that* bad," said Possibly-Trish. "Civilised. You can go to a *restaurant*, get your *hair* done." She glowered a bit at the countryside, as if the lack of salons was its fault.

"Oh, yeah, it's got stores and things," Chris said, "but it's fucked. The people in Deecee, they're crazy. Chasing their tails. They're not changing, just trying to do the same things while the waters rise around them. You know, the city used to be a lot further East than it is now?" He looked around, challenging his audience. "I'd rather we were based in Albany-New-York, or out on Westcoast, maybe in Spokane or someplace." He turned his gaze pointedly towards Lee, and Ken sensed the repetition of an old argument.

"Deecee's still got the best arts scene, and they've got most of the money," Lee said flatly.

"Westcoast's rich, and Albany-New-York's changing," Chris said. "Plus you're not stuck doing soldier shows off the back of a flatbed."

"Don't knock the soldier shows," Lee said. "They pay good money, and I don't care if you can't get your favourite mascara when you're travelling out to the front lines."

"Oh yeah, just trivialise things, like always." Chris shrugged.

"All right, this is the last time we'll go this far out, I promise," Lee conceded, then turned, brightly, to Ken. "Do you know when you'll be heading back East? Because when you do, I could give you guys tickets to see our show. Our real show, in a proper theatre. Let me give you my address..."

The sky darkened, the moon rose. A few performers made excuses and headed off to their trailers. Al concluded some kind of arrangement with one of the Bonsai Girls and they both disappeared together. Ken asked Lee about the war news, and traded information for a while, making careful notes on the maps as to their location and the last known position of the front lines. Manders offered to sit first watch, till midnight. Ken went back to the SUV, got out his bedroll and rucksack. He took out the Bunny Girl motherboard, looked at it. Then, digging further, he got out the data dot, looked even harder at that.

———————

Walking back to the camp, he saw the Bunny Girl again, off in the distance, waiting. White, skinny, bony.

"What are you for?" Ken wondered. The cyborg didn't reply. "I think you're part of a system," he said. "I think whoever built you, also built the pods out at the Detroit Line, and the castles. I think it's all linked. But why?"

He thought of Tina's brave new world, the different species of humanity co-existing. A designed ecosystem. People living in castles. "Perhaps that's what you are?" he asked it. "A new system someone's designed, for survival as the climate changes. They're testing it out here to see if it works?" The mask was silent. "If so, what are you?" But the cyborg had vanished again, and Ken was alone.

———————

When Ken came back, the rest of the performers had gone off to their trailers. Manders sat on a deck chair, rifle slung casually beside him, poking at the fire with a long stick. Ken sat down opposite him, propped himself on his bedroll. Took out his fieldpad, looked at it, thinking.

Al emerged from a trailer, strolled over to the fire, and flung himself down with such theatrical satisfaction that Ken couldn't help laughing.

"Enjoy your walk on the wild side?" he asked.

Al grinned. "I am not in love," he said, "but I am open to persuasion."

"I was in love once," Manders said. The sentence was so uncharacteristic that Ken at first couldn't believe he'd heard it. Al propped himself up on his elbows. The night seemed to grow fractionally quieter, as if an unseen audience had taken its place and was waiting.

"We met when I was at school," Manders went on. "I didn't know it at the time, but I think that was when I first fell in love with... with *him*," he said, a slight glance at Ken to check his reaction. Seeing no change of expression, the old soldier continued. His voice changed, got softer, more clipped. "He was older than me, and braver, and cleverer, and better at sports. I don't think he noticed me much at the time, but later, when we were both in our twenties, we ran into each other again by chance. I'll spare you the details, but that was when we moved in together, and we were happy for a while. Well, *I* was happy, it was always hard to tell with him. But I don't think he was unhappy, at least."

Manders paused a moment. Ken held his breath. It was like the moment when a feral animal decides to trust you, come close, eat the food you hold in your hand. "He wasn't easy to love. He was easy to worship, if you like, but harder to love. He liked danger, liked skirting on the edge. Liked testing his friendships to the limit, to see who would still stick with him after he'd done the unspeakable thing. And I did. I forgave, time after time. Was it love? I suppose in a way."

Another pause. "He was the one who wanted to join the army when war broke out in South Africa."

Al broke the silence. "The civil war thirty years back, you mean? The Boer Genocide?"

Manders smiled slightly. "I was less keen, but like I said,

he loved danger, and he could be very persuasive. I've never known him not to get his way. So he went, and I went, too." Another pause. "Got himself killed not long after. Shot."

"I'm sorry," Ken said, because he felt like he should say something.

Manders nodded. "It transformed something, though. I stayed alive. Learned to fight. Changed, stopped being the weak citified old thing I'd always been. When that particular war ended, I stayed in the army. Went to Belgium, France, Spain, all the European conflicts. When that ended, I got on a boat and came here."

Ken couldn't remember hearing about any war in France, or Belgium.

When Manders continued, it was more thoughtfully. "I've met a few since. Even lived with one or two, for a while, but it never lasted. Never had that fascination for anyone else that I had for him, crazy as he was." He poked the fire for a moment.

"I have to ask, though: would my life have been better if I hadn't fallen in love with him? And I have to say: yes. It'd have been a lot less exciting, more likely. But what I couldn't see at the time was that he was a sadist. I don't mean in bed." A sudden private, prurient smile, which on Manders was as strange a sight as a flowerbed in a quarry. "I mean, he liked controlling people, letting them think they were in danger, then revealing to them that everything had been all right all along. Liked knowing how much under his control I was, that I'd follow him to the war zone. Don't let anybody tell you that love's worth any cost." He suddenly fixed Ken with his gaze. "It's not. Thanks to him I've become the Wandering Briton. The Flying Old Etonian."

Ken remembered the term *Briton*. It was an old name for what was now England, back when the island was bigger and more full of self-importance. The other term, he didn't know.

"And what I mean is"—the soldier's tone changed back to Manders' usual directness—"sometimes doing the right thing, the idealistic thing, isn't actually right at all, not when you map out everything that's going to happen. I think you know what I'm talking about, Usagi. And if not, meditate on that." With those parting words, he stood, walked out of the firelight, and Ken could hear him getting his bedroll out of the back of the SUV.

Al rolled over onto his back, looked at the sky. "Moon's full," he said. "You can see the man in the moon."

Ken looked up. "Rabbit."

"What?"

"There's a rabbit in the moon. Not just a man. See? There's his ears, and there's his back legs, and his front paws." Ken pointed them out, remembering how his grandmother had shown him, back when he was small. "Man, rabbit. Depends on how you look at it."

"Huh," Al said. "Never heard of that before. That a Nunavut thing or a Japanese thing?"

"It's a lots-of-places thing," Ken replied.

"Goodnight, Usagi," Al said. "Rabbit in the moon man."

Ken stayed awake a while, thinking about the performers, the weird outpost of metropolitan culture out here among the deserted fields. When he dreamed, he dreamed of being pursued by men, their faces modified into those of rabbits, through a field of houses like shipping containers.

The next morning the performers struck camp with surprising efficiency, breakfasting, discussing their performance for the evening, and hitching the trailers up to a diverse array of cars and small trucks. Ken watched with interest, but was grateful that no one asked him to help. The Bonsai Girls briefly practiced a tumbling routine, their size and precision making the activity surreal. Ken wondered if Manders would refer to what he had said the previous evening, but he was back to his usual conversational efficiency.

"You can stay and see the show if you like," Lee said as they drove off.

Ken nodded, hoping they could. Strange though the performers were, it had been good to have company again. Al was likewise in good spirits, singing a popular tune as he drove after the convoy. The party stopped briefly for lunch, then drove on into the afternoon.

Then the convoy halted.

"Something's wrong," Manders said after a minute. Al stopped the car, and the trio got out, went over to where Lee was standing in conference with Chris and Lacey.

"The camp's supposed to be *here*," Lee said, gesturing ahead of them. "See, there's the river, like the map says. The ground's cleared. So where's the camp?"

The ground was empty, white, flat, like a saltpan. The earth was cracked and crazed, as if in a drought. The river was visible up ahead, running slowly through algae-rich banks. But there were no people, no animals.

"How big is it supposed to be?" Ken asked, feeling stupid.

"Few hundred soldiers, plus support personnel," Lee said. "Where'd they go?"

Manders went back to the SUV, returned with two rifles, one of which he tossed at Al, who caught it automatically. "Let's go, private," he said. Ken followed, with Tina, resplendent in pink shorts, keeping pace. He reflected that, in daylight, she wasn't bad looking, once you got used to the cartoonishly large muscles.

"There." Manders pulled up, pointed. Ashes marked the rough outline of a tent or temporary building. Up ahead there was the beginnings of a bridge over the river, blackened, ending in splinters. A couple of crows, or ravens, picked at something nearby.

"The Bunny Girl," Ken said. "It has to be. The heat flare."

"Why, though?" Al asked.

"Why does it do anything? I'd like to know." Ken's foot struck something, and he pulled back, horrified, when he realised it was a shinbone. A shinbone with rags of burned tendon and muscle attached. A minute later Tina was patting his back.

"Let it out," she said. "It's normal to do that the first time you see one, yeah."

"It's not my first corpse," Ken managed.

---

The last time he'd seen frogmen was after the really bad flood. The time his parents finally managed to book passage on one of the boats out. They didn't have visas to go to Nunavut, but were hoping they'd be taken in as refugees anyway. "We're skilled labour," his father said.

"They've got enough of *that*," his mother countered. "Don't you know they've got doctors working as janitors and lawyers picking garbage up there? And what about your mother, she can't stay down here. Do you think they'll take her, too?" Up ahead, in the distance, Ken saw the Seeing Tower, rising out of the water, jutting up over the houses and high-rises and pointing, like some prophet in mid-recitation, at the sky. Closer to, a couple of ravens circled an apartment building lazily.

They passed the makeshift camp which sprawled across Queen's Park and generated daughter-colonies extending onto College Street and down University Avenue, tents and shanties for the people made homeless by the last couple of floods, around the fronts of what had once been government buildings, hospitals, university departments. "We're not in one of those yet, at least," his father said.

"Yet," his mother repeated, setting her mouth.

Ken stopped, looking hypnotised at the pile at one edge of the camp. Bodies, stacked up like a cord of wood, like building girders. Pale and bloated. Staring, open mouths showing sharp teeth, fat hands with webbing between the fingers.

"Oh, Kennie!" His mother was suddenly holding him. "Don't look, Kennie. It's so sad, those poor people. No families, no one to claim the bodies."

"Huh," his father said. "It goes to show. All those modifications supposedly to help them live in the water, and they still die same as the rest of us when the floods come in."

---

"Okay, second, or third time." Tina cracked a smile. "It does get better, though. I was in the Seaboard Army a while, till they threw me out for having too many recognizable bodmods. You get used to it." She looked up ahead, where Manders and Al were quartering the ground, then back down to the shin. "That's weird," she said, picking it up and looking at it. "Looks like something chewed it before it burned up. See those marks?"

By the riverbank, Manders was waving. Ken and Tina headed towards him. Ken noted as they passed that the buildings and vehicles closer to the river weren't burnt; it was as if the area of the blast had been somehow protected.

Manders had found someone. A soldier, in rags still recognizable as a Seaboard Expeditionary Force uniform, curled up and rocking. His face was bleeding.

"Who is he?" Ken asked.

"Don't know," Manders said.

"The bears," the soldier said. "The bears came down."

"What bears?" Ken asked him.

"The prophet Elisha, when the children made fun of him for his bald head. He called the bears down and they ate... they ate..." the soldier whimpered.

"Seriously?" Ken said.

"That is, actually, in the Bible," Al said. "Two Kings, Chapter Two. Some kids made fun of Elisha, and he called on God for revenge, and God sent two bears which ate them all, forty-two kids." Ken and Manders looked at him. "I've got a few church-struck relatives," he explained briefly and noncommittally. "And no, none of it makes much sense. But that's the Bible for you, you're not supposed to take it literally. It's all symbols."

"Bears," the soldier explained urgently.

"What the hell sort of symbols those are, I really don't know, nor do I want to," Manders said.

Al reached in gently, checked the man's tags. "Ronald Wang," he read. "Gunnery Sergeant. Blood type O, who'd'a thunk? There's a data dot, probably you could scan it and find out who the next of kin are and whether he's made any arrangements for burial."

"We can't leave him here," Manders said. He helped the soldier up, and they headed back to the trailers.

"Well, that's a complete waste of our time then," Lee frowned. "The whole camp, destroyed? Like a giant bomb? Didn't think the Reds went in for that sort of thing."

"Not sure it was the Reds," Ken began, but Manders silenced him with a look. *That's more than enough, Usagi.*

"If it is the Reds, it's a game-changer," Lee mused.

"What about the one who's still alive?" Ken thought for a minute to remember the name. "Sergeant Wang?"

"He's in Tina's trailer," Lee said. "Seeing Chris freaked him out a little. I'd've put him in with Luke, but Luke likes his privacy, and that one's still talking non-stop, about bears and some girl named Lisha."

"Elisha, the prophet," Al whispered, but only Ken heard.

"Don't worry, we'll take care of him fine till we get back East," Lee finished.

"So, we're going back to Deecee?" Chris, who had been silent, put in.

"Temporarily," Lee said. "But I think you're right. These services gigs are getting too difficult. If they've started bombing..." Lee trailed off, left the thought unspoken. When the androgyne spoke again, it was louder, more decisive. "Once we've worked out our remaining Deecee contracts, we'll go North to Albany-New-York for a while, see what the performance scene is like there." Lee smiled at Ken. "If it doesn't work out there, we could go up to Iqaluit, shake things up a little?" Ken tentatively smiled back.

"I think you could really surprise them," he said.

Chris nodded, satisfied. "What about you three? Still going to look for the magic biotech?"

Ken nodded. "Until we find it, or until we find out

where it's coming from at least. And who's making it, and why."

Chris smiled, whiskers perking strangely. "Well, good luck to you." He put out his hand, and Ken realised that he'd had the skin thickened, and the nails treated, to resemble paw-pads and claws. He tried not to feel strange about this, blocked the memory of the frogmen rising in his mind. "Hope you do find it. You could do a lot of good with something like that. Tina's a little extreme, but she's right; something's got to change, if we're going to survive."

Lee nodded, smiled slightly. "Look us up when you're back in Deecee. Or, if we're not there, go North."

Ken wondered how far North they would go. If they would, really, go to Nunavut, and if so, whether people would ask them if they kidnapped children, ate dogs. He wondered if the refugee community would be glad to see them—a reminder of a lost aesthetic past—or hate them as cousins of the frogmen. Probably things were more enlightened now. In a place the size of Iqaluit, and with people everywhere facing the changing environment, he was sure there would be Carverites there now, or at least people willing to listen to the Carverite message.

*But*, he remembered, *the frogmen drowned, too, same as the rest of us.*

———————

"If we keep on going this way," Al remarked as they drove West, "you do realise we'll wind up in what the most recent map calls disputed territory, and what the Reds call theirs."

"We'll have to go through it at some point," Ken said. "According to the latest map, there's skirmishing through the Idaho territory, almost all the way to Westcoast. Can't we just try and slip through someplace quiet, and head towards"—he looked at the map—"California? The southernmost known sighting of the biotech? Head Southwest through those mountains there."

"OK, but it's a risk," Al said.

"Any more thoughts on what you're going to do with it, once you've got it?" Manders asked as Ken settled into the back seat beside him.

Ken shook his head. "I think a lot will depend on what *it* is."

Manders slit his pale eyes. "Some of it can, at minimum, be weaponised. Those were kids back there. Maybe a thousand of them. Most of them, not even the bones survived. And you think that might have been a single cyborg? What if there were thousands?"

"I know," Ken said. And even if not, he thought again of the future Tina envisioned, gilled fish-people and glassy-eyed frogmen and desiccated desert-people and giants like Tina, and he shivered. He felt echoes of his childhood fear of the strange people, a glimpse of a future truly alien. *Could I have an operation to make me look like that, Mummy?*

We've got to adapt, he thought, remembering the horse-people and Joe Qimmirjuaq's rabbits. Is it wrong to direct the adaptation a little?

The thought frightened him in ways he didn't understand.

# CHAPTER EIGHT: THE COLONY

ABOUT NOON, Itch found the jaguar. He did this by stumbling over it and falling down, swearing.

The rest of them gathered round the body. Already it was desiccated, spotted fur stretched over feline bones, eyes sunken in, ants and a few of the ubiquitous hairless mice nosing about underneath. With his walking stick, Totchli prodded gently at the black guiding-helm that sprouted from the cat's spine and covered its head; he could see the black cilia of its infrastructure poking out from under the matted dead fur.

"One of ours," he said, unnecessarily. Coyotl gave him a what-do-you-think-I-am look. No one else would be seeding pods around the North for animals to pick up.

"Well, now we know they lasted long enough to start collating the animals," Itch continued. "Want me to do anything with it?"

Totchli squatted, felt around the guiding-helm, identified the master control centre and, with a twist, jerked it free from the rest of the system. "We'll take this along for analysis, like the scout parts, but I doubt they'll get much," he said. The guiding-helms didn't record data, but if something went wrong with the system, there might be some way of identifying it. No real way of telling how the animal died, either. He stood up, as Coyotl, with a nod, returned to the journey.

After unsuccessfully casting about in the woods for a while, attempting to follow the scout's random path back to the point where a rational purpose to its movements could be discerned, they'd picked up a trail. Poorly maintained, but visibly something humans had made within the last few months. The trail had persisted, even as the trees grew denser and the shore further. Clearly, the colonists had been expecting some form of regular traffic between their site and the seacoast.

Not long afterwards, they saw a couple of small deer wandering along, helms on their heads. A third had evidence of growth along its spine. Totchli took out his scroll and transmitted a standard Axoxoctic Biotechnical Temple recognition code, but the deer continued stumbling randomly, looking for a signal they recognised.

"Creepy," Itch said, and Totchli knew what he meant. At the best of times, he found the use of helms on wild animals unsettling. Alpacas and capybara who had been bred to it were one thing, they were really not too different to the scouts, just with the balance of technological and organic material reversed. Like scouts, they could follow a pre-programmed pattern, or they could be more finely guided through a mind-link. Wild animals, though; they'd had time to develop identities and patterns of their own, and control could be erratic and difficult. He'd never operated a mind-link with one, mainly because he never wanted to, and generally made sure to avoid the possibility of doing so.

The scout, and now the deer, were disturbing him in other ways. The ghosts of technology, still following their last programming even now that their instructions made no sense, ambling around looking for what they wanted. Unable to think for themselves with the programme gone. Even to the point of being unable to feed. Perhaps that was how, and why, the jaguar died. An image flashed through his mind: Axoxoctic deserted, in ruins, lit signs switching on and off as their batteries recharged in the sun, automated signal posts transmitting data no one could hear, controlled animals staggering around on programmed paths until they collapsed, dead of starvation.

"Keep an ear out," Coyotl said, voice low. "If there were any survivors, they won't be too far off."

But they heard nothing apart from the urgent calls of birds, and the occasional rustling of animals. Which was why they had no warning when the trail suddenly opened up and they were inside the clearing.

Totchli's spine prickled and stomach clenched, a feeling like sharp stones piercing his intestines. The field appeared to have originated as a natural clearing within the forest, but, from the newer growth around the edges, the colonists had widened it, chopping down trees and clearing brush until they had an area about the size of two handball courts. He looked at the dozen or so black, sleek boxes that formed a rough circle around it—single-storey instahouses, with another one in the slow process of flowing up from the ground, forming its substance from the rocks and soil beneath the dwelling. Other instabuilt sites: covered bins for storage, and one that might have been a shared bathhouse. Outside cookers made of shining metal; roughly in the centre of the field, someone had built a large bonfire, now charred down to a mass of black sticks. A celebratory act, Totchli wondered, or a destructive one?

At the apex of the compound stood what looked like a melted or charred building, larger than the others. It seemed oddly familiar.

*A twisted grey path, one raven leading him on, another raven behind him, moving him forward, forward into the unknown, and on either side the twisted, black, molten trees against the stark white sky...*

"Reminds me of my namequest," he remarked.

"Is that normal?" Itch asked.

"What?"

"For a namequest."

Totchli looked at him. "Don't you know?"

Itch looked awkward. "Never had one."

"Why not?"

Itch looked even more awkward. "Couldn't go into the pod," he muttered. "Took the drugs, chanted the chants, climbed in, but when the lid closed I just, well, screamed."

"So your name is—"

"—my grandfather's, actually," Itch confessed. "I didn't see a dog. My family just suggested I take on the name Itzcuintli to hide it. It happens, people in the same family seeing the same animal."

So. No wonder the kid was superstitious about death rituals. Missing an adulthood ritual was bad luck enough. Totchli found himself feeling a little bit grateful that he'd managed to have his own vision, even though he'd been a little embarrassed by the banality of its content and the irritation of being saddled with a rabbit for a totem animal.

"Any survivors?" Coyotl whispered to Totchli.

"Can't see any," Totchli whispered back. The detached, scientific part of him had started making notes again. The area was clean, and superficially looked to be in use, as if the inhabitants would reappear in a second; tools were leaned against storage blocks, a string of clothes hung between two trees, waving gently in the wind; a pair of hard rubber work boots was placed by a door. A harder look revealed the thin films of algae on the outsides of buildings, the dust on the tools and boots. The clothing was faded and starting to run to rags. The bonfire logs were wet with rain. The lack of waste—packets, food scraps, work detritus—began to look less like careful maintenance, and more like something sinister, a telling absence. Totchli wondered why the animals hadn't raided the camp.

"Fan out," the warrior said, raising her voice a little. "Search building to building. If there's anyone still there, we can get some explanations; if there isn't, well, maybe there'll be some forensics. Scrolls out, and recorders on, the Bunker will want to see it all."

By unspoken consent, Totchli went first towards the large melted-looking building. Bioconstruction wasn't his speciality, but he did have some understanding of how the process worked. He was right, he realised as he got nearer. It was a control-centre, or the botched beginning of one, ragged spires reaching up but halted, somehow, before they'd had a chance to form a full structure. He touched it gently. Cold; the growth had stopped some time ago. He peered at it closely. No, he was mistaken. The black spires were crazed with shatter-marks, there were heat scars on the insides. The control centre wasn't half-finished; it had reached its full growth, then something inside it had burned it out. Or exploded.

Totchli swallowed, moved away from the burned spires. Looking round the corner, he saw the first body. Human, partly decayed, desiccated and gnawed. His stomach rose.

A noise made him turn abruptly. He saw, behind him, a live jaguar with a guiding-helm, a dead gull in its mouth. It locked eyes with him, then, still keeping eye contact, laid the bird on the ground and nudged it towards him, with an enquiring *brrt*. Totchli was absurdly reminded of his uncle's pet cat and suppressed a surge of frightened laughter. Instead, he crouched low and reached out his hand to it, as he would to the cat.

"Hello, are you programmed to hunt?" The jaguar sniffed him, then wheeled with a movement oddly like a shrug and trotted back into the woods, apparently off to look for more prey. This probably explained the lack of scavengers in the main camp; the jaguars must have been programmed to guard the buildings, though evidently not to protect corpses. Also, Totchli reasoned, this meant that whatever it was that had killed the man, had gotten past the guard animals. Or had been within the camp to begin with... He tried to think positively about this. "Some of the biotech's still working," Totchli said aloud, looking around for the warriors. "Keep an eye out for guard and servant animals around the place."

A shout from Itch. "Got one!" the boy was yelling from inside one of the instahouses. "A live one! Coyotl, Rabbit Boy, quick!"

By the time he reached them, Coyotl was already there with him, bustling around a stick-thin, fragile, shaking figure that Totchli vaguely thought might be male, clutching one of their biotech warm-blankets from the medical kit around his shoulders.

"It's OK," Coyotl was saying. "You're safe now. We can get you back home." The man looked worried, then gradually more relieved.

"It's really over?" he said.

"It is," Coyotl reassured him. "We're warriors. Up from the Bunker, to find out what's going on, get you back home. I'm Coyotl, this is Itzicuintli, and this is Rabbit B—I mean, this is Totchli, he's not a warrior, he's a biotechnician, but he's all right really." Her tone was unusually gentle and friendly, coaxing the traumatised man as his shoulders relaxed almost imperceptibly. "What's your name?"

"Z-zolin," the thin man managed. Then, sounding a bit more human, "Call me Zo. Everybody does."

"Warrior?"

Zo shook his head. "Scientist," he said. "Biotechnichs."

"Huh, one of yours, Rabbit Boy," Coyotl said, still maintaining a friendly eye contact with the thin man.

"Are there any others?" Totchli asked. "Survivors, I mean. People in the camp."

The thin man gestured vaguely. "A few," he said. "Maybe four, five. Stayed behind when Meztli left, with his people."

"Axotl?" Coyotl asked.

Zo shook his head. "Died," he said with a small sob. "Died."

"How?"

"Meztli," Zo said. "Director of the control centre. It blew. The ones in it died, the ones nearby..."

"Went crazy," Coyotl finished. "Yeah. A small control centre went down on the border about ten years back. Sent out a signal that shorted out the minds of anything sentient for a mile. So yeah, everyone here would be dead, or crazy. Meztli's lucky he survived." Zo looked at her fearfully.

"Mice," he said, as if it explained everything. "Mice. It was the mice."

"Course it was." Coyotl said, then, turning to Itch, "Search the houses. Look for hiding places." She bent down as Itch hurried off to comply, arranged the man's blanket, looking uncharacteristically maternal. Straightened, then said to Totchli, "Well, I guess that's it, then."

"What do you mean?" Totchli said, as Itch came back, leading an equally frail-looking woman, with short, tousled hair. Out of the corner of his eye he saw a rabbit hop up to the ruins of the control centre, then a small *banf* sound as its helm detonated. Someone had started the construction cycle programme. He closed his eyes in disgust. The animal construction cycle was only used in situations where the area was dangerous for humans to enter. The animals would gather minerals, then their bodies would provide the necessary biological starting material. He shouldn't find it disgusting: the same thing went on in normal construction, just that the added starting material had been killed beforehand. But he still did, in the same way, he supposed, that city-folks might find hunting, rather than buying your meat pre-killed in the market, distasteful. *To be hypocritical is human*, he remembered one of his fellow students saying.

But Coyotl was speaking. "We've found the camp," Coyotl said. "Found the people. Taken pictures and samples. Got some idea of what happened: breakdown of order, breakdown of biotech programming. Control centre destroyed and everyone goes mental. Meztli goes off into the woods with some unspecified number of people, never heard from again. So." She began counting off, gesturing with the fingers of her hand. "We say a prayer for the dead, then assemble the survivors, control any of the animals we can get to come with us, deprogramme the animals we can't, take a few more samples from the houses and control centre, take them back to the Bunker. Let Zorrah and her team figure it out."

"Shouldn't we do something about the corpses?" Totchli asked.

Coyotl thought. "What I'd like to do," she said, "is burn them. Have a pyre. But given the state of this place, I'm thinking that Axox' is going to want to send up some kind of forensics team, figure out what happened here in more detail. In which case, they'd be pretty poison-faced if we moved the evidence, let alone burned it. So yeah, I get what you're saying, but we'd better leave them for now. They'll get their proper funeral later. Come on."

Totchli shook his head a little. "What about Meztli?"

"What *about* Meztli?" Coyotl gave him a long look. "He's probably dead, and if he isn't, I don't want to find out. At best he's in the same state as these poor kids." She gestured to the survivors, who now numbered a total of four, and were huddling together in a small group by the remains of the bonfire, with Zo still earnestly trying to explain to a bemused Itch that the mice were not what they seemed. "And at worst, well, I don't want to think. Look at those people, I can't get over it. Scientists, warriors, technicians. Not stupid or resourceless people, and they've spent a good few weeks not even trying to find out if each other was alive, just hiding in the ruins like rats from the looks of it. And if Meztli was at the centre of it all, he'll have gone the full opossum."

"But we don't know," Totchli said. Then, surprising himself, "You can go back. I want to stay on for a couple of days, see if I can find the rest of them. Or what happened to the rest of them, anyway." Want to see, he thought, if the colony failed intentionally, or by design. "I'll go due East for a day, then back to the rendezvous with whatever I find. Just send Tot back with the boat. If he's not there when I come back, I'll wait."

Coyotl looked at him, looked away, thinking. "I ever tell you how I lost the arm, Rabbit Boy?" She moved the stump.

"No," Totchli said.

The warrior looked off into middle distance. "It was actually in battle," she said, "and not peacekeeping some riot, either. It was in the last major war we had, with the Southerners. You were probably too young to remember." She was right, sort of. Totchli had been about four when the Southerners gave in and were formally absorbed into the community. He remembered a few parades and celebrations. His father had taken him to the sacrifices, bought him a straw alpaca to throw on the pyre.

But Coyotl was still talking. "I was young, and stupid, and didn't duck fast enough. They offered me a redundancy package if I wanted it, but I opted to stay on and transfer to peacekeeping. Best job decision I ever took; seems I'm a lot better at logistics and supply than I was at dodging machetes, and I like working with kids like that one there." She nodded at Itch. "Reminds me of my own son, back in Axox'. Different breed, they are. Never seen a war, they think warrioring's all about rounding up drunks, rescuing flood victims and building irrigation systems for droughts. Not about killing people, or maybe getting killed yourself. And I get to thinking myself, it's been twenty years, not just since we've seen a war, but since we've seen *any* human beings outside of our own territories. Oh, yeah, we've got classical literature, movies, all that, but has anyone ever *seen* a European? Or a Taiwanese?" Totchli shook his head, involuntarily. "Far as we know, we're the only ones on the planet now," Coyotl continued. "And it's a hell of a big planet."

Coyotl fell silent, thinking. Totchli waited, not daring to move or make a noise. Over at one of the instahouses, two hairless mice cautiously emerged with scraps of fabric in their mouths, scampered away into the undergrowth.

"You can stay, look for the others," she said, finally. "Just one day, though. The boys and I'll wait by the coast. Strike out for half a day, come back. Take a bolt-shooter and some flare bolts, send them up if you get into trouble. If we don't see you at the boat site by tomorrow evening, we'll assume you're dead." She cracked a wry smile. "So, come back soon, Rabbit Boy. Don't keep us waiting too long."

lends a mild dubiosity; never it with a tape. a bit felt to their me, re's. Remmember anyone dig to keep with. on as ets lack for th others," she said finally." at sandy?

er get fifty lay. com a barg. Tak a frke hoofe and sure bare Lot used them up if you get into trouble. If not, if you at the booster, by a furry example, we'll meature put-nothdre. blown head's smalle. So one bolt the Rubbla Boy. Don't Lop's wldte too long."

# CHAPTER NINE: WHITE BEAR

"ROADBLOCK!" Al slammed the wheel to the left, veered crazily off the road into the meadow. Ken had a brief impression of shocked pink faces, red vests, shouted invective. Behind them he heard what sounded like fireworks, then remembered they were guns. The vehicle jolted through hummocks and ditches, the field which had looked so smooth from the roadside revealing its true nature. Ken crouched, fearful of a bullet passing through the window; he could see the side mirror, could see men in pursuit. Red-vested soldiers. *Reds*.

"Forest," Al concluded desperately, as they came to the edge of the treeline. With a look at Ken, Manders flung open the door, sprang out into the woods and took up a defensive stance behind the SUV's hood, pistol somehow at the ready.

"Run, Usagi," he said.

"But—"

"Run," Manders said, drawing a bead on something, or someone, Ken couldn't see. "You too, private. Keep him safe."

Ken swallowed and ran as fast as he could, between the black trunks of the pines. Al, moving surprisingly fast for someone so plump, passed him on the inside, gun drawn. Ken followed, lungs heaving and throat burning. He remembered belatedly that he'd left the fieldpad, with all its information, back in the car. Above them flashes of grey sky, threatening rain, showed through the dark cover of the pine trees. Rocks seemed to lurch out of nowhere and strike at his ankles, tree-trunks seemed to hurl themselves into his path. Small branches whipped at his sides. He could feel his feet getting cold and wet despite the heavy waterproof boots he was wearing. A raven cawed somewhere, a harsh mocking laugh.

To his left, he saw something white moving. Large, perhaps the size of a man, but slow, shaggy, ambling on all fours. Ken, surprised, checked his speed, then instantly regretted it.

He felt a hand grab his shoulder, pull. He fell heavily into the reeking cover of pine needles beneath the trees, the breath leaving him, and he struggled to rise.

A foot came down on his chest. "Don't try anything, kid," a voice said, conversationally, almost paternally. He focused on its owner, a Red partisan, a slightly overweight White man in his fifties, smiling at him even as he leveled his rifle. *I'm going to die,* Ken thought abstractly. The Reds didn't bother with uniforms, mostly, except on formal occasions. To fight, they just wore red vests over normal work or hunting clothes, and this one, in jeans and flannel, reminded him surreally of the men, refugees from the South, who used to go fishing on weekends, back in Nunavut. *I'm going to die. This smiling, fatherly man is going to shoot me.*

But the man didn't shoot. "Name? Rank?" he barked.

"K-kenichi Usagi," Ken managed. The reality of it still wasn't sinking in. "Civilian. Embedded Journalist, Iqaluit Online News. With the Seaboard Expeditionary Force. Citizen of Nunavut." Reminded, and slightly emboldened, he said, "I claim journalistic immunity under Article 234 of the Neutral Parties Act," just like they'd told him he'd probably never have to say, during the briefings for Embedded Journalists back in Deecee. As he said it, he felt a twinge of betrayal, knowing the other two couldn't claim immunity. He hoped they'd got away.

"An act only applies so long as people are willing to respect it," the man said, but he pointed the rifle away from Ken, who suddenly remembered how to breathe again. "Get up then, Embedded Journalist, Iqaluit Online News. We'll get you to local HQ, they can decide what to do with you. I can't say I've ever heard of an Embedded this far out." He marched Ken back through the woods, out to where the SUV stood.

As they approached, Ken saw Al Benjamin standing at the edge of the woods, hands on his head, a mutinous expression on his adolescent face. Ken's gut sank. Nearby, another Red was frisking Manders, none too gently, a small pile of hardware accumulating next to him. "Hey, Loot' Rennert," his captor said, marching him over. "This one's an Embedded Journalist."

"Really?" The apparent ranking officer—he had some sort of pin the other Reds didn't have affixed to his vest—frowned at Ken. "Can you prove it?"

Ken moved his hands slowly downwards towards his chest, keeping his eyes on the officer's. He reached in, pulled out his press pass. Rennert glanced at it, snorted. "I don't think I've ever seen one of those before," he said.

"He's claiming journalistic immunity under the Neutral Parties Act," Ken's Red said, straight-faced.

"Is he, now?" the officer said. "Maybe I'm claiming he's a spy, and not liable to international treaty protection." Ken swallowed. It was a bit too close to the truth, in a way; certainly, looking for biotech in Red-claimed territories probably constituted some form of hostile action. If they asked him questions... well, they wouldn't believe the truth, but... then there was the information on the fieldpad...

"I'm fucking with you, journo," Rennert said, smiling a little nastily. Ken remembered Steve Tulugaq and the other bullies at school. "Names?"

"Kenichi Usagi," Ken repeated.

"Henry Manders. Captain," Manders said bluntly. He had a black eye, but Ken noticed that many of the Reds also had visible injuries. He wouldn't have wanted to have been the one assigned to take down the old soldier.

"Albert Mumbuto, Private First Class," Al said. Manders gave him a look but said nothing. The Reds apparently didn't challenge it.

Ken's internal journalist had taken over, was making dispassionate notes. The entire unit were White, and there were no women. There were stories, which Ken had mostly flagged up as rumours, that the Reds wouldn't let women into front-line positions, or, according to some accounts, even into the army. Other stories that they wouldn't let women do any sort of paid jobs at all, just kept them in the houses and made them wear veils when they came out, so as not to strike men down with lust... they couldn't *all* be true. Ken thought of all the ridiculous things people said about refugees in Nunavut, or Northerners in Deecee. *I suppose,* Ken thought wryly, *I'm going to get the chance to find out how much of it's true, if I survive this.*

"Better off getting them to HQ where we can find out who and what they are. Two Seabees and an Embedded in an SUV driving through the war zone, no unit around? Don't add up."

"Maybe there *is* a Seabee unit..." one of the other men suggested. "They could be an advance party, scouts? Or maybe they lost their way."

The officer furrowed his brow. Ken realised suddenly that Rennert was young. Perhaps younger than him, even. His dark-red hair and snub nose, under the peaked hat, added to the general sense of eerie boyishness.

He appeared to reach a decision. "Two of you, take that Seabee heap and drive it to HQ. I claim it officially in the name of the government of the United States of America."

"You can't do that," Manders said suddenly. "This is technically disputed territory."

"It's US territory if there's US soldiers there. And there's five good men dead because of *you*, you Seabee tree-rat—" Rennert looked for a moment as if he was going to hit Manders. Ken held his breath, but nothing happened. After a moment, the two Red soldiers nodded and climbed into the SUV—a little dented and scratched from its encounter with the treeline—started it on the second attempt and drove off.

Ken felt a short, sharp pang. They would take the SUV, and everything in it. Their clothes, Ken's fieldpad, the pieces of Bunny Girl, Patel's data. He hadn't felt that attached to any of it before, but the sudden prospect of losing it made him strangely sad. He'd noticed the Seaboard soldiers had a general fondness for tattoos. *I suppose it's one thing you can't lose, even if you wanted to,* Ken thought.

"Bayer, Woolf, and I'll take them to the HQ," Rennert said. A large, bald-headed Red soldier, with a florid and bulgy face that suggested a history of alcohol or possibly rosacea, and a skinny pale teenager with a gigantic nose, gripping a rifle like he was afraid it would turn into a snake, both nodded and moved closer. "The rest of you, fan out and run a search to make sure these are the only ones. I'll text the change of plans to the captain." He took out a small black fieldpad, typed rapidly on it with his thumbs for a minute, looked at the screen, frowned, then pocketed it. "Go on."

Ken's captor gave him a paternal wink. "I'm sure it'll be OK for you, kid, if you're really a journo and all," he said, then joined the rest of the patrol. Ken looked back helplessly. The Red soldiers all avoided his eyes, as if they were afraid of acknowledging their common humanity, that what happened to Ken might, someday, happen to them in turn.

"Move," the Red named Bayer ordered, gesturing with his pistol. Ken took his place behind Al and Manders, walking forward through the meadows, back towards the roadblock.

---

"What happens now?" Ken whispered to Al. He was still trying to get his head around the situation. They'd briefed him on the possibility that this might happen, of course, but the reality was hard to grasp. *They hadn't handcuffed us,* he thought, and then scolded himself for his stupidity. Why should they? They were unarmed, and even Manders would find it hard to escape, running across unfamiliar territory.

"In theory," Al said, "they take us to their headquarters, question us, then ship us off to a camp somewhere near Salt

Lake City until the Seaboard government pays the ransom, or does a prisoner exchange, or something like that."

"In practice?"

Al lowered his voice. "I'm Black, you're a journo, and the captain just killed five of them single-handed. If I was them, I'd make sure we got shot trying to escape."

Ken breathed. The air was cool and smelled of pine. It made him think of camping trips, of shops around Christmastime.

"Aw, don't worry, Usagi, it'll be OK," Al said. "That's a worst-case scenario, and you know they never happen."

"Either way, though, no more biotech," Ken said.

"You win some, you lose some," Al said neutrally.

"That's enough talking," Bayer said.

Ken realised that they were almost back at the main road, heading in the same direction the SUV had been taking when they hit the unexpected roadblock. He reflected that if they'd gone on driving, they'd probably have found the Red headquarters before long. *Either way, we were clearly due some bad luck.*

"That's strange." Rennert hesitated as they approached the roadblock. The post was deserted, the yellow-and-black striped poles knocked aside. Glancing at his officer for permission, Woolf approached it, poked around the margins and ditches. Silently he held up the torn remains of a Red vest, then a peaked cap soaked black with blood.

"Know anything about this?" Bayer asked Manders, who shrugged.

"Not my doing," the old soldier replied, harshly. "How could it be? I was too busy holding off your lot."

"Maybe you've got some friends." Bayer was threatening.

"Friends that attack roadblock gangs without making a

noise?" Woolf rejoined them, a slightly sceptical look on his face. Bayer looked like he was trying to figure out if the youth had been insubordinate or not.

Rennert called out, listened. Nothing.

"Maybe they got away from whatever it was, joined the patrol?" Woolf asked. Rennert shook his head.

"We'll find out more on the way," he said, moving them out along the side of the road.

At least, Ken reflected, the road was paved, and the walking was easier.

A little further on, they found the bodies of the Reds from the roadblock. One lay nearly torn in half, sightless eyes staring upwards. Ken noticed, in the way that one does at times like this, that he needed a shave. The other one was represented only by a forearm and a leg, jeans and boot still attached.

"Something's chewed that," Woolf said, pointing to the leg. He sounded frightened.

Ken remembered the shinbone up at the Seaboard camp. *Tina was right*, he thought, *it does get easier*.

"Scavengers could have done it," said Bayer.

"That soon after?" Woolf shook his head. "I ain't been hunting as long as you have, Ray, but that's a fresh kill."

Rennert was texting again, thumbs flashing over the fieldpad. "Well, at least we know it wasn't Seaboarders, unless they've somehow raised a zombie army," he said, pocketing the device. "You three"—he gestured at Ken, Manders and Al—"pull them off the road. Make them as presentable as you can."

Ken tried not to gag as they did as they were ordered,

pulling the body parts onto the side of the road, closing the eyes, waving away the flies that were beginning to cluster. He stood hating himself and the Reds as Rennert said a few incongruously pious words over the scene, then they walked on again.

---

Some time later, the clouds thicker and the smell of rain heavier in the air, they found the SUV. By now, the fields had given way to sparse forest, with denser forests further up the hills. The vehicle was deserted, the windows smashed, lying half in the ditch beside the road. There was no sign of the Reds who had driven it.

The party halted. Rennert went up to it and had a look while the others stood guard.

"What did that?" Ken asked, feeling even worse.

"Same thing that got those two men back at the road-block, clearly," Manders said, his pale eyes narrow. *Usagi, don't be a complete fool.*

"I know that," Ken said. "But what is it?"

"Some kind of animal, maybe," Al said, more calmly than Ken felt. "Could be a bear?"

Ken remembered Sergeant Wang, his story about Elisha and the bears.

"No," Woolf said. Ken looked at him in surprise, but the young man's desire to show his knowledge had apparently got the better of his reticence. "I'm from round here, up by the Westcoast border. We got a lot of black bears up there. And there's no way one of those guys could do that. Even if they wanted to, and they don't usually want to. They only attack if they feel threatened, and they only feel threatened if, you know, you walk into their territory, or if it's a female with cubs, or if it's wounded, or—" He realised he was running on, stopped and looked a little embarrassed. "Anyway, no bears. Can't think of *anything* that could do that much damage."

"Several bears?" Al asked.

"They're solitary, too," Woolf said. "Looks like an animal, but can't be."

Ken suddenly recalled the word *Wendigo*, after a minute remembered, too, what it meant. A spirit, a great invisible animal that tore away everything in its path with huge rending claws and teeth, eating people after tearing them apart. The teachers in Native Cultures class had told them about it. Even though it wasn't an Inuit monster, but a Southern one, for weeks afterwards the Inuit kids lorded it over the Southerners by talking about the monster the way kids had talked about the frogmen back in Toronto: *Watch out or the Wendigo will get you.* Ken even remembered a horror movie, seen too young on television one night and fueling nightmares for weeks until his father learned the cause and bought him a book on special effects. *See? Not real, just computers and puppets. Not real* was what the teacher said, too, with barely suppressed ridicule, when someone—probably a Southerner—asked if the Wendigo really did eat the unwary.

The grown-up Ken was beginning to have his doubts.

"Or could be some new Seaboard weapon?" Bayer asked, glaring at his prisoners. "Maybe you're out here testing it on our guys?"

Ken was shocked back to reality. *Of course*, he thought. *Not ghosts and spirits. Biotech. Just good old unfamiliar biotech.*

Rennert re-emerged. The fieldpad came out, he texted briefly, looked at the screen.

"Any new orders, sir?" Woolf asked.

Rennert seemed distracted. "No... just stick with the plan. Back to HQ."

Ken wondered if he should say something. If it was biotech, it could be some new manifestation of the Bunny Girl, but then, it didn't look like anything one of them had ever done before; they went in for explosions and light flares, burning, not tearing, and having fought one close up —albeit a weakened and weaponless one—he didn't see how its arms and legs could cause that sort of damage. *Great*, he thought. *Something new, and it looks like it's out to kill us.*

———

Then it crashed, roaring, out of the woods. *It* is *a bear*, Ken thought, and then saw what it had on its head, neck and shoulders. Black plastic, like the foxes and coyotes at the Detroit Line, but bigger and corrugated or faceted, like a fly's eyes. Part of his brain took dispassionate notes, while other parts folded up screaming.

Something cannoned into him, breaking his reverie. "Fucking *move!*" shouted Manders in his ear, pushing him along. Ken ran, following Manders, aware that the Reds were also running with them, prisoner and escort roles temporarily forgotten, through the sparse pine trees and scrub bushes, into a suddenly exposed clearing. Ken saw boards, bricks, the rusting shell of a pickup truck, realised there'd been a house there once.

"In there," Manders panted, gesturing to what looked like an abandoned garage or shed, overgrown with weeds, set back from the ruins of the house. The rest of them pushed past the door, into the dark space.

"Help me wedge it shut," Manders said, and they fell to,

pushing pieces of wood, broken furniture, rusty metal, anything they could find, against the door.

Outside, Ken could hear the bear moaning, battering against the door. He gritted his teeth, pushed his nails into the palms of his hands, thought hard about something nice... *waking up in a hotel back East, all expenses paid, croissants and coffee at the door, morning sunlight streaming in through immaculate white curtains...* until the animal gave up the fight and wandered off.

"Name of Jesus," he heard Woolf whimper.

"Don't blaspheme, soldier," he heard Rennert reply sternly.

A light flickered; an LED torch beam shone. "Everyone OK?" Al asked from behind it.

"What the hell was that thing?" Rennert asked. Ken could see his face, reddened and sweating, eyes frightened in the torchlight.

"Usagi, that device on its head. That was like the pods up around Detroit, wasn't it?" Manders said.

"Yeah," Ken replied. "Different, though. Biggest thing those pods ever got was a deer, and even when they got a predatory animal, it didn't attack people. Just did building work."

"What about the ones who ran into groups and detonated?"

"They were confused," Ken said. "That bear wasn't confused, it was angry. And I don't think it was trying to detonate, either. It seemed to be out to fight, not to find a castle."

"Could it be a mistake?" Al suggested. "You know. Like the animals detonating in the wrong place. Some of the pods infecting the wrong sort of animal."

"Could be," Ken said. "It's plausible. Making them crazy, attacking people."

"So this *is* some kind of Seaboard weapon?" Rennert came in again.

Ken met Manders' eyes. A moment of agreement. *OK, Usagi, but be careful.* To Rennert, all Ken said was, "No, not Seaboard. Things like it have been attacking Seaboard troops, too."

"Elisha and the bears." Al nodded. "Reckon one of those might have done that camp up near the Prairies?"

"Makes sense," Ken said. He felt almost relaxed, despite their predicament. Bears with pods, however threatening, were something more familiar than being taken prisoner, or monsters from Native Studies class. "Or more than one."

"If they explode like the foxes, too, it could explain the bomb damage," Al went on speculatively.

Ken shook his head. "My money's still on the Bunny Girl for that. We did see one not too far away from the site, after all. And if this is biotech gone rogue, it wouldn't make sense, them detonating there. Nothing tall or warm to attract them."

"The camp?" Al suggested.

Ken thought. "Possible. Add it to the list of hypotheses." He thought how strange it was, discussing the bears scientifically while they huddled in a damp, mouldy shack waiting to be sure the way was clear.

"You *know* about this stuff." Rennert leaned forward, slit his green eyes. Ken was suddenly shocked back into remembering his previous predicament. "You know what they are, what they do."

"Not really," Ken said, but Rennert had collected his wits.

"Is that why you're out here? It is, isn't it? You're a scouting party, looking for these."

"I wouldn't say we were looking for *these*—" Ken began, but Rennert cut him off.

"Right, just remember, you're my prisoners, and you're going to have some very interesting stories to tell them at HQ."

"If there *is* still a HQ, have you thought of that?" Manders said, looking away from Ken, then turning his narrowed pale eyes onto Rennert. "Had any texts from them recently? If we're right, just one of those bear things might have wiped out a camp of close to a thousand Seaboarders, so taking out a little Red HQ unit would be nothing to them."

Rennert hesitated, then set his mouth. "We're going anyway."

"Sure that's a good idea, sir?" Woolf wondered desperately.

"Got any better ones?" Rennert glared at Woolf, and the thin man quietened. "At least there's shelter there, and other men, with guns. Enough to seriously worry those bear things. We can make a stand, and you"—rounding on Ken—"can tell us what you know about this."

They headed back towards the road, cautiously, but more boldly as nothing came roaring out of the woods.

"Reckon we beat it?" Bayer asked Rennert, who shrugged.

Ken shivered. The sky was darker now, slate-coloured overhead, and there was a smell of rain and damp pine needles; the countryside was green and black under the trees. He kept seeing movement in the shadows. Again he thought he saw something white between the trees, stumbled.

"I don't know," Woolf said quietly. "Like I said, bears attack when they feel threatened. If that thing on its head is telling it we're a threat, then I don't see it giving up any time soon. I think it's gone to regroup."

"Whose side are you on, Greg?" Bayer complained.

"I'm on the side of not getting murdered, Ray," Woolf countered.

And then, inevitably, they came roaring out again.

———

There were three of them this time, Ken realised with the calm, abstract part of his brain. Two bears and some sort of large cat, a mountain lion, he supposed. Bayer screamed, high, a surprisingly feminine sound. Ken saw red, saw the man fall, eyes squeezed shut as if he was about to cry. Beside him Woolf stood momentarily hypnotised. Without thinking, Ken pushed the young man out of reach just as a clawed forepaw slashed down, but didn't stop to make sure he was all right. The youth blasphemed again, but nobody told him off this time. Ken ran as hard as he could, hearing other footsteps behind him and alongside.

He collapsed beside a small cliff-face, gasping. The others joined him. *Better to be eaten by bears than nibbled away by rabbits*, Ken thought hysterically, and began to laugh. Manders glared at him and he got himself back under control.

"Can't—keep—doing this—sir," Al panted.

"Working in groups." Manders turned to Ken. "That's different, isn't it?"

"Very," Ken said.

"Look, will you just tell me what the hell is going on?" Rennert looked at Ken with terrified eyes. "I got off a round just now, it only made the thing madder. What the hell are they?"

Ken looked around, made a decision. "Okay. We've seen something like these further North," he said. "They were part of a construction system—no, it'd take too long to explain. It wasn't bears there, it was coyotes, foxes, small animals. They were drawn to clusters of large objects. Trees, rocks, that sort of thing, and when they got there, they'd explode, and that would trigger a biotech cycle that would grow a building out of locally available materials. Now, the headpieces on the bears are a little different, and we've never seen anything larger than a deer, but this is a different environment. I think it's gone rogue. Latched on to the wrong kind of animal, screwed up the cycle, made it attack people." He thought of the pod-animals detonating under vehicles and in groups of people, heading for things of the right temperature and/or size. Clearly the biotech wasn't above being fooled. "But if it's the same pods, it's going to follow the same cycle."

"So you think if we lure them in to..." Rennert appeared to come to his own decision, nodded. "...we could trigger the mechanism? Make them explode?"

"It's your territory," Ken said. "Clearly the trees here are too low to trigger them, or they'd've done it. Is there some place with a stand of trees, or something like that, which is much higher? We'd be safe there."

Rennert considered. "Yeah. About a quarter-mile from here, deeper into the pine forest, some of them get pretty big. We'll head for that."

He came to a further decision. He took two of the guns

he'd confiscated from Manders, handed one to Manders and the other to Al. "Best we don't lose any more men," he said.

Woolf shouldered his rifle, grinned. He stepped forward to walk beside Ken. He seemed more than a little relieved not to be a guard anymore, just one of a group of human beings, trying to survive.

---

"This it?" Al asked.

"This is it," Rennert confirmed. Up ahead there was another clearing, then a forested area where the trees were tall, broad, much larger than anything Ken had ever seen before. It was like being in the prehistoric world, he thought, imagining dinosaurs stalking through the trees, lean and quick, their footsteps like rhythmic peals of thunder.

"Quick, down," Ken said. He saw one of the pod-wearing bears heading towards the forest.

"Heading for the taller woods, like you said." Rennert sounded almost triumphant in his relief.

"Look, sir." Woolf pointed. Three small coyotes, backs covered by pods, trotted alongside the bear and ahead.

"What's it mean?" Ken wondered. He heard wet explosions from inside the forest, winced. So, the small-animals system applied out here, too. In that case, what were the bears for? They couldn't be rogue biotech, after all.

"Look at that one." Al pointed again. A bear, but smaller than the others and white, the dark pod material in stark contrast to the creamy fur, ambled quietly towards the woods. "Ken, is it a polar bear?"

Ken shook his head. "There aren't any outside of zoos,

and anyhow, they're a lot bigger, and have smaller heads than that," he said. "This one looks like a black bear, but, uh, white. Could be an albino?"

"Kermode bear," Woolf said.

"What?"

"Kermode bear," he repeated. "They're supposed to be spirits or something—at least, that's what the locals used to say." He crouched up cautiously. "Like I told you, I grew up around here. The old folks talked about them, but no one ever saw one." Woolf looked a little bit enchanted at the sight of the bear, like Manders with the castle up on the Detroit Front. "They thought they were extinct. Seeing one's good luck."

Rennert nodded. "After it," he said.

The five men inched after the bear, into the forest.

"Well," Manders said after a moment, "that's *your* theory conclusively blown, Usagi."

---

The trees in the middle of the forest had been flattened, burnt away. In their place stood the biggest biotech castle they had ever seen; huge, black, glittering, almost taller than the highest trees, rising to a twisted point. It seemed to shimmer, to move in the dim light.

"Reckon that castle's grown up," Al said. "What we saw before, they were just little ones, babies."

Around it, bears, cats and a few large, antlered deer wandered.

"They're patrolling!" Rennert said, and Ken realised it was true. The animals were walking regular beats. Others were walking out to the forest, running wider patrols.

"A defense system," Ken said. "They're here to guard the castle." He thought. "Means the bears aren't rogue." He indicated the patrolling animals. "They're doing what they're supposed to."

"So who's controlling this?" Rennert asked. He checked his fieldpad again, frowned.

But Ken wasn't finished putting things together. "I think I know how the Bunny Girls fit in, now," Ken went on. "Those things dangling from its arms, like grenades. Maybe they're not grenades, they're pods. Maybe, when it detonates, it seeds the ground. Explains what happened at the camp." Ken remembered the blasted circle, the sole survivor. "The Bunny Girl clears the ground. Give it a day or two, there'll be coyotes and ground squirrels bringing raw materials, and a few days after that, a castle will grow. Then the bears activate, defend the place."

"What about that sergeant, Wang?" Al wondered. "Said he saw bears. And you said you and Tina found chewed bones."

Ken shrugged. "My guess is, colonisation is sequential?" he hazarded. "Once a system's established, it sends out a new colonising force. Bears *and* Bunny Girls, to back each other up."

Al shrugged. "I suppose that'd make sense."

They watched the castle, the patrolling animals, for a few minutes.

"Right," Rennert said, with a new confidence. "I'm claiming this thing for the United States."

"Are you nuts?" Al said. "This thing's bigger than the Reds or the Seaboarders. Do you really think you can just walk in and take it over?"

"Why not?" Rennert said. "We can figure out how it

works, especially since we've got an expert here. I've texted HQ about it, they should be sending someone after us."

"Heard anything back?" Manders asked, again.

"None of your business," Rennert retorted.

"See," Manders said, "as I said earlier, I don't think there *is* a HQ. Not anymore. These bear attacks, I've got the impression they haven't been going on very long?"

"Couple of guys disappeared a few days ago," Woolf confessed, ignoring Rennert's sharp look. "One of the scouts said they saw a big, strange animal. We thought he was drunk or high, from the description. So yeah, putting it together, maybe four, five days. But I have to say, we've seen nothing like this."

"And you're also not hiding very well the fact that you haven't had any replies to your texts to HQ," Manders continued to Rennert. "I've got a hypothesis of my own, Usagi. I don't think the bears are just defense, I think they're offense as well. I think they've been going on raids. Clearing the territory," Manders finished. "Getting rid of the opposition."

"In that case," Rennert said, "we have a duty to engage it."

"Seriously?" Woolf turned to him.

"You nuts?" Al cut in at almost exactly the same time.

"No," Rennert said. "It's a hostile force, attacking our men. With HQ out, it could take days before a rescue party comes. In the meantime, we need to take this thing on, secure the area."

"Secure the area with *what*, exactly?" Manders looked sceptical. "In the first place, as prisoners of war, you can't exactly compel Al and myself to fight alongside you, and secondly, do you really think four men with pistols and rifles can fight off a couple of dozen bears?"

"We could arm Usagi," Al suggested.

"Don't be a fucking idiot, private," Manders said. "The odds of him being able to hit that castle at ten paces are pretty long. No offense, Usagi."

"None taken," Ken said, feeling near-hysterical laughter welling up. He wondered if the castle-builders were exercising their right to arm bears. The thought brought the laughter out. Al and Woolf gave him peculiar looks, moved away from him.

Rennert, who had been sunk in thought, brightened. "We could set fire to the trees," he said. "Smoke them out."

"That's crazy," Al said, frowning. "No way that could work."

"Might do," Woolf put in. "See, a lot of the trees around there are pines, and the dead ones catch fire real fast. Be a distraction for them."

"And what about the castle?" Al looked at the building. "Seriously, look at that thing. I don't trust it. What if it's got other defenses?"

"I think it's moving," Manders added.

"Look." Al pointed. Ken saw the front of it part like a curtain, the thick plastic opening up an entrance to the building.

"It wants us to go in," Manders said wonderingly.

"That's disgusting," Al said with a strange weak tone, as if he was going to faint.

Rennert found a dry pine branch, dug around in his pockets, held his lighter to it. "Right," he said, brandishing it, "everyone who's not with me, into the castle."

"You crazy?" Al looked around desperately. "Not going into that thing, it might eat me."

"*You're going*," Rennert growled. Ken was shocked at

the vitriol in Rennert's voice. He looked at Al, fully expecting him to lash out at the Red officer. Al, though, was backing up, hands in front of him, with exaggerated fear as he moved towards the castle. "You, Woolf, you're with me."

"Do as he says." Manders also sounded frightened. *What the hell?* Ken thought. He would never, after their travels together, have believed that the two soldiers would have been afraid of the castle, or of Rennert. What did they know that he didn't? Feeling afraid, too, he joined them at the castle.

Looking up at the entrance, Ken saw the smooth opening giving way to a small room, with no other entrances or exits. *Like a Venus flytrap*, he thought. Swallowing down his revulsion, he crept into the smooth black vestibule, watched as Rennert and Woolf set fire to dead trees and pine needles.

The animals scented the smoke. A deer stamped, blew. Others turned, made little running darts back and forth.

"It's working, sir," Woolf called. "They're scared, I think they're going to break." A few of the animals turned and ran. The smoke got thicker. A tree caught, then another.

Ken could feel the air on his face, from the forest, burning with heat. Inside the castle, though, the air was warm, pleasant, slightly plastic-scented like the inside of a new car, or a hotel room. *Maybe Manders and Al weren't so stupid after all*, he thought.

Then, as they watched, a small phalanx of bears emerged from the burning forest. A few had sparking or burning patches on their coats. They stood for a moment as if awaiting orders, then, as one, turned and surged onto Rennert. There was a scream, a snap, and the Red officer vanished under a tide of fur and claws.

Woolf looked around, panicked, flung himself into the castle. He crouched there, panting.

Al began to laugh triumphantly. "Born and bred in a briar patch, Bre'r Fox!" the youth shouted in the direction of Rennert's corpse. "Born and bred in a briar patch!"

Manders smiled wickedly. "Born and bred in a briar patch, indeed, Bre'r Rabbit."

Ken realised. "You mean... you were setting Rennert up?"

Al nodded, smugly. "Reverse psychology," he said. "Plus, the not-too-unreasonable hypothesis that the bears weren't going to let anything happen to the castle. Or anyone *in* the castle."

Woolf shook his head. "Phew."

Ken could hear the wet crunching sounds from the location of what used to be Rennert. He swallowed, but reflected that it was, indeed, getting easier all the time, and wondered what that made him.

———————

The four men watched from their position of safety as the forest fire raged. They retreated further back as the air outside got hotter and hotter, and yet, the atmosphere inside the castle did not change, stayed the same pleasant warmth.

"It's protection," Ken remarked. "Some kind of dwelling or workplace, built to provide shelter for, well, whoever it's for, whatever the conditions."

"I'm just amazed the general managed to blow one up," Al said, conversationally, as if they sat inside a black plastic fairy-tale castle, watching a forest burn, every day of the week.

"That was a newer and smaller one," Ken pointed out.

"Maybe it wasn't fully developed yet. Certainly, it didn't have a defense system."

"Even so, I bet she used up her year's allocation of blasting material on that thing," Al remarked.

———————

As the flames died down and the day turned into night, the atmosphere cooled outside. The other animals began slowly to return, and incredibly, as Ken watched, began putting out the last of the fires, knocking down the burning trees, rolling them over with no apparent sense of fear. He suppressed a laugh as a wolf or feral dog incongruously wandered over to a burning twig and urinated on it.

"I think it's safe to move now," he said.

"Question is," Manders said, "how are we going to get out past all those damn bears?"

Ken looked up, pointed. "Over there."

In front of them, just on their side of what was left of Rennert, the white bear stood still. It made eye contact with him, peering out from under its headpiece. It turned, walked away a few paces, stopped, looked back.

"Follow it?" Manders was skeptical.

"No stranger than anything else," Ken said. He started after the white bear, and the others followed. Behind them, the entrance to the castle sealed shut. Ken glanced back, saw the shape of the castle slowly rippling, as if it was gradually changing form.

None of the other animals looked at them as they passed.

———————

At the edge of the now-extinguished forest fire, the white bear seemed to lose interest in them, and wandered back into the woods. Ken breathed a little easier, and the others seemed to relax as well.

"Look at that," Woolf said. He indicated a rough area, denuded of vegetation, about ten feet wide. The bare earth was raked thoroughly, as if by large claws.

"The animals," Al said. "They made a firebreak."

"How'd they know how to do that?" Woolf asked, then smiled. "I know, something's controlling them."

"They've probably got certain defense routines programmed in," Ken said. "With any luck, we'll find out how it works eventually."

"So, what do we do now?" Woolf asked.

"We," Manders said with careful emphasis, "go Southwest." Casually, as if blowing his nose or scratching an itch, he raised his gun and fired. The thin youth dropped.

Ken stared at the corpse, the neat hole above the peaked nose, the wide green eyes in the white face, the lips slightly parted as if in surprise.

"We couldn't take him with us," Al said, putting a hand on Ken's shoulder, as Manders dispassionately searched the body, confiscating any weapons, ammunition and useful small tools. "And we couldn't leave him to tell the Reds what he knew. Or get eaten by any surviving bears."

Ken said nothing. He knew Al was right, and Manders was right, but he couldn't accept it.

"Come on, let's see if we've still got a vehicle," Manders said.

The SUV was where they had left it, leaning into the ditch by the side of the road. A light rain had blown in through the broken windshield and left the seats damp.

Al climbed in, attempted to start it a couple of times, then climbed out, raised the hood. "Fuel line," he said a minute later. "Chewed through for some reason. Don't know why, they can't know how it works. Maybe they just liked the taste." He examined the machine critically. "Plus, both front tires are flat. We've got one spare, but not two. I don't think we can use it, sir."

"We'll just have to walk, then," Manders said wearily. "Probably for the best, actually—engines attract Reds, and around here they'll also attract bears. They left us alone for a while, but I don't know how long the protection of the castle, as it were, is going to last. Are the rucksacks still in the back?"

They were, along with most of the remaining food and medical supplies. The Reds had appropriated some of the medicines and tools, and none of them thought it worth searching the woods for them. The bags were mostly unrifled. Manders' fieldpad had a broken screen and flashed feebly when he tried to switch it on, but Ken's had apparently survived intact apart from a couple of dents in the casing. The Bunny Girl chips had disappeared—probably, Ken thought, fell out of the rucksack when the bears attacked the SUV, as he couldn't imagine why the Reds would want to steal them—but the motherboard was still present.

They spent a few minutes dividing up what they could still carry, and figuring out which way was Southwest.

"How long do you reckon it'll take us now, sir?" Al asked pointedly. Manders didn't bother replying, but looked at Ken.

"Reckon you're OK carrying that, Usagi?" Manders said, almost kindly.

Ken nodded.

They walked for a few minutes in silence.

"We do these things, so you don't have to." Manders' tone was neutral, gentle, but unapologetic.

Ken nodded, but still couldn't meet his eyes.

# CHAPTER TEN: COMMAND AND CONTROL

TOTCHLI SPENT a couple of hours examining the remains of the control centre and looking for the guiding-helm apparatus. Eventually he found the control box; the connections appeared to have been gnawed through by some kind of animal, but he patched it together, linked it briefly in synergy with his mind, and spent a few minutes wandering through the patchy system until he figured out how to return the pods to dormancy and to switch off the detonation cycle in the smaller animals, the obedience controls in the larger ones. Any animal with the helms was likely doomed to a shorter life than normal out in the wild, he reflected sadly, but at least they could return to some semblance of a normal existence. The technology had been developed by the warriors, to obviate the need for carrying supplies and bringing domestic animals, allowing for quick and stealthy takeovers of territory, but there hadn't been nearly enough refinement on the technology since. Totchli reflected that if they were going to make a large-scale go of colonisation, it would be a good idea to find something less invasive.

He turned off the box, shook his head to clear it. Realised he was face-to-face with the jaguar he saw earlier. It looked at him, clear-eyed and uninterested, then turned and wandered into the forest, shaking its ears. Totchli felt a little sad to see it go. Hoped, irrationally, that it would be all right.

Having seen to the animals, he went through his baggage, separating out only what was necessary for a few hours' journey and leaving the rest in one of the insta-houses. His plan was to strike out for a few hours, come back, overnight in the colony site, conduct another foray next morning if necessary, and then return to the meeting point the next day as promised. The thought of sleeping in the colony site was disturbing, and he certainly wasn't antic-ipating an easy rest, but it made the most sense from a secu-rity point of view.

He spent some time pondering the small bolt-shooter that Coyotl had insisted he take. He wasn't keen on carrying it. He wasn't exactly trained in weapons use, and could foresee too many accidents happening. But he decided to take it anyway, as it might be useful against hostile wildlife. Shouldering his small pack, he set off in what the survivors had indicated was the direction the breakaway group had taken. There seemed to be a rough path through the forest, machete cuts against trees, suggesting that people had been this way fairly recently, albeit not often.

Almost unexpected, a second control centre loomed out of the forest at him; the size of a small temple, this one was pyramid-shaped. Black and shining, instabuilt fairly recently. He could see it over the trees, in the distance. Far enough from the compound that the trees had hidden it until now, but close enough to reach easily from there.

Totchli stopped in his tracks, looked up at it. Felt a sense of foreboding. He checked the plans and reports on his scroll; the camp was only supposed to have a single control centre, the destroyed one at the apex of the compound. So what was this one doing here?

The problem with control centres, the dry, disinterested part of himself was lecturing away uncontrollably, was that they needed people to work properly. At least one person, linked temporarily with the structure as a director-mind. Without one, they lapsed into dormancy, then ultimately decayed. So, if there was a full-sized control centre out here... who was running it? Was *anybody* running it? If they weren't, what was it doing?

Another piece of information from his biotech lectures. An untenanted or dormant control centre would emit a faint pheromonal signal, trying to attract a suitable person to go inside and run it. Totchli holstered his scroll, looked critically at the centre. Was it doing that to him? Or—had it done that to the others?

It was unlikely to be the first option; he was a qualified scout operator and could run a mindlink competently enough, but he had never been identified as having any particular skill or sensitivity for it, unlike some; he remembered the instructor saying that he had no talent whatsoever: a diagnosis which had come as a relief, as it meant he could get someone else to do the difficult work. The thing could be blasting its pheromones at the top of its vents, and he would still likely miss the calling. If it was the second option, why weren't they responding? They had to be aware of his presence.

His attention was caught by a rustling in the bushes as a couple of brown bears, of a kind he'd never seen before, emerged from the forest. He tensed, then relaxed at the sight of their helms, then tensed again—with the control signal off, they could still be wild. He remembered Coyotl's bolt-shooter, wondered if he would be able to use it, pictured himself being torn to pieces by an angry, injured animal if he missed. Then he remembered that it was stashed away safely in his pack, and berated himself for his stupidity.

But instead of attacking or threatening, the bears showed no sign of hostility or fear. They ambled over to him and nosed his hands, like tame dogs or alpacas. Totchli relaxed. Not wild ones, then.

As if in answer to his unspoken thought, they gently nudged him along the rough path, in the direction of the pyramid.

So, clearly they were under the control of *that* centre, whether it was tenanted or not. "It must be on a separate control circuit," he said aloud. "Somebody, possibly Meztli, destroyed the original control centre, set up a new one. Why?" The bears looked uncomprehending. One paced in front of him, stopped, looked back.

"Well, all right then," Totchli said. "But if it wants a controller, it's out of luck, understand? I'm not remotely competent to run one of those things for more than five minutes." At the same time, he reflected that it might, actually, be a good idea to go up to the control centre, find what answers he could, and then get out of here. Assuming the bears would let him—and assuming, he realised as a chill struck his abdomen, that he wasn't being lulled by the pheromone signal...

The sun was low, heading for the horizon. Beams shafted through the trees. Totchli thought he could see a cliff-face further away, then realised it was smooth, man-made. A building perhaps, or a segment of wall, or perhaps —he thought he could make out some regular yellow markings—part of an overhead roadway system, like in the movies. He felt a stab of curiosity, desire to find out more, mingled with nostalgia for his side career in archaeology. He wondered idly what it would be like to come up here, away from the towns and the floods and the chaos, and spend a lifetime discovering the ancient cities and roads. Imagined himself setting out with his tent and gear, making camp, mapping the terrain and identifying likely dig sites. It was a strangely comforting, mundane fantasy, in a world populated by mad biotechnicians and intelligent helmed bears.

The trees were thinning, and Totchli realised they were close to the pyramid. It was situated at the centre of a clearing half the size of the compound, the only building visible. He could just see it through the forest, huge and dark.

A figure loomed up against the sun, as if out of nowhere. It took Totchli a moment before he realised what he was seeing, then recoiled with horror. The bears jostled him, puzzled at his reaction.

A tall, thin man, clad in a warrior's quilted tunic and trousers, dirty and wearing out. Above, like a parody of a warrior's helmet, a guiding-helm. The man's eyes were blank, sharp, the sort of programmed intelligence that shone from the eyes of helmed animals.

Totchli retched.

"We have to change to survive," another voice said. Totchli turned to the newcomer, then recognised him from his picture, just barely.

Meztli was a tall, pale man. Totchli found himself thinking abstractedly that the name *axotl* might have suited him better than his superior officer. He'd lost some weight since the picture Totchli had seen on his scroll, but was still paunchy, his face and stomach hanging with loose folds of skin that were somehow more grotesque than fat would have been. His head was bald, with a close-cropped remnant of hair around his ears, his eyes pouched with shadows, like the markings on the moon. He was wearing summer gear despite the cool spring weather, a light sleeveless tunic and loose trousers, filthy and unwashed, but not ragged or torn. His feet were bare and calloused.

"What—happened to him?" Totchli managed.

Meztli shrugged his big shoulders. It was, Totchli realised absurdly, as if he found strangers wandering along the path to the control centre every day in the company of bears. "We have to change to survive," the man repeated. "Some of us have to become like the animals. Some of us will have to grow new skins, new eyes. The technology will be the catalyst. But we will all be changed. He"—indicating the helmed man—"has become a bear, a lion, the true warrior he could never be in his other shape. I have become a snake, and slipped away into the jungle. Evolved into a monkey."

Totchli nodded crazily. Meztli had turned, was walking towards the pyramid, with the two bears and the helmed man following him, leaving Totchli staggering behind. Totchli noted that Meztli, whatever he said, had no helm, no indication that a pod had latched onto him anywhere.

"It's good to see someone new," Meztli said, conversationally. Then, "You're Totchli."

"How—" Totchli frowned. Had it been the control centre, the one in the centre of the field? How did it know? Had it been the mindlink he'd managed to patch through at the compound? Had the two control centres been in contact? How? Could it have told him? How? Why?

"I know what you're here for," Meztli said.

"Do you?" Totchli said, almost on the verge of hysterical laughter. "Because I don't."

"You're here," Meztli said, "to bear witness. To see the different things we must become in order to survive, and to tell the others."

"I am?"

Meztli turned, smiled. "You are," he said, and his voice had become gentle, friendly. Avuncular. "Come, it's all right. It's all going to be perfectly all right. Look. I'll show you."

# CHAPTER ELEVEN: MOUNTAIN LION

"I DON'T KNOW, SIR," Al said. "It looks a bit run-down to me."

"You're a city boy, private," Manders remarked. "It's clean, the whitewash is fresh, and someone's mended that fence recently."

"I thought you said you were an Old Etonian," Al retorted. "What sort of Old Etonian pontificates on farmhouses?"

"One who misspent his twenties breaking into them, for the sheer hell of it," Manders remarked, "and don't you know the minor aristocracy always have a house in the country?"

"What the hell is an Old Etonian," Ken said, "and if it's something English, how do *you* know about them?"

Al looked hurt. "I'd done one year of English Literature at Cornell when I got called up," he said. "*You* can explain about Eton, sir, you're the authority."

"It's a school, for the rich and the well-connected," Manders said through thinning lips, "and we'll say no more about it. Returning to the problem at hand," he continued, "we *are* running low on supplies, and it would probably be a good idea to see if we can barter with one of the few remaining local farmers for some portable goods. And possibly, do a hunting stop."

Ken's heart sank. On the one hand, despite the lack of supplies, they had been able to feed themselves due to Manders' hunting skills, acquired, or so he said, during his sojourn in Africa. On the other hand, every so often Manders insisted on stopping for a day or two in one place to set snares, so as to save on ammunition. This required either finding an abandoned building they could shelter in for a while, or a farmer willing to let them stay on the property in exchange for barter or, as their supply of tradable goods dwindled, labour. Twice, also, Manders had insisted on smoking some of the meat, to make it portable, which meant a longer stay.

Ken could not argue with the logic, and it did break up the journey as well as providing time for tending minor injuries and mending torn and broken kit, but it slowed them down. There was also no guarantee that the things trapped would indeed be edible, or, if they were edible, tasty. Ken reflected that when, or indeed if, he ever got home, he was going to subject someone he hated to a dish of slow-roasted iguana—or worse, to smoked dried iguana. Manders had attempted to teach his deeply unenthusiastic fellow travelers how to hunt with snares. Ken, remembering a few cursory lessons from boy scout camping trips, had some success, but Al was hopeless. Otherwise, the weather was increasingly hot and humid, and Ken was discovering that there were far more types of biting insect in the world than he'd ever thought possible.

At least, Ken reflected, they hadn't had any more encounters with Red troops. They'd managed to make it across the Westcoast border at some point—nobody seemed entirely sure where Westcoast began and ended, not even the compilers of the maps on Ken's fieldpad—and since then it had been nothing but farms and the occasional small community. These they were generally avoiding, due to their lack of acceptable currency. Some places did take Seaboard money, but that portion of their funds which hadn't been appropriated by the Red soldiers had now been almost entirely spent.

Ken had also noticed that the population was becoming sparser, and the towns fewer and further apart, the farther South they travelled. This farmhouse had been the first inhabited building they'd seen in days.

"All right, then," Ken said. "Who rings the bell this time?"

"You're probably the most innocent-looking, Usagi," Al said. "Not everyone loves a man in uniform. Don't worry, though, we'll be behind you, with guns."

This did not particularly improve Ken's spirits. The house was low, flat, with small windows, white paint, and a red tile roof. He associated the look with the Spanish, with old Hitchcock videos watched at university, an icy blonde woman saying to a frowning, uncomprehending man, *I died here*. A worn-out sign by the door read *Thule*. Ken spent a minute wondering what it meant, and how it was pronounced. Then, standing taller, he went to the rounded wooden door and knocked.

The door opened cautiously, then widened. Inside was a small chamber, like an airlock. A thin, young Black woman with a cloud of hair and cream-coloured skin, dressed in jeans and a loose sleeveless shirt, looked out at him curiously, but not warily, a well-worn paperback book in one hand. Ken was able to make out the title *Castle Keep* on the cover. "Hello?"

"My name's Ken Usagi," Ken said. "My friends and I are traveling, and we need someplace to stop and replenish our supplies. Could we, er, trade with you?"

The woman looked beyond him to Al and Manders, nodded. "Come in," she said, then, cryptically, "I'll get the spokespeople." She slipped gracefully away, leaving the three of them alone in the airlock-like room, with Ken reflecting that this was not really very safe of her.

"We could just rob this place," Al said, echoing Ken's thoughts.

Manders shook his head. "If she's OK with leaving three strangers alone here, then the place has some other defense system. I bet there's a sniper on the roof right now."

Al snorted, but didn't contradict him. Instead, he adopted a slightly more difficult-to-hit stance, angling himself sideways in the doorway.

The young woman came back with two people in their sixties, a Black man, cheerful and tall, with prematurely white hair and beard, and a White woman, with dark curly hair and a smile as if she was thinking of a private joke. Both were dressed in jeans and folk-art shirts.

"We're the spokespeople for the group here, today," the man said. "I'm Ibex."

"And I'm Lioness," the woman said. Al raised an eyebrow and she smiled wider. "Most of us take on animal names when we come to live here," she explained, "and that one, well, it was that or Cougar, and I'm not sure I could take all the jokes."

"Then I'm Puff, the Magic Negro," Al said. He laughed at the look of shock on her face. "I'm Al Benjamin," he added, placatingly. "This here is Ken Usagi, and back there is Henry Manders." Ken noticed the lack of titles.

Ibex frowned, but not unpleasantly. "You're wearing Seaboard uniforms," he said. This was a slight exaggeration. Ken was wearing the durable clothes which the clerk at the camping store had assured him would stand up to all weathers (thus far, this seemed to be broadly true). Al, due to the summer heat, had given up wearing his jacket and shirt, walking around in a worn green tank-top, and even Manders was in carefully mended shirtsleeves. The soldiers' clothes were, however, still recognisably military issue.

"We've lost our way," Manders said, following Al's lead.

Lioness nodded. "We've got a few here who've found their way South from the war zones," she said. "There's no sides here. Reds, Seaboarders, all that's off topic if you want to stay."

"Excuse me, but," Ken said, realising how awkward he was sounding, "you have a, well, community here?"

Both the spokespeople nodded. "Some people stay a long time, some a little," said Ibex. "They come from all walks, and for lots of reasons. The only reason we won't accept is conflict, you understand? No fighting. Even if somebody here was a Red, even if he personally killed your best friend, you have to treat it as past history. OK?"

Manders and Al looked at each other. "OK," Manders said. Ken wasn't sure he personally would be able to, given their recent experiences, but said nothing.

Ibex relaxed. "Good. A lot of soldiers can't agree to that, even deserters. The other stipulation is that, while you're here, you've got to help out. Work in the fields, help with repairs, cook, whatever you can do."

Ken looked at the two soldiers. Al shrugged, Manders nodded cautiously. "That's fine, too," Ken said.

"The house is full," Lioness said, "but we've got a couple of domes free if you like."

"Uh, domes?" Ken asked.

Lioness smiled. "I'll show you." Glancing at Ibex to make sure he agreed, she left the house, indicating for them to follow her. The Black girl, who had been perching on a bench near the door listening to the conversation, stood up in a fluid motion, like a dancer, and joined them. "This is Swift," Lioness said by way of introduction. She led them all around to the back of the farmhouse.

Following her gaze, Ken noticed that, dotted around the field behind the house, there were small, cottage-sized geodesic domes on short piles. As he watched, a young White man with a scraggly red beard wandered out of one, naked to the waist, yawned and stretched.

"That's Coyote," Lioness explained. "You'll meet him later, I'm sure. The domes don't look like what you're used to, I'm sure, but they're warm and environment-proof, and about half of our people live in them."

Beyond the field with the domes, Ken could see other fields, cleared and cultivated. In a small enclosure near the house, some animals that looked a bit like llamas idled. "Alpacas," Swift explained. "Wool, meat, also they're good if you need something heavy carried and there's no road." There was a wooden barn and a few other storage buildings close by. Around the farm, the forest grew, enclosing the community.

"I'm sure we'll be all right," Ken said.

Lioness smiled. "I've got to get back to work. Swiftie, do you mind showing these men where they can stay? You know which domes are the empty ones."

Swift nodded. "Come on."

While they stowed their rucksacks in an empty dome, large, clean, bare of furniture, with an unpainted wood floor, and smelling faintly of sawdust, sweat and old foam rubber, Swift explained the system. "If you're going to stay a couple nights or more, you go on the duty roster. Everybody has to do a couple hours of work a day. Usually it's just things like cleaning or mending, but do any of you have any useful skills or experience?"

"I can hunt," Manders offered.

Swift shook her head. "We're OK for game, thanks," she said.

"I know a little bit about cars," Al said.

Swift nodded. "That's a bit more useful. We've got an old tractor, converted to run on alcohol, needs a tune-up, maybe more. I'll see you get assigned to it. Will you need electricity?"

"I've got a fieldpad, but it has a solar charger," Ken said.

Swift nodded again. "We generate our own. Usually there's enough but sometimes there isn't, so you have to ask permission if you want to use any. See that building over there?" She pointed to a large shed. "That's where we keep spare furniture, you can help yourself to whatever you find. Beds, desks, anything. You might have to mend some of it. There's a battery lantern you can use up there—" She pointed to one hanging from a hook from the top of the dome. "If you need more lanterns, just ask." She straightened, seemed to listen to something they couldn't hear, then moved to leave. "Dinner's at five, and since the weather's good we'll be outside the house. I'll see you there."

Behind the house was a large, paved area, a patio, Ken supposed. Someone had set up tall arches to hold grape vines over it, and these draped over and around the structures, affording shade. A couple of long wooden trestle tables were set up on the paving under the vines. Behind, a door and long, low window revealed a large kitchen inside the house, also with expansive tables.

"When the weather's bad we eat in the kitchen." Swift appeared at Ken's elbow, noticed his interest.

"How old is the house?" Ken asked.

Swift shrugged. "Old enough that it's big enough," she said, annoyingly cryptic.

The population at dinner was about twenty people of various ages from infancy on up. As they approached, Lioness smiled and gestured them to three places she'd been saving; she introduced them briefly to the others, and vice versa. Ken found the names bewildering and occasionally, though he didn't want to admit it, a little ridiculous. He could just about understand names like Coyote or Mouse, but who the hell, he wondered, would choose a name like Mustang or Frog or Wren? He reminded himself to be polite.

Most of those present, it seemed, were more or less permanent residents. A couple of others were deciding whether to stay. The permanent residents, Ken noted, all had animal names.

"Tell me about this place," Ken said to Lioness. He realised he'd left his fieldpad back in the dome, but carried on. He could always make notes later. "How'd it get started?"

"Ibex and Crane bought the farmhouse about twenty-five, thirty years ago," Lioness said. "They were both programmers up in Westcoast, young and burned out, wanted to give up the city life and get back to the land. Then a couple of their friends decided to do likewise. After the earthquakes and tsunamis to the South, more and more like-minded people came up from the South, you know, California? Then we got even more from the North, after the war started, refugee families, deserters, though less and less since the fighting's spread to the Rockies."

Ken remembered the refugee boat, with his parents and grandmother. The rabbit falling into the dark water. *Never mind, Kennie, you're a big boy now.* He'd missed that rabbit during the days that followed, a spare government facility with what seemed like thousands of people crammed into a warren built for hundreds. He hadn't felt remotely like a big boy. If anything, he'd felt smaller, diminished, infantilised by the abrupt officials who spoke English slowly to him, made him take babyish tests of math, writing, computer skills, smiled patronisingly at his scores. If someone had offered him, or his parents, a farmhouse in the mountains, during those cold days, they would have taken it.

"What about you?" Ken asked.

Lioness smiled. "Nothing that glamorous. I came here about seven, maybe eight years ago. I'm from Westcoast, a place called Eugene. I was going through a bad time. I lost my job, my partner left me. I'd always liked camping in the mountains, so I came out here to lose myself for a while, and found this." She passed them a dish of stewed beans. "Went back long enough to sell the house and say goodbye, then went South again. I was an architect, in Eugene. The domes here were my idea. I'd been working to develop sustainable housing, back in Westcoast, but the government ran out of money to support the project, so it was a good way to put it to use. They're built from local materials, easy to repair." She ate for a moment, then went on, "I love it here.

Growing our own food, living off the land, like the pioneers did. *This* is the way of the future, not cities, not wars."

Manders looked mildly sceptical. "There's been cities as long as there's been farms," he pointed out.

"Things are changing now." Coyote, sitting to Manders' right, leaned in. "If you don't know that, you'll find out soon." He looked as if he was going to say something else, but Lioness shot him a look.

"Way of the future," Lioness repeated. "Try the bread, I made it myself."

Manders leaned forward. "I was wondering," he said. "Would it be all right if I did a little hunting? Set a few snares in the wood out back?"

Lioness exchanged a few looks with Ibex, Crane and a couple of other permanent residents. "Shouldn't be a problem," Ibex said heartily. "So long as you stick to the downhill woods, the ones to the North of the farm. Plenty of small game. I don't hunt myself, but some of the younger people do when we run short of fresh meat. We've got deer, too, if you want to try shooting, and there's a lake a couple miles out."

Manders shook his head. "Deer, maybe, but ducks are too much trouble," he said. "Why only the Northern woods?"

"Bears," Crane, a plain dark-haired woman, said mildly. Ken jumped a little, remembering their encounter a few weeks back—*the corpse torn almost in two, the red and white thing that used to be Rennert, Bayer screaming high and scared like a woman, Woolf's startled face, looking up at the grey sky around the dark red hole in the middle of his forehead*—but controlled himself. He'd had enough bad dreams since then that he was used to the images. "No, really," Crane continued, clearly taking his reaction for surprise at the news. "There's a few of them in the woods to the South. They don't bother us and we don't bother them, but this is the time of year when the females have got cubs, and they're more than usually excitable. So far as we know, they don't go in the Northern woods."

Manders raised an eyebrow. "First bears I've met that respected boundaries."

Crane shrugged. "Who knows why?"

Frog, a small White man of about thirty-five, leaned across the table eagerly. "So, you hunt?" he asked. He and Manders were soon deep in a conversation about guns, types and calibers and history and manufacturers, which Ken found mildly disturbing in its intensity. Al chuckled a little at the sight, caught Swift's eye and smiled. Ken turned back to his plate of food. It was, he reflected, nice to eat cultivated, prepared food, set out on a ceramic plate on a wooden table, with a glass of wine to drink: apparently home brewed, but if there were any problems with this, he certainly couldn't tell. And people having silly conversations about the things that interested them all around. He reflected that no one had asked him any questions about Deecee, or Nunavut, or the war.

The absence felt good.

———

"So, what do you make of them?" Ken asked Al the next day. They'd both been working all morning, watering, hoeing and pulling the insects off some sort of plant Ken didn't recognise, but he'd been assured it was edible. The work was not difficult, but was very repetitive, and he was developing some appreciation for the concept of agrotech, particularly irrigation and insecticide. However, under the rules of Thule (as Al put it), the pair of them were now free to spend the afternoon and evening as they pleased.

"It's the principle of the post-scarcity society," Frog had explained to him earnestly as they worked in the fields. Frog didn't seem to ever say anything less than earnestly. "Hunter-gatherer tribes work for only a couple of hours a day; the rest they spend making art, writing songs, all that." Frog himself spent his leisure time mainly on archaeology, it seemed. He had a small dig over at the corner of the house, where he'd identified something he called a midden. "You'd be amazed what you can find in one of those," he said, showing Ken pictures of brown ceramic fragments. "When we get a satellite signal, I upload pictures and reports to a buddy up in Vancouver, at the university there. He writes the papers and puts my name on some of them."

"Frog?" Ken hadn't been able to resist asking.

Frog smiled, a gotcha look. "Actually, kind of. I use my old name, Kent McGee, but now it's Kent F. McGee. Know what I'm saying." Ken laughed at the silliness of it, and Frog laughed, too.

Manders hadn't joined them in the fields. He had been assigned to the afternoon work shift, and had spent the evening setting snares, in the northern part of the woods. He had gone off early in the morning, before the other two men were awake, and had taken one of the rifles, so Ken assumed he was spending the morning building up their game stores again. Now Ken and Al were sitting (well, Al was lounging) in the field between the domes, enjoying the sunshine, watching a few children of various ages playing something vaguely resembling football with a strange-looking puffball mushroom, which had grown in triangles, like a natural version of the geodesic domes. Ken had managed to get his fieldpad working again, and was attempting to upload his finished stories to the Iqualuit Online News servers for editing, but the faint satellite signal he thought he'd picked up earlier seemed to be an illusion. *Oh well*, he thought, *it's not like I particularly need to get paid right now. Nothing I could spend it on out here, even if Thule would so much as recognise my credit.*

Al shrugged. "Lioness seems OK," he said. "So does Swift. They're all OK until they start to talk about how wonderful everything is here. Then they get a bit weird."

Ken nodded. "Well, we don't have to stay long. Just a few days, to build up our reserves and gather information."

"Look, here's the captain." Al propped himself up and waved at Manders. The old soldier was approaching with his gamebag under his arm, and a grim look on his face.

Manders slung the bag down in front of the younger men. "Trouble," he said.

Ken opened it, pulled out a couple of limp-necked quail and a slightly bloodied pika. The pika had smooth, black plastic folding over its eyes and ears, and extending down its spine.

"It's here," Manders said.

———

"So, what do we do about... the pika?" Ken asked when they were back in their dome. The offending animal lay between the beds, untouched, while Manders efficiently denuded the quail of their feathers in front of the entrance.

"How do you mean?" Al asked.

"Shouldn't we, uh, warn the people they've got an infestation on their doorstep?"

"So they can blow it up, like the general did?" Al snorted.

"We don't know that it's hostile," Ken said.

"We don't know that it's *not*," Manders said. "There's plenty of black bears in the mountains here. You heard what that woman said last night, and whatever she said about them staying in the Southern woods, I saw quite a few signs of bear in the Northern woods when I was out last night and this morning. What if one of the people here stumbles across a fully formed castle and trips the security system?"

"They seem peaceful," Ken said. "If we just explain to them to stay away..."

"Would they believe you?" Manders asked. "And if they didn't, or one of them didn't, and got hurt? Peaceful people can get pretty non-peaceful when threatened, that's my experience."

Ken sighed. The other two seemed to be, once again, looking to him for a decision on this. "The castles take a while to grow, and it can't be too big yet or these people would have noticed," he said. "Let's give it a day or two, see if we can find it, figure out what to do. We can also talk to them some more, figure out the best way to tell them about it." Al raised an eyebrow. "They're not stupid people," Ken said. "They're educated, rational." Perhaps that wasn't quite the word. "Calm," he tried again. "It's not like those Red soldiers. I'm sure we can find some way of explaining it all to them."

---

The next day, Ken was back on hoeing and watering duty, this time on what was recognizably potatoes. Al, as promised, had been co-opted to work on the tractor. From the field, Ken could see him, shirt off and dark-bronze body glowing with sweat, as he dug around under the rust-speckled, faded hood. Swift, who was apparently on her time off, was sitting perched on the top of the machine, chatting to him. Ken was too far away to hear what they were saying, but from the smiles and headshakes, he knew he was watching another of Al's courtship dances play itself out. *Oh well*, he thought, as Al went around behind the machine, looked critically at its exhaust system, then spread himself out under it and began tinkering invisibly. *More room in the dome if he starts sleeping somewhere else.*

Ken stood straight, took off the broad-brimmed hat Coyote had lent him (it looked ridiculous, he thought, but it was better than sunburn), stretched his cramped muscles, then stopped. The tractor was moving. On its own. Slowly, but—

"Clear!" The tractor began to roll faster. Al pulled himself startled to his feet, jumped, raced after it. Swift clung to the roof, eyes wide with fear, but not screaming. Her cloud of hair blew behind her. Ken ran towards them, shouting an incoherent warning to the other fieldworkers, noticing as he ran that Swift had that peculiar, distracted look again.

A bear came crashing out of the woods, roaring. A black bear, with the corrugated headpiece fully in place. It rushed in front of the tractor, stood still, took the impact of the rolling machine on its body without a whimper. The tractor bounced back an inch, comically, and stopped.

Swift slipped down from the tractor as Ken and Al ran up. Al flung himself into the cab, set the handbrake, then stared down at the young woman. Unbelievably, she reached up to the bear, caressed its face. "Thank you," she said to it.

"The hell?" Al said, while Ken babbled, "Those things are dangerous, get away from it now."

Swift turned, one hand still on the bear's face, just under the black headpiece. "Oh, they're not really dangerous," she said. "Not if you know how to talk with them."

"We don't usually tell new visitors about it till later," Lioness said. "Not until we're sure we can trust them. But you say you've seen the animals and the alien houses before?"

Ken nodded. "One in the Rockies, one up near the Great Lakes."

"They're that far North!" Lioness raised an eyebrow in what seemed to be pleased surprise.

They were in the farmhouse, in the main living room. It had a large stone fireplace and hearth, plain whitewashed walls, and a simple wooden floor. Making up for this simplicity of construction was a variety of intricate wall-hangings and paintings of fantastical animals and birds, and a wildly assorted set of colourful, comfortable chairs, sofas and stuffed large pillows scattered about the place. Various craft projects were scattered around the walls. Baskets of knitting, a small foldable loom, a half-finished rag rug.

Lioness was sitting on a wooden chair that seemed to be as old as the house itself, covered with a handwoven rug. Al and Ken sat on an orange sofa, Ken perched on the front, Al, properly dressed again and with the engine grease washed off his chest and hands, slumped against the back, head down against his chest, like a child expecting a scolding.

Now Al sat forward. "Alien houses?" the young man asked.

"That's what they are," Lioness said. "At least, that's our

theory, and the most sensible one we've come up with so far. It's some kind of alien terraforming device, preparing houses and communities for the aliens, when they come."

"Looks pretty human spec to me," Al said.

Lioness shrugged. "There's theories about that, too," she said. "Some think the aliens look a lot like us. Some others think they're going to change to fit Earth parameters. Caribou thinks they're not technically aliens, but humans from the future or from another dimension, but I think that's a little far-fetched. Wherever it came from, though, it's technology, invented by something intelligent and built for something about our size and humanoid. A lot of us are ex-programmers, app designers, pad builders and repair-people, and some of us have been studying it."

"How?" Ken asked.

Lioness looked careful, as if she was thinking what to say. "In the farmhouse. The lower part, the one that we think used to be servants' quarters back in the day. Mouse, Mustang and Hyrax have got a whole lab set up in there, gathering data about everything to do with it. The rest of us chip in as and when we feel motivated, but for all of us, part of the duty roster involves checking on the woods, seeing what the house is doing, keeping a rough count of animal numbers and species. Obviously, we leave newcomers out of that until we're reasonably sure they're a good fit for the community"—she smiled—"and they're going to stay a while."

"So let me get this straight." Ken was finding this all a bit difficult to take in. "You've got a full castle?"

Lioness nodded cautiously. "If that's what you call it. Out back of the white barn. In the Southern woods. Yes, that *is* the real reason we didn't want your friend hunting there; I guess it's perfectly safe if he knows how to behave around bears and alien houses, but we were worried he'd find the house, panic, frighten the bears, get hurt. You can see it later, if you like, and once the bears are used to you."

"That's another thing," Ken said. "What exactly was that trick Swift pulled with the bear? It was like it knew she was in danger, was trying to protect her."

Lioness nodded. "It was," she said. "Swift's a bear-speaker. Not all of us can do it. The young people can do it easier than the older ones. We're pretty sure all the little kids, the ones born here or brought here when they were small, can. They all seem much more at home with this stuff than we do. Same with any new technology, I guess." She smiled, as if making a private joke, then became serious again. "But some of us, like Swift, can talk with them. Tele-pathically, kind of. I can't do it myself, not one of the lucky ones, but the ones who can say it's not like sci-fi telepathy, it's more a sort of sharing concepts. The bears don't have language, but they do have feelings in common with us, understand some of the same things, and that's where the communication is." She smiled apologetically, spread her hands as if sorry she couldn't make it clearer. "You'll have to ask Swift, or maybe Mustang."

"It all seems pretty incredible," Ken said.

"It is." Lioness smiled again, this time joyously. Ken thought strangely of Red evangelists he'd seen on video, choirs of women bursting into carefully manufactured praise songs. "It's incredible. And when I think of what you say, that there's more of these out there..." She began to sound almost messianic. "I think—I know I'm being mystical and illogical—but I really believe now, from what you've told me about your mission, that you three came here for a reason. I think you're going to go back East and tell everyone about this; you're going to take the alien tech to

Deecee and show them how we can all change. And when they've changed, the Red States will follow, the Prairies, the North, maybe even send it by boat to Korea and Taiwan. Everywhere they've been touched by the climate. It's the right way. I mean, think about it. Our community's survived I don't know how long, because of the tech. When the harvest's bad, the animals feed us. Something about it protects us, too. We had bad weather and earthquakes before, but not now. You know, we're right on the Sierra Nevada Fault. It's why Ibex and Crane could get the land so cheap in the first place. People have abandoned places not too far South of here because of earthquakes, but we're just fine."

"It all sounds very nice," Ken conceded.

"It is," Lioness said, missing, or ignoring, Ken's tone. "It's exactly like what I wanted to do, back in Westcoast, with the domes. Sustainable living for a new climate. We'll show you everything while you stay here, and you'll see."

---

The castle—no, it wasn't a castle, Ken realised, it was a pyramid. It was small, irregular, but definitely coming to a peak, and it was the biggest one Ken had seen. He thought back to the one in the Rockies, remembered how it had seemed to be changing shape. He wondered if this were what it would look like, now.

"It's big," he said.

"It's getting bigger," Lioness replied. "We don't know how big it's supposed to get. There's other ones, too, smaller ones, further up the hill, but that one's definitely the mother."

"And it doesn't... do anything? Just sits there and grows?"

Lioness nodded. "The bears were a bit hostile at first, but then"—she seemed to be choosing her words a little—"it's hard to explain, but we sort of tamed them. Explained to them that we were on their side, that we weren't a threat to the castle, that we could help them, even. They stopped attacking us, began working with us. They don't mind us coming here and looking at it, even measuring things. They just leave us alone." As if to prove her right, a mountain lion, corrugated headpiece in place, trotted up to them; Lioness held out her hand and the creature, like a tame cat, whuffed it briefly, made a sort of curious *brrt* noise at them, then began walking its beat around the pyramid. "And sometimes, when we ask them, they help out."

———————

"So, biotech utopia," Al said. "Manna from heaven, or maybe from Mars. Wait till the captain hears."

"Mm-hm," Ken said. He was sitting on his bed, his back against his bedroll, looking at the screen of his fieldpad without really seeing it. He was flicking through some of the pictures he and Patel had taken of the castle on the Detroit Front, back and forth through the sequence.

"You're thinking about Hase, aren't you?" Al said. Ken said nothing. "You're wondering whether to tell him what we know about the biotech. We could do it. Send up a rocket, bring in the Marines. We know roughly where to send them, and we could go back East, job done."

Actually, Ken had been thinking about the Carverites, and how they compared to Lioness, but he nodded anyway. "True."

Al sat down. "The captain doesn't think you should send it."

Ken nodded again.

Al sighed. "The captain's a mercenary," he said. "He doesn't like the word, but that's the long and short of it. He's got his principles, sure, but he fights because they pay him, not 'cause he got drafted. He's not from the Seaboard, doesn't have friends or family there. Never grew up there. I'm from Massachusetts. There's a lot of American history there, goes right back to when the first Europeans landed. You ever hear of the War of Independence, up in Nunavut?" Ken nodded again. "Well, it started in Mass-achusetts. Place that's underwater, now, but the rest of the area's still got the spirit. I like where I grew up. I'd like it to go on, and if, like Lioness said, that means changing, well, it'll change." He paused. "The other thing we're known for, though, is our philosophy. We say that if the government's wrong, you shouldn't obey it. It's been abused; the Reds took it as justification for secession, back in the day. But it's still not a bad starting point." When he next spoke, he sounded like he was quoting. "The enemy is not either side. The enemy is something in between. You've got to make up your own mind if living with the biotech is bad or good."

"If I activate the app, there'll be a cost," Ken said.

"Ain't there always?" Al smiled, back to his usual unse-rious self. "Look at these guys, they figured out the costs and benefits for themselves. You do the same."

---

Lioness had clearly spread the word, because the community members were now very keen to tell Ken all about their experiences of the biotech. He was now, once again, the biotech expert, but this time, he was an expert in the company of other experts, people who studied it as much as he did, who didn't treat him with the mixture of deference and contempt he'd encountered at the Detroit Front, or the slightly creepy enthusiasm of the Circus of Form. While not all of the community were intensively involved with the biotech, all of the regulars and most of the sojourners had enough experience of it to want to tell their stories.

Over the next few days, the local biotech experts and Ken went into a flurry of information sharing. Swift attempted to describe how it felt to bear-speak, though eventually gave up, saying you had to experience it for yourself. Coyote showed him some of the black substance, which his infant daughter (by Mouse, apparently) had moulded through brain impulses into complicated spirals. "The littlest kids," he said proudly, "the ones who grew up alongside it, they've got an intuitive understanding of how it works. Maybe it's just exposure to the technology, maybe it's something about a child's mind?" Hyrax, a grizzled, squat, badgerlike man with an unplaceable accent, showed him four alpacas, with the corrugated bear-headpieces, housed in a small barn near the Northern woods. "It was an experiment, originally, to see how the headpieces take," he explained, "but it turned out pretty handy. With the bear-speakers, it means you've got a work animal that knows what you want it to do, where you want it to go, and you can call it in an emergency. We tried it out on a rabbit, too. Wanted to see if we could get it fetching metal scrap for us —it's more useful than you might think, out here. Didn't work so well. The damned critter did fine for a couple of weeks, then trotted off to the woods and we never saw it again. But the alpacas are just great."

Ken tentatively touched the warm velvety muzzle of a large brownish-black animal, feeling an odd disconnection. Weeks before he'd been running from the biotech, now he was among people who treated it like a useful pet.

Mustang, an incongruously small and skinny White man with an oily smile and thin moustache, who had apparently been something very big in app technology years ago, showed Ken the lab, as promised. It was a converted kitchen or workroom, the same low, plain construction as the rest of the house, full of samples, pads, notebooks. Mustang showed him files of data, analysing the chemical composition of the black substance, detailed notes on the life cycle of the pods, notes on the condition and behaviour of the experimental alpacas. Ken couldn't help but think how much Patel would have wanted to see all this. With a pang, he wondered if she was even still alive.

"What's back there?" Ken asked, indicating a locked door at the side of the room.

"Junk." Mustang shrugged. "A few things we were playing around with, didn't work out. I'll show you later if you like, but there's not much to report. Couple of dissections, a box Mouse tried to rig up to run an emulator app. Here," he said, "that reminds me. Look at this. We used to have an EEG, got it from an old hospital. Broken again now, but when we got it, I fixed it up and put it on when I was talking to a bear. Check out the spikes."

Days passed. The three of them worked their shifts in the fields, or on repairs, or gathering mushrooms, or anything else needed. In his spare hours, Ken spent his time in the biotech lab or out in the woods with the bear-speakers, trying to understand. He had tried to interest Al, but the teenager was largely bored by the science, and spent most of his time pursuing Swift, and occasionally, to Ken's mild surprise, Lioness (who, to Ken's further surprise, rather encouraged this).

Manders kept to himself as usual, slowly growing the stack of biltong near the front of their dome, responding monosyllabically if at all, but he seemed contented enough, occasionally making trips out to the castle to peer at it curiously, and observe its growth. He'd discovered that the community had its own smokehouse, which he used in his meat-curing experiments. One of the women, a recent arrival who still went by the name of Carol, was conducting a project to revive the art of tanning hides and took an interest in Manders' hunting activities. Only once did he express a firm opinion.

"There's something funny about this place," Manders said, when they were alone one evening in the dome, looking out at the sunset and sharing a bottle of what purported to be tequila. One of the community's homebrew experiments had matured, and most of the members were sampling the results, which at least contained enough alcohol to match the description, even if the flavour was more than a little wrong.

Al snorted. "Course there is," he said. "They're idealists, true believers. Want to make the world a better place. People like that are weird, even if they're nice."

Manders shook his head. "Not talking about the people. I mean the demographics."

"What *do* you mean?" Ken asked irritably.

Manders shrugged. "Just that, if there's been a community here for maybe thirty years, and there's been two floods of refugees—one from the South fleeing the earthquakes, one from the North fleeing the war—then where are all the people?" He let this sink in. "There should be a whole town here, not just a couple of dozen in a field."

"They probably all moved on," Al said. "You remember what Lioness said. Most people stop for a while and don't stay."

Manders shrugged. "Ought to be more people, that's all."

"Huh. Know what *I* think's funny," Al said. "That many people here, and not one of them knows how to fix an engine."

"Not everyone in the world is a gearhead, private," Manders said wearily.

"Yeah, but you know? Where I come from, at least a couple of guys—and some of the girls, too, come to think of it—would know what went on under the hood of a car, enough to change the oil filters. And I grew up in a *suburb*." Al emphasised his point with a stab of his finger.

"Ever ask why?"

"I asked Swift once," Al said.

"And?"

"She said there'd been someone here who'd known how, but he'd gone away. No, that wasn't quite it." Al frowned. "There was a strange way she'd put it. Said he'd found other things to do, then gone away. Either way," he said, "you'd think one of the others would have figured it out, smart people that they are, but they've got no interest. No interest at all."

Ken put both complaints down to cultural differences, and the subject never came up again.

Days became weeks. The two soldiers gradually abandoned their uniforms, the three of them dressing from the community's store of work clothes. Manders looked even more like some kind of ancient frontiersman, dressed in lumberjack shirts and work trousers. Al was sporting a new range of brightly coloured sleeveless T-shirts, sewn for him by Swift in her spare time. He'd made her a bracelet out of some spare tractor parts, which she seemed to like and wore every evening. He was beginning to slim down, Ken thought, get a firmer jaw, look less like an overgrown baby and more like a finished adult. Al stopped shaving his head, grew a neat crop of black hair. Ken let Hyrax cut his hair back to a more fashionable collar-length, felt civilised again. Their dome began to acquire furniture: old beds and chairs, brought out of storage and fixed, a makeshift bookshelf.

Ken reflected that he wouldn't mind spending some time here. Years even. The physical work wasn't hard, and the challenge of trying to understand the biotech took up his spare time and attention. It was good to be able to live under a roof, have regular meals, not be continually looking over his shoulder. More than that, though, was the conversation. He hadn't really thought about it much in the field, but now that he had it, he realised how much he'd missed being able to talk with people who weren't soldiers, about something other than war or survival. He hadn't been able to talk with Manders about much else, apart from during those two or three brief moments of self-disclosure. Al had been a little different; he'd been to university, they had read a few of the same books, seen a few of the same movies. But he was nineteen, and the number of interests they had in common was fairly limited.

Out here, almost nobody talked about the war, or plain survival. He did learn, at one point, that Coyote was a former Red soldier, though not by birth; he was a foreign volunteer like Manders. Coyote had come up North from Texas, a young man bored with his life and eager to be a part of something bigger.

"Then," Coyote said, "I discovered that the bigger thing I wanted to be part of wasn't the war, so I deserted. Claimed sanctuary in Westcoast, traveled South, came here. Now I've got a lady to share my life with, and two kids. Things couldn't be better."

It was easy to talk to Coyote, about the biotech, about life in Thule, about painting and videos and music. Same with Mouse, when she wasn't busy with children. Same with Frog, and even Lioness. The last time he'd had that sort of relationship with anyone, Ken reflected, had been Patel. There'd been a real joy in gathering data, examining it, developing and rejecting theories, back up North. Frog had, with barely concealed pride, shown him some of his journal articles; now Ken sometimes imagined his own name being used that way, a pioneer of biotechnology, someone working to change the world.

He got out the Bunny Girl motherboard; showed it to Mustang. The man was delighted, turning it over in his thin hands. "Amazing," he said. "We've been able to extract some control units from the animals, but nothing this big or detailed. Mind if I borrow it, make some scans?"

"Sure," Ken said, "provided I can have copies."

"I'll get to work on it with Mouse," Mustang said. As far as Ken could tell, none of the community members had seen a Bunny Girl, and they were all interested in adding the information to their store of knowledge about the pyramid and its system. "*If* it fits with the rest of the system," Mouse said, when they were discussing the issue over dinner, "we could be dealing with two separate types of biotech here."

"It makes more sense if we're just dealing with one." Coyote leaned across the table. "Occam's razor."

"Then why haven't we seen any?" Mouse countered. "We've seen the builders, the defenders, what does this thing do?"

"I'm pretty sure it's a seeder," Ken said. "Finds a good location, scatters the pods, moves on. It fits with the behaviour of the first one I saw, in the Arctic. Trying to seed, but the ecosystem up there's not suitable for construction. At least not in the winter. And if I'm right, when the pyramid gets mature enough, it'll generate others, and they'll go out, with bears, and colonise more sites. *Then* you'll see them."

Ken began to decorate the walls of the dome with charts, sketches, printed-out photographs. Had fewer nightmares about the Red soldiers dying in front of him, then eventually had none at all. Tried to learn to play the guitar (with electricity rationed, people here tended to make live music rather than play recordings, except on special occasions), but eventually Mouse declared that he had no feel for the instrument whatsoever and suggested he stick to the tambourine. He thought of an animal name: *Rabbit*. Considered using it. It was only his surname, after all. A Japanese person would think of him as Ken Rabbit.

Sometimes, he'd feel an itch, a pang of guilt, things he ought to be doing. He knew he should be trying to find the source of the biotech. It seemed nobody, even here, had much of an idea where it all came from. They agreed with him that it was probably to the South, and not all that far away, but exactly where was unknown since they hadn't had any real communication with California in almost a decade. He should be trying to spread the word, should activate the app, be getting back in touch with the Seaboard.

Bring in the real experts. Go back to Deecee, maybe get Embedded somewhere else, or go back to Nunavut, hand in his notice and work on getting the biotech to adapt to the North, make itself useful. The augmented alpacas made him think that something similar could be done with dogs, perhaps, develop smart rescue teams.

Ken knew he'd have to leave Thule eventually, with or without Al and Manders. But he kept on putting off the day, saying he could always leave later, that it wasn't the right time, that he didn't know enough yet about the castle, the bears. He'd just gather a little more data, try out a couple more experiments. That he'd know when the right time was, the point when he'd have to make his move.

When the time came, he nearly missed it.

———————

Ken had been working the late afternoon shift. He'd been tasked to clear the guttering on the farmhouse, a messy job which had taken a lot longer than he'd expected. He'd been alone, lost track of time, and by the time he'd finished, he realised the sun was setting. He'd missed the evening meal. Not that this was a problem, cold leftovers were always kept in the kitchen for people who'd worked through the official mealtime, or who just weren't in the mood for company.

Ken put away the ladder in the storage shed, washed his hands at the water barrel under the guttering, looked over at the rising moon. It was full, and gigantic on the horizon. Al and Manders, he reflected, would have had dinner, and they would probably be back in their dome. He thought almost nostalgically, longingly of the place. Unless Al was off with Swift again. Where the pair of them got the energy, given the pace of work around the community, Ken didn't know.

*First, get some leftovers from the kitchen,* Ken thought, *then back to the dome and look over the Bunny Girl data.* The previous evening, Mustang had returned the motherboard and a data dot containing everything he'd been able to figure out from it so far. "You might want to take a look at the 'geography' section," Mustang said. "One thing I've managed to get, there's some kind of homing data on the board, seems to indicate a return location, someplace it's supposed to go. We're pretty close to finding out where." *Or maybe sleep,* Ken thought, contemplating the sheer amount of data Mustang and Mouse had managed to generate. *Sleep might be good.*

On the way to the kitchen, he passed the lab. Heard someone speaking. He opened the lab door, thinking to have a word with Coyote or Mustang, but the lab was empty, the lights off. Puzzled, he looked around the room. *Must have been an illusion.* Birds under the window, maybe.

Then Ken heard it again. A couple of voices, speaking indistinctly. There was a rhythm to them, like someone reciting poetry. He thought, perhaps, that one of the pads had accidentally triggered a recording, went deeper into the room. *No, not one of the pads.* The voices were louder now, and he could trace their source.

The locked door.

He tried it. Still locked. He tried to remember if anyone had mentioned where the key was kept. Looked in a few drawers, on the windowsill. Finally, he found a plain unmarked key under the monitor stand of the box Mustang used most often. It had a large painted stencil of a rearing horse in blue adorning it, in case anyone had doubts about who had first claim.

Ken held it, tried it in the lock.

It worked.

The room beyond the door had clearly once been a storeroom, but somebody had added beds, a latrine. Food bowls. Water bowls. The windows were high and narrow, and someone had put several layers of chicken-wire over them, on both the inside and out. Like a prison. Or a mental hospital. Or a zoo.

Ken stood in the doorway, stared, tried to make sense of what he saw.

Three figures, two male and one female, wandered around the bare, white-walled room. Their heads and shoulders were all covered with controlling pods, black and plastic, but lumpy, misshapen, rough-surfaced. He couldn't tell if they were fox-pods or bear-pods. Some parts were smooth, others corrugated, others held different textures he'd never seen before. The woman had raw, red patches where the filaments extended into her backbone.

As he looked, she raised her face, made eye contact below a matted blonde fringe of hair. "Bow your head, my darling dear, can't stare down a mountaineer," she said cryptically.

"Ken, I'm sorry," said a voice behind him. Ken turned, saw Lioness. "We didn't want you to see this at first. They're normally quiet, so it was easy to hide—but they do tend to get talkative at the full moon. We think it's the light."

"What is this?" Ken managed.

"We were going to introduce you to them later, when you'd really integrated. I know they seem frightening, in their way. But you know enough, you understand—you know what they are—don't you, Ken?" The last was sad, almost pleading.

"You—" Ken couldn't get the words out. A sea of ideas was roiling in his head, clashing against each other. "You tried to merge humans with the biotech, didn't you? But it's not built for humans."

Lioness nodded sadly. "We take care of them, give them what they need. Honour their sacrifice, if you like. Don't get the wrong idea," she added quickly. "It's not some Frankenstein experiment. All of these people, they volunteered. Cat did it first." She indicated the woman. "We didn't know what she was planning, but then we found her out by the alien house. She was a bear-speaker, one of our best. Probably *the* best, and that was the problem. She wanted to get closer to it, become one with the system. Then Gecko, there, he was going out with her. He volunteered to do it under experimental conditions, thought we might be able to find out what had gone wrong with hers, through him. Shark, I think he just thought he'd be lucky. Always was convinced of his own immortality, that one." She shook her head.

Ken breathed easier. "OK," he said, "I understand." It was crazy, but then you always did get lunatics, obsessives, and having seen Swift, Coyote and Mustang bear-speaking, he could imagine that it might become addictive, something you wanted to try for yourself. *Like the Carverites*. The woman, Cat, began speaking again. He quickly shut the door to the room, locked it. "A tragic story," he said, putting the key away and following Lioness out into the hall. "People trying to understand the technology, become part of it."

Lioness nodded. "It wasn't for nothing, though. We found out through them that it's the wrong way," she said matter-of-factly.

"The wrong way," Ken said. "That suggests there's a right way."

Lioness smiled joyfully. "There is. Again, something we

weren't going to tell you about till later, but it's clearly the right time now. Let me show you."

———

The sun was almost down, but the moonlight made up for it. Ken stared up at the giant pyramid, wondered, *has it grown bigger, since I last saw it?* The biotech seemed to glow faintly in the moonlight, pulse and gleam like a dim firefly.

Lioness was intent on the structure. She passed a couple of black bears on guard, which ignored her. She stood in front of the smooth surface. As with the castle in the Rockies, the front of it parted, its substance opening up like a curtain on an inner chamber, and there were...

*...people inside...*

Ken blinked and stared. Not just an antechamber. The room they were in extended all the way up to the top of the structure. He could see the whole interior of the pyramid, layers and layers flayed open and exposed. The entire space was hollowed out, riddled with passageways and tunnels. Inside the pyramid was an intricate maze of levels and connections, with dozens of people walking around, silent, that same distracted look on their faces.

Ken remembered, when he'd been at school in Toronto, a teacher who surprised them with a thin tank full of sand. Inside were tunnels, and insects busily running back and forth along them, looking for food, mending broken walls, tending larvae. "It's an ant farm!" the teacher said with delight. Ken had been mildly horrified at the sight of all those little creatures rushing about, blindly but with a purpose. Hadn't been sure whether to be sorry or glad when the entire tank succumbed to some insect plague and the experiment was quietly abandoned, no more said. He felt that same feeling now, as when he first saw the ant farm, with its incomprehensible denizens.

His mind went back to what Manders had said, a few weeks earlier, about the demographics. *So, this is where all the people went...*

"They're talking to each other," Lioness whispered, indicating the human figures walking about the interior. "In their minds. That's what the bear-speakers say. And in here... even I can hear it, a little bit."

Ken could, too. Sensed, on some level, the life of the pyramid, the lives of the people, the bears, the small animals, all moving together.

"See what I mean? It's the way of the future," Lioness whispered. "We'll all go there eventually. For the moment, it wants some of us outside, bringing people into it, communicating its wishes to the human world. But when everybody knows, then I'll go in, join them. I'm looking forward to it. Wouldn't you?"

Ken backed away towards the entrance.

The entrance was closed. In fact, there was no entrance anymore.

Lioness smiled. "It wants you," she said, with certainty. "It's telling me. It wants you. Likes you. It's got your scent."

"From when we went into the other one, before?" Ken managed.

*Maybe*, Lioness said, without saying anything. *Once it's come to know you, it's not going to let you go.*

Ken felt darkness, a rushing. He couldn't breathe. He pulled a utility knife out of his pocket—he'd borrowed it from Al a while ago, kept forgetting to give it back—struggled to open a blade, shoved it in where the entrance had been, twisted, shoved again. Felt the system hurting, but kept on. *Let me go. Just let me go and I'll stop hurting you. I'm not ready. I don't want to be with you. Let me go and things will be fine. Don't let me go and I'll hurt you more.*

The entrance parted again, and Ken fell out into the woods. He stumbled, half-ran, through the darkness, back to the lights of the dome.

"We've got to go," he blurted, falling in through the dome entrance. Manders and Al both looked up, startled. Al was lying on his bed, reading one of the crumbling paperback novels that circulated around the place. The front cover had a picture of an old-fashioned biplane flying over a sprawling Japanese-looking building constructed against the side of a mountain, and the words *Lost Horizon* blazed above it in lurid gold. Manders was seated cross-legged on the floor, scraping a large deer hide.

"Pack quickly," Ken said, doing so and clumsily trying to explain what he'd seen. The other two sprang into action, began rolling sleeping-bags, stashing dried meat. The novel went flying, knocked one of Ken's photographs off the wall.

Something roared outside, in the distance. "Now," Manders said. He hoisted his pack, unholstered his pistol, shouldered his way out of the dome. The others followed.

The edges of the sunset were fading away; the moon was climbing, bright and silver. The sky was clear, a translucent dark blue, faint stars visible around the edges of the moon and the sunset. The field behind the house was eerie, washed with blue, the grasses moving gently in an evening breeze. Ken could see lights on in the farmhouse, a few others winking from the windows of the domes. *Strange,* he thought. *The bear-speakers must have warned them by now. Why aren't they doing something?*

Manders turned in the direction of the lake, clearly expecting the others to follow. Wordlessly, Ken and Al fell in behind him, keeping up a steady pace across the fields, away from the farmhouse, the woods, the castle.

When they reached the edges of the forest, Manders stopped, bit back a curse.

Two bears blocked the way, Swift standing behind them, one hand on each hairy back. Tense, poised as if she were trying to fly away.

"They want you to go with them," Swift said, an agonised look on her face, a painful tone in her voice. "They're asking me to tell you. You've got to join them. Go to the alien house with them."

"We know too much," Ken said.

"No, you don't know enough," Swift said. "You have to learn more, then you won't be afraid of it."

"That's what I'm afraid of," Ken said. "Let us past."

The bears growled softly. Swift shook her head. "They can't. I can't. You've been in one before—it's changed you, made you more like us. If you go in, the house will show you everything. Everything you need to know."

"The source?" Ken said. "The makers? Where it came from, what's it for?"

"Everything," Swift promised. "Even things it hasn't told us, yet. Then, when you know everything, you can come out, go back East again if you like. Just do what it wants." The last was said almost weeping.

Ken heard something zing past his head. Swift made a soft painful noise and crumpled.

"Run," Manders said coolly over the muzzle of his pistol. The bears were turning, nosing around Swift, who was whimpering, a dark stain spreading across the thigh of her jeans.

Al let out a wordless cry, started towards her.

Manders grabbed him, turned him around, pushed hard

on his chest, almost sending him sprawling. *"She's not on our side, you little idiot,"* he snarled at Al's shocked face. He pushed him again. "Now *run.*"

Ken, horrified, ran. Heard footsteps behind him. Human ones, not animal. *Thank God.*

They didn't stop moving until almost dawn.

---

"I think we've lost them," Manders said, as they stopped, panting, by a shallow river. The sky was clouded over now, the sun a red smear at the bottom of a dark grey sheet; sheet lightning played across it like strobes.

"Or they're not interested," Ken said. "Or they're playing a long game. Who can tell?"

"Either way, they're not following us, and that's what's most important," Manders said. He pulled a cloth from a pocket, wiped the sweat off his brow. "If they're playing a long game, we'll find out about it later. When we're prepared."

"Swift," Al said, almost a moan.

"She'll be OK," Manders said, "unless she's very unlucky. I shot to wound. The bears would have gone for help. And those fools back at the farm, whatever else they are, I reckon they know what an antibiotic is."

"Sir, I know you're right, but just for the record, sir, I hate you for it," Al said. "Sir." He threw down his pack, walked to the river, sat down, took off his boots and socks, and thrust his feet into the current, scowling. He was wearing one of the shirts Swift had made for him, Ken noticed belatedly.

Manders looked after him, a little sadly. He shrugged, put down his own pack, extracted his canteen and some water-purification wafers, and went down to another stretch of river.

Alone, Ken breathed in, breathed out. Looked at the sky, the river, the trees, the mountains. Somewhere, something cawed; another bird, one Ken didn't recognize, sang a brief sequence of notes, over and over.

Ken pulled the SIC data dot out of the inside pocket of his rucksack, stared at it. He imagined Deecee taken over by black castles and pyramids, people walking antlike around it. Imagined the Arctic, villages abandoned, black-girded grizzlies and husky dogs patrolling the tattered and torn agrotech facilities. Remembered Tina and her assertion that the world was going to have to change itself. He thought, *be realistic, be progressive, be open-minded*. He shuddered, dropped the data dot on the ground, spat on it, ground it hard under his heel until there was no way the app was scannable. He picked it up, walked to the river, threw it in, watched it float away on the current. He walked back slowly, looking at the gravel.

"Ready to move on?" He looked up, saw Manders sitting on his rucksack nearby.

Ken sighed. "Yes," he said shortly.

"Someone needs to confront the horror, stop the horror," Manders said. "But if someone's not disturbed by the horror, then there's no point for someone like me, is there? I told you before, I kill so you don't have to. That's got a lot of meanings, and not all of them are bad."

"In an ideal world," Ken retorted, "no one would have to kill."

Manders snorted. "Look at the community, back there," he said. "The farm with the pyramid. That's what an ideal world looks like. Ideal worlds are dangerous. Best to live in the real one. The real one's got good and bad. But they're in a balance, more or less."

"Humanity doesn't deserve to exist," Ken mourned, thinking of Lioness, of the people in the room.

"Perhaps not," Manders said. "But it's not a question of deserve, or don't deserve." He pointed to the sheet lightning, fluttering across the horizon, paling in the dawn. "See that? The Earth did that long before there were humans, and it'll do it long after there aren't any. You understand?"

Ken nodded slowly. "I think I do."

Manders waited for a minute. "Do we go back, up to Westcoast and send up a rocket for the Seaboard rescue party? Or do we carry on South?" he asked.

Ken thought. "I don't know about you," he said, "but I want to keep going South. I want to find out where it came from and what it is. Not for the Seaboarders, not for Nunavut, not for Lioness and Ibex and the community, but for *me*. I want to meet the biotech-makers on their own terms, ask them why."

Manders nodded. "Me, too," he said. "Let's get Al—"

"—if he's speaking to us," Ken finished.

Manders cracked a rare smile. "The private and I have been working together a while. He knows the score. Come on, you stupid journo, let's go South."

# CHAPTER TWELVE: THE COLONISTS

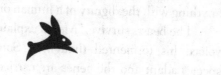

THE SPACE at the middle of the compound, around the control centre, looked simultaneously like nothing on Earth, and strangely familiar. After a minute Totchli figured it out. European horror, he thought. The Codex Serafinatus, with its animal-object hybrids, like strange parodies of the familiar gods; the Garden of Earthly Delights. A brief rescued clip of an orgy of animal-headed humans, believed to come from a film by the great director Hammer. The beast-headed humans found in rows during one excavation he'd been hanging around in Mexicociti. They looked like grave-markers, but had been inside a building, no remains with them, just ranks of black statues with lion heads and bird heads and alligator heads. Totchli told his mind very sternly to stop babbling, but it carried on, seemingly for its own comfort.

The pyramid rose tall, black and gleaming sinisterly. Around its base, animals and humans with helms moved twisted, slow. Beasts trying to walk on two legs. Humans with the same blank-yet-intelligent creature eyes as the man he'd met on the path. He realised he'd never asked the man's name. Hadn't even wondered, tried to put the face together with the images on the scroll document. Like he was an animal—no, less than an animal, how many times had he admired someone's pet or work beast, asked *what's his name?* Like a scout, or a boat, or a mechanical puppet. Not anything with the dignity of a human or animal.

"The beasts survive," Meztli explained, as if Totchli had voiced his tormented thoughts. "Some die off, but the species adapt and the genes are carried on. To survive, we have to become like the animals."

"Is that why you killed Axotl?" The words were out, too quick for thought. Totchli cursed himself. Bluntness wasn't just going to cost him a social network, it was going to cost him his life, the way things were going.

Meztli halted and gave him a long look. Totchli cursed himself.

"I didn't," Meztli said eventually, sounding a little hurt.

"Then who? And why?"

Meztli shrugged and moved on. "The mice," he said, as if this made perfect sense.

"The... mice," Totchli said. He'd already figured out the man was crazy, destroying the control centre. But blaming the *mice* for it?

"The mice," Meztli nodded, as if he were talking about something normal. "That's when we discovered the truth. This is mouse country. They run it. They own it. They don't want us here. That's why expeditions up here keep failing."

"They destroyed the control centre."

"They did."

"How?" Totchli's mouth ran away with him again. "Did they talk to you in the night, give you instructions?"

Meztli turned and frowned at him. "We don't know

how they did it," he said, as if explaining something to a very stupid child. "All we know is they did. One minute it was there, the next, they were in it, the next, it was burning."

"All right, I believe you; the mice destroyed the control centre."

"They did."

"And this has to do with Axotl... how?"

Meztli nodded, back on track. "After we learned about the mice, and what the mice were capable of, we... quarrelled about the direction the colony should take. He was all in favour of adapting the land to us. Tools, terraforming. But that's what we've been doing for centuries. That's what's changed the climate, brought the floods." He was proceeding through the orgy of twisted animals, ignoring them. "That's what frightened the mice. I knew differently. If we're going to live with the mice, we have to coexist with them."

"All right." Totchli nodded. "So what did you do then?"

"After the destruction, we both agreed we needed a new control centre. Somewhere we could defend it. It was agreed that I was the best qualified one to make a new one, since Tototl had been killed—she was linked with the centre when the mice came—and Cuiatl had gone away, no one knew where. I came out here, set up the growth. When it had grown, I linked in. I tried to fix the mouse damage. I changed the programming of the pods."

"So they'd attach to humans?" Totchli was simultaneously repulsed and interested. "How'd you manage to do that?"

Meztli did not share. "Axotl was frightened. We fought for control of the centre. I formed the gestalt."

Totchli nodded. The control centres operated through

linking with a single mind, the director, who could then link other humans together into a gestalt-mind, either a large group temporarily, if a lot of computing power was needed, or in small groups over longer periods, for ongoing operations.

Meztli was continuing. "But the gestalt wasn't unified. Axotl broke. What was left of the people scattered. I came here to form a new gestalt."

Totchli scoffed. "Sorry, with *these*?" He gestured at the crowd.

Meztli paused. Totchli realised they were at the door of the centre. "No," he said.

The door opened.

Totchli looked in. He knew what he would see in a normal pyramid. A director, a few operators, moving briskly around the pyramid on autopilot, minds in the gestalt. Inside this one he could see bears, jaguars, rabbits, swaying and moving around like they were trying to be human.

"It needs the right sort of mind," Meztli said. "I tried to be director again, but burning the last one changed something, I can't do it anymore. It needs you."

Totchli belatedly tried to get away, but the bears blocked his path. Shoved him towards the door with their muzzles.

He turned to Meztli. "It can't be me," he babbled. "It can't. I'm no good. I'm not intelligent, I'm not really talented at mindlinking. I'm barely qualified to run scouts, you have to understand. I'm not who you want. Who they want. Let me go. Please, let me go."

Meztli shook his head. "It wants *you*," he said. "It's told me. It wants Rabbit Boy."

"*Rabbit* B—" Totchli felt as if he'd been struck. "How the hell did it know—what in the name of the fornicating

*Serpent* have you *got* in that control centre?" His mind was casting back to campfire stories about control centres that had become independently sentient, or which had learned to read people's minds out of mindlink. Stuff to scare kids. This—this was like being out in the field, hearing someone tell the story about the crazy vagrant who had murdered an entire archaeology camp, and then coming back to find the rest of the dig personnel massacred and a vagrant standing in the middle with an axe.

Totchli realised that he'd been pushed into the entrance of the pyramid. Meztli gave him a final shove in the middle of the chest. He collapsed, sprawling, inside it, cried out as the doors sealed shut. The air was hot, smelled of sweat and hair. He struggled to his feet, tried to run for the door, but his legs wouldn't move.

He felt his mind linking, without intending to, into the animal gestalt.

It was... big.

He was a cell in a body. He was a droplet in a river. He was... no, he was a sugar crystal dropped into a supersaturated solution. He was the breaking barrier between chemicals in a light. He was the signal that triggered, telling the body whether to develop cancer or not.

He was everything.

Part of him, the still-Totchli part, saw movement in the corner. Through the gestalt, he focused with many eyes.

Tiny, hairless mice, running deep into the centre of the pyramid. One paused, looked at Totchli. The intelligence behind its minute black eyes was calculating, human. Weighing the odds.

Totchli realised he couldn't hear its mind. Couldn't control it, couldn't link with it. An animal physically in the control centre, but not part of the gestalt.

The not-Totchli, control-nexus part of him sounded an alarm, but the Totchli part of him was too interested by the paradox to allow a response. The animals froze in perplexion.

Something in the pyramid, deep inside, exploded.

As one, the mice turned and fled. Totchli could, for an instant, feel a brief echo of their triumph from outside the animal gestalt—*an intelligent mind, a groupmind, a rival gestalt, who is this?*—before he began to feel the animals screaming, inside him/the gestalt and out.

Totchli/not-Totchli saw flames, collapsing bodies. Something near him—a bear—died, and he felt it.

The death left the Totchli part of him temporarily free. Feeling himself alone in one body again, he pushed quickly towards the door, only for the large, pale figure of Meztli to block the way.

*How in hell is he in here?* "Let me through," Totchli begged.

Meztli didn't move. Suddenly Totchli surged with anger.

"Let me through, damn you!" Fear and wrath and pain gripped him, and he found himself grabbing something fist-sized and hard off the floor, *a stone, a component, the corpse of something, not sure.* Fought off the edges of the gestalt reasserting itself in a wavery, sick feeling, hurled the object. It bounced.

Meztli didn't move.

"You don't know what you're doing. Let me through!" Totchli shouted desperately.

Meztli drew breath, then stiffened. Fell to the ground, a single dark hole formed at the base of his skull, like the early stages of a helm. Blood pumped out in sluggish bursts onto the black instagrowth floor.

"The horror," he whispered, and died.

Totchli turned to see Coyotl, framed in the now-open doorway, face set, a bolt-shooter in her hand. Against the bright flames and the dark night sky, her stocky, blunt profile looked heroic, a legendary figure.

*Or a god, even. Smoking Mirror*, he thought hysterically, almost laughing. *Killer of the Serpent. Only the Serpent doesn't die, they just keep killing each other over and over...*

"How—" He couldn't manage to finish the sentence.

"Got worried about you," she said, walking over and kicking Metzli into a face-up position. She looked at the corpse, her expression neutral but with a slight edge of distaste.

Somewhere behind Meztli, a support structure gave way. Coyotl holstered her shooter, grabbed Totchli's arm, wrenched him out into the clearing, pushing and shoving through the ring of half-mad animals moaning and shaking their heads around the control centre, back to the edge of the treeline. As she let go, Totchli sank to the ground, his chest heaving and gasping with the contradictory impulses to draw breath and to vomit.

Coyotl leaned against the nearest tree, resumed talking as if nothing had happened, though her stump was twitching slightly, as if with nerves. "Got to thinking," she said conversationally. "People like that big fellow back in the pyramid are crazy enough to survive, when anything normal would just curl up and die. Didn't think a city boy like you stood much of a chance with people that possum-shit. Got Itch to take the survivors back to the boat and turned back, followed your trail." Totchli wasn't sure if it was her tone, or the hyperawareness of the gestalt wearing off, but he seemed to receive a mental underlying, *trail so bleeding big and obvious, he might as well have planted torches along it, Serpent knows the kid's no woodsman, but that's just as well...* "Good thing I did!" Coyotl went on aloud. "Found that big thing in the woods. I'm expecting you've got an explanation for what I saw, but it can wait..."

Totchli looked back at the pyramid. The exterior was now in flames, melting like the one in the compound had melted, like an oversized candle. He couldn't see the animals—or, thank God, feel their minds. Bits of the experience were starting to come back to him. He looked up at Coyotl, leaning on her tree, watching the fire.

"It was the mice," he said. "They did it. Destroyed the first control centre, and this one, too. They've been following us. Listening to us." *It wants Rabbit Boy... how did it know I was Rabbit Boy...?* "I think... they might be sentient."

Coyotl raised an eyebrow, but didn't laugh or contradict him. "That poor fool back at the colony said the same thing."

Totchli nodded.

"That means," Coyotl said, "either you're as crazy as he is or else he was telling the honest truth."

Totchli nodded again.

"We'll figure out which it is later," Coytol said with finality. She extended her hand to help him up. "Come on, Rabbit Boy, I'm taking you home. Or out of here, anyway."

# CHAPTER THIRTEEN: MOUSE TRAP

ON THE THIRD day of hiking through the fruit jungle, Al's machete caught on something, twisted. A sudden thunder of vines fell off what hadn't looked like a man-made structure a minute before. Now a strange grotesque, round-eared, skinny-legged, leered at them, pointing with one of its obscenely bulbous hands. *This Way to the Happiest Place on Earth! 25 Miles* the sign read.

"What's a mile, sir?" Al asked.

"A couple of kilometers, private." Manders studied the sign a minute. "What do you make of it, Usagi?" the old soldier said, his strange European accent harshened by the damp weather.

Ken studied it, feeling uncomfortably on the spot. In their months of traveling together, going from the Seaboard States towards the Southwest looking for the origin of the biotech, and especially since leaving Thule, the civilian-military distinction had blurred, under the influence of Al's general air of insubordination and Manders' practical attitude to life. Although Manders occasionally wore his military clothing, and still insisted on referring to Al by his title, he had abandoned all outward signs of rank and insignia. Al had not worn his uniform since leaving the community, instead choosing the loud, splashed, tie-dyed shirts that Swift had made for him, perhaps as a reminder of happier days, perhaps just for practical reasons. The atmosphere was becoming less and less like a military expedition, and more like some kind of ancient colonial voyage of discovery, searching for a lost tribe out beyond the reach of civilisation.

Occasionally, though, Manders liked to remind Ken that he was a journalist, and thus both a lower form of life and one which was expected to be a font of cultural knowledge, and this was apparently one of those times.

"It's an old version of Mickey Mouse," he said. He remembered a children's book, pages worn thin, in the library of the small Nunavut town where he'd spent half his childhood, a scratchy DVD, a vaguely remembered reference in a documentary, a prized antique ceramic figure rescued from the family home in Toronto, but given away after his grandmother's death. *Tacky*, his mother called it, although quietly, so that his father wouldn't hear.

"The Japanese cartoon?" Al asked.

"Didn't used to be Japanese," Ken clarified, reflecting that Al was nineteen, his university education interrupted by military service, and so probably didn't know his media history. "Back twenty or so years ago, Disney used to be, well, round about here. Somewhere in the South. It owned this place where it ran this big... kind of like a fairground, for people on holiday, called it the Magic Kingdom or Disney Land or Epcot or something." He remembered his grandmother, her hands and head keeping up a gentle shaking, but her eyes bright as she talked about the Theme Parks, clean shiny places that children were taken to on holiday. Remembered sitting with her as she showed him a video file with strangely lurid colours, maybe a hundred years old, children riding in whirling giant teacups and hugging giant plush animal-grotesques, gazing in wonder at fireworks exploding over a castle with pointed turrets. There'd been one near Toronto once, she said, but the climate had forced it to close before Ken was born, and anyway it hadn't been very good. "The Americans are always so much better at Theme Parks," she sighed, her English almost, but not quite, accent-free even after all these years. "To see the exciting things, you must go South."

When Ken was small, he'd believed her promises that if he was good he'd be taken to one, too, but he'd rapidly come to realise that Theme Parks, like Movie Multiplexes and Shopping Malls and Television, were things which now only existed in the minds of people as old as her. And after they made the journey to Nunavut, his questions were met with visible disapproval by his teachers. They were part of the decadent past, frills that had no place in the austere, practical society which was going to survive the climate change. Only his media history professor in Whitehorse showed a genuine interest, showed him scans of brochures and print advertisements, asked Ken if his grandmother was still alive, was disappointed when Ken said she wasn't. "Pity," she'd said. "We need to record people's memories of that sort of thing, or they get lost. You're *sure* she didn't tell you any more stories about it?"

"Huh," Al said, startling Ken back to the present. "I thought you said the biotech-makers were somewhere around here, too," the teenager went on, a skeptical look on his slightly rounded dark-bronze face as he returned to clearing the path. Ken sympathised as he fell back into line. They hadn't seen a single human being since they'd fled the community in the mountains with its strange, halfbioteched, half-primitive lifestyle. Indeed, since they entered the dense jungle, any traces of humanity were only discovered, like the mouse sign, by sheer accident or careful observation under the layers of plant life.

Manders didn't seem to mind, but Ken, for one, was finding it hard to get used to.

"All we know is that thus far, the trail of biotech has pointed South, and mostly West," Ken said. "Patel's data. Everything Thule had. All the sightings we've been able to find, up to the border of the jungle. Even the fact that the castles and pyramids are apparently earthquake-proof. This part of the world used to be famous for biotech, back in the old days, so it made sense to look here for them."

"Even with the jungle?" Al raised a thin eyebrow.

Ken shrugged. "Whoever's making this stuff doesn't want to be discovered. A jungle's a good place to hide a secret facility. It adds up. There's got to be someone out there."

"Or some*thing*," Manders remarked, his lined leathery face deadpan. "After all, we're not sure if the people we're looking for are human people, are we?"

"So you think it's down to the aliens, sir?" Al said disingenuously. Getting no reaction, he continued a few machete strokes later, "Lioness was right?" He tried again. "Reckon all the people here got abducted?" After waiting strategically, he added, "Maybe they're all off enjoying a good probe?"

"Don't push it, Benjamin," Manders muttered. Al settled back into a slightly more contented silence. After the initial strangeness of their environment—the prolific, seething grape vines with wisteria-like muscular trunks, the dark groves of almost luminous citrus, the giant flying cockroaches, the heady, sweet, rotting smell of the vegetation—

the fruit jungle had rapidly become a boring twilight slog, meaning that the main daily entertainment was, for Al, needling Manders, and, for Ken, watching Al needling Manders. At least the dried food, and the stock of ammunition, were holding out enough that Manders wasn't insisting on any long hunting stops. Ken thought that spending a couple of days in one place in the jungle would be simultaneously boring and disturbing.

For the next hour or so, as they walked under the same grey sky flashing with the same primeval lightning that had accompanied them since leaving Thule, Ken reflected on Al's last jibe. He didn't particularly believe in aliens either, not like Lioness had. They were the stuff of Seaboard States mythology, FBI agents carried off by owls which were not what they seemed, giant warehouses of flying saucers hidden in the desert, humanity created by mad genetic engineers experimenting on ramapithecenes. As a child of Toronto and citizen of Nunavut, he retained a deeply ingrained stereotype regarding the credulousness of his southern neighbours. The other foreign Embedded Journalists back in Deecee used to collect stories about the outrageous things Seaboarders believed, tried to top each other's tall tales in the journo bars on weekends as they waited for their postings.

Ken had initially dismissed the idea that the strange, part-biological technology which had spawned the pods, the bears, the Bunny Girls and castle-pyramids, could be alien in origin as similar mythologising. However, while the trail of biotech the three of them had been following since they left Deecee had clearly indicated that there really was someone to the South of the Red States who was capable of building these sorts of things, Ken was, like Manders, occasionally wondering whether that someone was actually human. He'd been wondering more and more since his encounter with the pyramid back at the community. Surely no one human could have thought up a system like that, let alone devised and implemented it. And, whatever he'd said about the local expertise back in the past, it did seem as if the historical biotech scientists of old California had given up and gone North to Westcoast or East to Texas, a long time ago.

Finally, as the sun approached the horizon, Manders suggested they make camp.

"Can't we see if we can find another building?" Al asked. The previous night, one of the vegetation-covered mounds they'd passed had proved, with a bit of excavating, to be some kind of restaurant, yellow and white plastic tables and chairs, no-longer-shiny deep fryers and stoves, benches with rotting foam padding. They'd spent a relatively comfortable night for the first time in days, though Ken had nightmares about the hideous effigy of a grinning plastic man, white face and blood-red hair, which was moulded into the restaurant's doorway.

"Light's going," Manders said, and that was that. They settled into their now-familiar evening routine, Manders heading off in search of game while Al foraged for firewood and edible fruits, and Ken tried to clear the chosen campsite of brush and rocks, remembering the boy scout expeditions he'd hated as a child, boring old Inuit men tediously explaining how to live off the land. Now he was vaguely wishing he'd paid more attention. He reminded himself that humanity had lived like this for millennia, and that Manders had, by his own brief account, gone very quickly from a citified sophisticate to someone who could bed on cold ground without a complaint, but Ken had to allow that, despite all the practice he'd been putting in, he himself would have made a terrible hunter-gatherer.

Remembered again his grandmother, in lucid moments, railing against what she considered their primitive life in Nunavut, no apartment buildings, no fashion designers, no privately owned cars, the coming and going of rationing season as the snow came and went. Her insistence that food from agrotech facilities somehow tasted fake, despite the assurances of the agrotechnicians that it was, if anything, better than anything they'd been able to grow naturally in the United Prairies. Ken had made fun of her behind her back, until his father caught him at it.

By the time Al and Ken had the fire going, Manders returned with a dead chicken and a slightly perplexed expression beetling his brown eyebrows.

"Look at this," he declared, brandishing the fowl.

Ken took it. "What am I looking for?" he asked.

Manders spread its wings. "They've been clipped. And it's been fed. Well fed. It's domestic, not feral."

"Really?" Ken knew he was right, though. They'd mostly been living off feral chickens since they got into the fruit jungle, the offspring of livestock abandoned when the farmers had gone North to better climates, and significantly more stupid than the feral pigs which they also occasionally managed to catch, or at least, less good at figuring out what a snare or a gun was. *Those* chickens were rangy, spotted, lean and gamy creatures. This one was fat, golden-feathered, with a huge breast and a startling coral-red comb hanging rakishly over its face. It looked almost like something from a Seaboard egg-farm, an expensive one, with free-range hens rather than cube birds.

Manders nodded. "Tame, too. I didn't have to waste my

ammunition." He lolled its head about to show what he meant. He'd broken its neck.

"So, there's people?" Al said, dubious.

Manders shrugged. "Primitive tribes?" he suggested. "Small farmers? Not exactly sophisticated biotech, this bird. If its owners come looking, we'll offer them a trade."

————————

By full dark, the owners of the chicken having failed to materialize, Ken was seated against an orange tree, trying to find a map to the coast on his fieldpad. They'd all agreed that skirting the shoreline would be easier than hacking through jungles, and there was also the possibility of being able to find a seaworthy boat that they could use to sail down the coast. Benjamin, nearby, poked the embers of the damp and smoky fire, and Manders did something complicated to his semiautomatic rifle. All three of them were ignoring, but conscious of, the occasional wildlife noises. Something cawed tunelessly. Rainless thunder muttered warnings overhead.

"Any luck?" Manders asked Ken.

"Not much," Ken said, squinting at the screen of his fieldpad, a little bit worried about the condensation forming under the screen. "Before we got out of range, I downloaded everything I could find for the entire continent. Problem is, there's no recent maps of this area, not since the satellites started falling, and it seems nobody's got the people to spare to send out cartographers to map the terrain. I'm having to apply thirty-year-old data, and back then, this place seems to have been urbanised." The maps he had were grids of fruit farms, towns, leisure parks, marinas, wildlife preserves. No jungles, no wild animals, no strange old buildings and signs under vegetation. A world his grandmother would have recognised, maybe even had visited as a girl. He tried to remember how long it had been since the mass exoduses from San Diego, San Francisco. He reflected that it really didn't take very long for the wilderness to reclaim the land, once the people left.

Al threw aside the stick he'd been using to prod at the ashes and groaned.

"What, private?" said Manders wearily.

"You know," Al said, "I reckon that even if we do find where all this biotech is coming from, we won't find anybody there. I reckon they all died out, or left, years ago."

"Pessimistic of you," Manders observed.

"Just realistic," Al said. "Think about it. *Nobody* else has that kind of tech anymore. Population levels are dropping. Remember what we saw on the Prairies? Remember how few people we've seen since getting out of Red country? I don't believe for a *minute* anything anybody in Deecee or Iqaluit says about achieving sustainability, and neither do you."

"What about—" Ken began to weigh in, when they heard the noise almost right next to their ears; an angry, burbling howling, wordless, like a ghost baby crying or an old woman keening. All three, including Ken, were on their feet in seconds. Ken heard the report of a gun, then something fell from a tree with a faint leafy crash.

"Ah, fuck!" Al exclaimed. "Sorry, sir. It was just a cat."

"Waste of ammunition, private," Manders remarked, as the three of them bent to look.

It was indeed a cat. They'd seen quite a few around the jungle, sleek, feral things perched gleaming-eyed on branches, or trotting busily through the undergrowth, and, on one occasion, staging a noisy orgy in close proximity to their campsite. The animals seemed to have adapted well to the new environment, and both they and the cats had pretty quickly concluded that they posed no threat to each other. With that in mind, Ken felt a twinge of regret as he looked down at the flexible, long, tabby body, still warm. Back North, he'd often wished he could afford to keep a pet cat, but they were rare, expensive to acquire and to keep, well beyond the means of a refugee family, or a junior frontline journalist for a struggling website. This cat seemed, like the chicken, better fed and healthier than the jungle cats they'd seen along the way, and Ken fancied its head was larger. Certainly its legs were, strange powerful back feet, bunched like a rabbit's.

"What's that?" In its mouth, something was squirming. Benjamin prised the locked jaws open and extracted an obscenely naked, wrinkly, wriggling thing, like a foetus.

"A mouse?" Manders looked dubious.

"A cancer-mouse," Ken said, peering closer.

"Come again?"

"They used to breed those little hairless mice for medical research," Ken explained. "In those biotech facilities I was talking about. They were good for studying cancer, Parkinson's, things like that. Old-people diseases. Probably some of them went feral, like the cats and the farm animals." He was a little surprised that something without fur could survive even in the warmth of the jungle, but then again, it had no less hair than many humans. The little creature had stopped struggling and was now looking at Al with an oddly speculative glint in its eyes. Ken found himself again remembering his grandmother, towards the very end of her life, so old she'd forgotten speech, small, wrinkled and balding, but still gazing solemnly out at the world, measuring and considering, judging and finding wanting.

Condemning it for its lack of Movie Multiplexes and Televisions and Theme Parks, for making her spend her last years in a tiny house with her son, daughter-in-law and increasingly alienated grandson, her final days in a bare new-build palliative care ward, surrounded by people speaking alien concepts in alien languages. Never saying, but always somehow implying, that it would have been more honourable to have stayed in Toronto, gone down with the ship, as it were. Also remembered his mother, complaining softly but with an edge of sharp hysteria about the lost labs with their bald mice, how you would have thought they would have cured all these diseases by now, saying the things his father, staring out a window stoically with a muscle twitching in his neck, would never say aloud.

"Put it down, Private, you've scared it enough," Manders said, and Al obeyed, putting it down gently on a patch of moss. It sat there, unmoving, apart from a slight quiver to its whiskerless nose.

"You've traumatised it," said Manders.

"No, it's waiting to be introduced," Al said. He faced it dramatically, bowed like a swashbuckler. "Greetings, noble mouse! We come in peace, from the strange lands of the waterlogged North. I am Flora, this"—he gestured at Ken—"is Fauna, and this"—indicating Manders, whose lips were getting dangerously thin—"is Merryweather."

The mouse considered this, cocked its head to one side, and scampered off. "Well, I reckon *that's* the closest thing to a human we're going to see out here," Al remarked, settling back down in front of the fire and picking up his stick again.

Ken found it harder than usual to sleep that night. He lay awake watching the sheet lightning through the dark leaves of the orange trees, the seemingly interminable light show that had followed them down the coast like an evil spirit, feeling as if his own motivations had been laid horribly bare by the day's events. He had been sure, when the trail of biotech seemed to lead Southwest, that they would find its origin around here. Now, he wondered if he had really been thinking objectively, if he hadn't been influenced by his memories of his grandmother's stories of magic kingdoms, his mother's about miracle-working research labs, all looking for an answer in the past.

Perhaps the answer *is* in the past, he thought. Perhaps the biotech-makers *are* all dead, and the things which have made their way North are just like the map-making satellites, robots blindly following a program until they break. Perhaps, he thought, we should give up and go back. They had enough information about the biotech systems and how they worked, enough so that real experts, cyberneticists like Patel, perhaps, could take over; did it really matter whether or not they found out where it was coming from?

He thought about Patel. Hoped she was still alive, hoped she'd managed to finish her tour of duty and get back to the work she wanted to do. Remembered the desert fortress, all the people around it, with all their lives going on, regardless of what happened with the biotech.

Ken decided. Sojourn over. Time to return. Once they found the coast, once they had a means of going back North to Westcoast and trade caravans and civilisation, he'd tell the others.

The next morning, Ken realised they were being followed. He knew the signs. The subtle, almost imperceptible movements in the jungle alongside or behind them, the animal instinct that tells you when you're being watched, the sound of unfamiliar breath or steps. He waited until he was sure before telling Manders, who was currently taking his turn on point.

"Again?" Manders frowned.

"Not like the Bunny Girl," Ken said hastily. Remembering the stalking terror in the mangrove swamps of upstate New York, that set them on the trail, the guiding will-o'-the-wisp that led them to the Circus of Form near the Prairies. Ken thought of the motherboard, now back at the bottom of his rucksack, the data files Mustang and Mouse had deciphered, wondered if they'd ever manage to get anything useful from the bits of memory they'd managed to extract from the remains, or if it was all just lines of code. "Look behind and to the left. See what I mean."

Manders looked. His eyes widened. Behind them, but keeping pace with strange ease, was a hairless mouse. Forepaws crouched, ears flattened, hopping like a tiny kangaroo. Ken fancied the expression on its face was quietly determined.

"Same one as last night?"

"Think so," Ken replied. Al looked, too, laughed.

"I *thought* it was a girl mouse. Reckon it's fallen in love with me," Al said. The animal did not seem fazed by their scrutiny. It stopped when they stopped, keeping its distance in case they made any hostile moves, but also clearly not regarding them as any kind of threat.

"What is it with you and women?" Ken wondered.

Al shook his head, grinning. "The ladies can't resist me. Even the rodent ones."

"We'll outdistance it," Manders said, putting a firm end to the conversation.

---

But they didn't. By nightfall, it was still with them as they made camp in the shelter of what Ken thought might have once been a highway underpass, now almost beautiful with trailing vines dangling from its edges, making a curtain around the interior, like some kind of magical pavilion.

As Ken managed to get the fire going, he saw it. Sitting near enough to them to enjoy the warmth of the fire, far enough to make a break if it needed to. Al tossed the creature bits of biltong, which it caught and nibbled delicately, turning them over and over in its paws.

"Don't encourage it," Manders said.

"*Her* name is Weena," Benjamin retorted, flicking another shred of dried meat in the mouse's direction. "And she'd appreciate it if you used it."

Ken, who was perusing the maps on his fieldpad again, trying to identify this particular highway underpass in its former state, laughed. "She looks more like a Morlock than an Eloi." Then, responding to Al's glare, "Seriously. A tiny Morlock."

"Don't encourage *him*," Manders said to Ken.

"That's the last of it," Al said apologetically to Weena, holding up his hands to show her the lack of food.

In the absence of any more biltong, the mouse continued to sit in front of the fire, eyes half-closed, paws raised to the heat. Ken was strangely reminded of watching football matches at his high school, how the players would warm their hands at long pipes of hot air before going back into the game.

"I reckon she's good luck," Al said. "Didn't we find this shelter to stay in? And didn't it take us, like, five minutes to find dinner? We owe her a bit of jerky."

"If she can find us a fast route to the coast," Manders said, "I'll fucking *marry* her."

---

The next day, still as grey as ever, but with a new sharp oppressiveness in the air, Weena seemed to have vanished, but then, as they set out on their route, turned up again, hopping determinedly behind them, paws tucked up, ears back. This sight cheered Al up no end, and he would periodically address remarks or questions to the wizened little animal.

"What do you make of those birds there, Weena?"

"Should we take the left or the right path, Weena?"

"Know where we can get a good map of the jungle, Weena?"

"Reckon there's aliens living to the South of here, Weena?"

Which was, Ken reflected, at least a change from the Manders-baiting. But not much of an improvement. Manders kept silent, ignoring the performance.

When the clouds were at their brightest, Manders ordered a halt to consider the best route.

"That way seems clearer," he remarked.

Ken checked the map collection. "It looks like it's the path of an old highway," he said. "Overgrown, but not as badly as where there's earth all the way down. Might get us to the coast faster than cutting through the jungle."

"Then we'll take it." Manders shouldered his pack and started off along the clear route, the other two following.

They hadn't gone far when there was an eerie, high-pitched noise, like an opera singer in distress.

"What—" Manders checked, crouched.

"It's that damn mouse," Ken said, just as Al said, "It's Weena. She doesn't think we should go that way."

The mouse had stopped in the middle of the path, feet planted, wringing her paws and howling, tiny jaws open and quivering on a tragic note.

"Well, she's out of luck, then, isn't she?" Manders scowled, continued forward. The mouse stayed put, intensified its keening, but Manders strode forward and the others followed. Eventually the sound faded away.

A couple of hours of walking later, the path ended in an asphalt cliff-face, stormy colour matching the sky. Painted white and yellow lines, and the twisted remains of hand railings, indicated nakedly what it had once been.

"Looks like there might have been an earthquake here," Ken remarked, feeling silly as he said it, and sillier as Manders favoured him with a slit-eyed look of weary conde-scension.

"See?" Al crowed. "*Told* you Weena was good luck. If we'd followed her, we wouldn't have wasted all this time."

They turned and trudged back, along the path. When they reached the junction where they'd left Weena, she was still there, sitting quietly, grooming her pink flanks. She looked up, sniffed the air, then, as they struck off into the jungle, resumed hopping along behind them, with what struck Ken as an unmistakably smug expression.

Manders dropped behind. "I can't believe I'm going to say this," he said to Ken in a low, peculiar tone, "but Usagi, I... don't trust that mouse."

Ken resisted the urge to laugh. "I know what you mean," he said. "It's probably not what it looks like, though. I think it might have evolved some sort of homing instinct, or it might have a territory that it's patrolling."

"Or it's yet another modified animal that wants us to go somewhere," Manders countered. "I tell you, I've had my fill of being pushed around by things with four legs."

"She hasn't got a headpiece," Ken pointed out. "And we've never known the pods to colonise anything that small. In any case, not all of the converted animals were hostile; remember the Kermode bear?"

"Still not sure that one's intentions were entirely friendly," Manders said.

Ken shrugged. "I'm running out of possibilities. Maybe it's imprinted on Al, thinks he's its mother?"

"Or maybe he's rescued the Princess of the Mouse People and she's now got him under a magic spell," Manders said sarcastically. "Whatever's going on, we need to watch it. *And* him." Unspoken, the final encounter with Swift and the bears hung between them.

"Still, it doesn't seem any less accurate than any other means of finding our way through this," Ken said. "It doesn't seem to be trying to stop us reaching the coast, and when it does, well, I don't think these things can exactly swim very well."

The mouse kept up its hopping pace, still covering the same ground as its much bigger traveling companions. At one point it halted, went off to one side of the path, disappeared into the undergrowth. Then they heard the shrill keening noise again. Al, with a glance at the other two, followed. Manders shrugged—*why not?*—and he and Ken went along.

They found the object of the mouse's distress in a small

clearing of berry bushes. It was the corpse of a dog, or coyote, or some hybrid of the two, old and desiccated into a tangle of fur, ligaments and scattered, jumbled greyish-white bones. Off to one side, the skull sat, looking strangely large and knobbly.

"It's dead, it can't hurt you," Ken said to Weena, feeling slightly whimsical. The mouse didn't listen, if indeed it understood (Ken was ruling nothing out at this point); it stopped keening, and instead began to poke around in the remains. What it found evidently satisfied it, and it hopped off again.

Manders paused and poked around in the same spot with his machete, tentatively then with more purpose. Looking, Ken thought, for pod matter, for any evidence the animal was part of the system. He himself looked around the grove, looked for the tell-tale moving cilia, black plastic lumps pulsing up out of the ground preparatory to achieving critical mass and forming a castle. Al leaned against a tree and watched them work, not offering to help.

"Anything?" Ken asked after a couple of fruitless minutes of searching.

Wordlessly Manders held up a small harness, woven out of copper wire, shaped to fit around the dog-creature's body.

"Biotech?" Ken said dubiously. He took it, felt around it with his hands. It just seemed to be copper wire; carefully woven in a tight braid, but nothing more than that.

"None of it's black," Manders said, "and the biotech has never been metal before."

"Could be a different sort of rig?" Al suggested. "An earlier type? A version for the jungle?"

"I just don't know," Ken said. He took a couple of pictures, put the rig in a side pocket. They moved on.

"I've got a theory," Ken said as they hacked through a particularly dense stand of young trees.

"Can't wait to hear it," Manders replied.

"Domestic chickens." Ken counted on his fingers. "A cat, maybe not a tame house-kitty, but definitely bred to look the way it did. A dog with some kind of harness, like for a leash or for pulling small things. Carts or sledges. And a homing mouse." He waited to see if the others would make the connection, then continued, "Those research labs. What if there are still people around there? Carrying on breeding programmes." Curing all the diseases. Defying old age, population collapse, rising sea levels and changing climates.

"Maybe the biotech makers *are* actually still here somewhere?" Al raised an eyebrow. "Might make sense. Or perhaps the local people know the biotech guys."

Manders was silent, and Ken waited for a mocking or sarcastic remark, but instead he pointed. "Notice how we haven't had to clear anything much for a while."

"You're right," Al said. "It's a path! A proper path that someone's keeping up. We'll be sleeping in beds tonight."

Ken refrained from saying the obvious—Al knew as well as he did that the people might not be friendly—but the thought did put them all in a much better mood, even when the sun went down, and the promised beds failed to appear.

"Never mind," Al said. "The rain's still holding off, and the ground's clear."

After the evening meal, Ken took out the fieldpad, began to go over the Bunny Girl data, hoping it might provide some connection with the mouse, some explanation of what they were looking for. He started with the folder marked *geography*, the one where Mustang said he might have identified homing data for the cyborg. Tentatively, not really understanding the more technical sections, Ken began to read, to make notes.

————————

The next day started more or less as the others, grey with occasional flashes of lightning, but before noon a wind got up, sudden gusts bursting through the forest. Between the rustling fruit trees and the alarmed noises of the birds, Ken initially missed the rushing, pattering sound, then put it down to the long-expected onset of tropical rain.

He heard Manders shout, turned. The old soldier was balancing on one foot, twisting to avoid a sudden huge flood of wrinkled, pink flesh. Like a river of human skin, swift muscles bunching convulsively underneath, surging along the path. Ken couldn't move fast enough to avoid it, looked down in astonishment as he felt hundreds, thousands, of tiny feet pattering over his boots, rebounding off his legs, a huge stampede of...

...*mice*...

...and just as suddenly, it was gone, flowing ahead of them. Manders began to run after it, followed by Benjamin and then, a second later, Ken.

Weena had vanished into the seething course of flesh, moving and darting as one, like starlings before a rainstorm. It twisted and turned along the path. Ken found himself suddenly emerging into a clearing before splashing into a shallow watercourse, noting with a kind of absent-minded shock that it was a man-made watercourse, lined with discolouring blue-green plastic, tripping over a fallen aluminum strut, nearly running into, *of course*, a giant teacup, mold obscuring the pattern on the side, running and along a wide path up to...

Ken stared in detached disbelief, as the surging horde of mice, *tiny Eloi or tiny Morlocks*, seemingly rose on itself and, at incredible speed, spiraled up the heights of the huge, vine-entangled castle with pointed turrets that suddenly loomed in front of him out of the jungle. He thought he vaguely recognised it from the old movie of the children, from the stylised image at the start of some Japanese cartoons. Crazily, he wondered if he had indeed been a good boy, if his grandmother had finally found some way to take him to a Theme Park. Then the squealing flesh-form was gone, vanished into the windows, only an eerie, keening river of chirping noises emanating from the castle betraying its continued presence.

Ken was startled to hear someone laugh, realised it was Al, on the other side of him. "This way to the happiest place on Earth," he said. "We've found the magic kingdom, Ken, *there*'s the people you were looking for."

Ken nodded, still in shock. Nearby, he saw a tall metal pillar, evidently a streetlamp of some kind. Peering closer, he could see pink mice inside it, chewing away at the wires, stripping it down to the usable copper. As he watched, one emerged with a length of wire in its mouth, scurried across the short length of ground to the castle. "I suppose the mice must have some human DNA in them, from the labs. Or maybe they're more products from the biotech makers, an engineered mouse civilisation."

"Or it's just evolution." Manders' harsh voice cut into the humid gloom. "Ants domesticate other insects, monkeys and birds use tools. With no humans around, something's going to take their place. Has to take their place."

"Life goes on," Al said, his tone strangely serious.

They continued to stand in front of the castle, thinking.

"Reckon she was using us," Manders said after a minute.

"What?"

"Protection. From those cats, or from enemy mice." Ken resisted the urge to laugh as Manders continued, "She was clearly some ways out of her territory. We were traveling the right way, we could take out the cats, protect her from attacks. We could be manipulated into going where she wanted us to go." He glanced slyly at Al. "What's the biggest trap built by a mouse?"

"Very funny, sir," Al remarked noncommittally.

They stood for a few more minutes, listening to the mouse chatter and the vague rumbling from behind the flashing clouds overhead, watching life go on, seeing, perhaps, the future of life on Earth. Ken reflected that his grandmother would have appreciated the joke.

"We carry on South?" Manders asked Ken.

Ken nodded, got out the fieldpad. "I figured something out last night," he said. "Wasn't going to say until I was absolutely sure, but it's worth mentioning now. I was looking over the geographic data Mustang was able to get out of the Bunny Girl motherboard. Now, if he and I have managed to interpret it correctly, then"—he called up a couple of files—"the thing's got an in-built homing device, that points to a location in Southern Mexico. Not exactly sure *where* in Southern Mexico, but somewhere in this region."

"So..." Al frowned. "That means we might actually *know* where the biotech makers are, or were?"

"If we assume this is some kind of emergency recall, telling it where to go," Ken said.

"Big assumption," Manders said.

"Even if I'm wrong, there's got to be a reason why they want the Bunny Girls to go there," Ken said. "Maybe it's a warehouse of Bunny Girls? Either way, though, it'll be useful."

"So we stick with the plan, find a boat?" Manders asked.

Ken nodded. Never give up. Keep following the trail. "If this area here is Disney Land, then..." He held up the map. "If we go due Southwest here, we're no more than twenty klicks from the coast. I expect the mice have kept the roads up."

"Reckon they've kept the boats up, too?" Benjamin asked.

"We'll find out, won't we?" Manders took point again, Al following slowly.

"You really going to marry her now, sir? She *did* find us a clear route to the coast..."

Ken joined them under the thunder-flashing sky, heading out towards the ocean.

# CHAPTER FOURTEEN: THE SHIP OF FOOLS

ZORRAH LOOKED as if she was going to speak. Instead, though, she leaned back in her chair and raised an eyebrow almost to her hairline.

Totchli knew she was trying to make him feel awkward, but felt it anyway. "Um... any questions?" he finished. He'd downplayed the role of the mice as much as he could, but he still had the feeling he'd come across as a complete lunatic.

Zorrah shook her head. She sat forward again, placed her arms on the table. "Next boat to the city with any space on it won't be going for a couple of days," she said, straightening up. Her tone was pleasant, neutral, as if Totchli hadn't spent the last couple of hours telling her some sunstruck tale about madmen, control centres and sentient mice with hive-minds. Totchli wasn't sure if she was humouring him. "You can stay here till then. Longer, if you like and provided you don't get in anybody's way. Afraid it's not exactly a recuperative environment, but apart from the weather, it's quiet. And there's plants."

"You'll be shipping the samples...?" Totchli asked.

Zorrah grinned wolfishly. "Already done. The boat

South went yesterday, while you were sleeping it all off. The Temple sent up a special emergency boat for the survivors, too. A speeder. That went South while you were still up at the colony, helping the team gathering the forensics. So don't worry, you won't be sharing your trip back to Axox' with a half-dozen of the traumatised."

Totchli nodded. "I see," he said, since she seemed to expect him to say something.

Zorrah stood to indicate the audience was over, gestured to the door. Totchli preceded her out of the bare, windowless meeting room. She nodded to him and strode off along the busy corridor.

Totchli, for his part, hesitated. His briefing done—and it seemed like it would be the last one, at least for a while—he didn't have any place to go or anything specific to do. All around him, warriors and technicians bustled about on errands. He could go visit the fields again, he supposed, but he wasn't even entirely sure how to find the door out of the Bunker, and he didn't think anyone would be willing to drop what they were doing to help him out.

"Hey," said someone behind him. Totchli turned. It was Coyotl, cleaned up and with her burns dressed. She smiled slightly. "Came to see if you were all right after your meeting with the She-Wolf. Want a walk?"

Totchli nodded. "If we can go outside," he said. "Getting a bit cramped in here, for me."

Coyotl nodded in return. "Weather report's for overcast, no unusual wind or rain," she said. "So if we don't go too far out, we'll be fine."

Once out of the Bunker, by unspoken mutual consent, they both wandered towards the experimental cultivar beds. Looking at the neat layouts, Totchli felt calmer, reassured. Order was prevailing. They reminded him of the chinampas and terrace gardens of home. There were no scouts in them today. Totchli was irrationally grateful for this, he wasn't feeling too keen on cyborgs at the moment. Just a wire-rigged irrigation system keeping up a gentle rain of water into the fields.

One of the more religious warriors had discreetly taken him aside yesterday, shown him a room in the Bunker—an ex-storeroom by the look of it—where someone had set up a rudimentary altar to the Serpent and the Mirror, with a few pictures and rough sculptures of more esoteric deities on shelves about the room. Had mentioned to him that if he wanted to spend time in it, get himself right with the god of his choosing, no one would think any the less of him. Totchli had thanked her politely. At least she'd taken the trouble to speak to him, where most of the warriors just avoided him, as if he, too, had been inhabited by the madness which had gripped the colony.

Totchli tried to avoid the thought that perhaps they were right.

It was easier to do that out here, among growing things. Easier to find a way back to normal life. Totchli had never been particularly religious. He'd done his namequest when he came of age, of course, but he'd never regarded the visions as connected with gods. A way of accessing of the subconscious, or communication with parallel worlds at best. Like sacrificing paper animals in the bonfires. A symbol of community and gratitude, not some kind of magic gift to a capricious deity. Looking at the cultivar field, he had a similar feeling. That the question of whether or not there were gods to get right with was moot, that the real spirituality was in the earth, the plants, the animals. The strange miracles of evolution that allowed the existence of maize, humans... and hairless gestalt-minded saboteur mice. Totchli closed his eyes, felt the sun on his face.

"What you going to do now, Rabbit Boy?" Coyotl asked.

Totchli shrugged. "I'm still technically on corvee for the next month. Flood season's almost over, so I doubt they'll want me back sandbagging. I'll probably wind up reassigned to damage assessment, bridge repair, filing, something like that. Can't say I mind, really. Not particularly wanting to go back to splicing genes for a while."

Coyotl nodded.

"You?" he asked her.

"Same as usual," Coyotl said. "Courier duty, logistics, the sort of thing I've been doing for thirty years now." She thought for a minute. "Just before we left, though, I put in for reassignment to the inter-city run. I've had it with trips to the Bunker. Given how bad the floods were this year, chances are they'll give me disaster relief duty for the next season or so. Maybe we'll run into each other?"

"Could be." Totchli wondered what it would be like to run into her again and wasn't altogether happy at the idea. He'd like to forget what he'd seen, forget the colony and the Bunker and the helm-headed animals and humans and the mice and the fat man and the probable fate of humanity. "Itch and Tot?"

"Staying here. They were assigned, and no reason to move them. In fact, since they've been upcountry and know what we're up against, even less reason to move them than before." Her tone softened a bit. "Don't worry about them, Rabbit Boy. They're young. No sense of their own mortality. They'll forget what they've seen, and be all right."

Totchli made a noncommittal noise. He supposed he owed his life to them. Coyotl for insisting on stopping, going back and following his trail, Itch for taking charge in her absence, Tot for sending an emergency message to the Bunker, calling in the rescue team.

The colony site, and the compound site, had been crawling with activity when he and Coyotl had left it, rescue personnel and forensic specialists combing every inch of the place, isolating every fragment of bone or chip off a guiding-helm, though he strongly suspected they wouldn't find any trace of the hairless mice. After Coyotl had rescued him from Meztli and the rogue control centre, they'd returned to the boat, only to get the message from Tot: the Bunker had responded, told them to stay there and await the team. They'd spent an uneasy, disturbing night and day in the camp, with Totchli dreaming of bears on fire and Coyotl—well, Totchli wasn't sure if she'd slept at all.

The arrival of the investigation team had, however, brought a wave of refreshing banality to the site. Like the sun coming in suddenly through a window in a dark store-room, exposing the terrifying monster as nothing more than an old and cobwebbed chair. A dozen brisk, efficient people, measuring, recording, taking soundings. Picking up samples of everything, berating the warriors and Totchli for having had the temerity to move things about, wanting to know everything they could. About what time had they found the first survivor? When had he encountered the bears in the woods? Could he identify the man with the helm? At first, they hadn't believed that part of his story. Then, after one of the investigators, sifting through the wreckage at the second control centre, had found a human skeleton with the tell-tale signs of helm grafting around the skull and spine—followed by another, and another—they'd begun to treat him with a bit more respect. And then they began to analyse the helms on the larger animals, and that was when they stopped acting as if he'd made it all up.

Though, come to think of it, that was also when the air of nervousness and fear had begun to creep into people's conversations with him.

Over the next few days, he'd told the story of what had happened at the compound more times than he cared to think, the investigators becoming a parade of blank faces asking the same questions, pinching and prodding and sampling. Whatever; it was out of his hands now. He wasn't alone anymore. He'd done his job. The medical investigation, admittedly fairly rough and ready, had also shown that he had no lasting ill effects from the time he'd spent in the control centre, beyond the inevitable stresses and strains anyone might get from going through a strange ordeal. "The mice won't be talking to you again," the doctor had said, thinking he was making a joke. Totchli had made himself laugh, just to prove he was on the way back to normality.

"Zorrah say anything much?" Coyotl asked after a moment.

"Yeah," Totchli said. "Kept asking about the colony, and the compound. Mostly the same questions the others asked. But strange thing is, I couldn't really tell what she wanted." He thought about Zorrah's manner during the interview, then said slowly, "It was like she'd been expecting the colony to fail—but also like she was gathering information. As if she was planning a second go."

"Probably is," Coyotl said. "She kept asking me about the geography, the location. As if maybe she thought it was something about the environment that brought it all down."

"Environment." Totchli spat the word like it was a curse.

Coyotl looked at him in surprise.

"The environment's the source of all our trouble. We can't live in civilisation anymore, the floods are getting longer and more frequent, the water levels rising. So, what do we do instead? Do we colonize the North, cut down the forests, enslave the animals, kill off the mice?" he went on, while part of him marveled detachedly at his own fury. "Do we stay in civilisation and try to fix the climate, accepting that it may be unfixable? Do we try to change ourselves, adapt to the new conditions? Do we do nothing and accept that if we don't miraculously evolve, then we'll just go extinct as a species? That's the problem," he said. Suddenly feeling weak, he sat down heavily on a storage box. After a moment of regarding him silently, Coyotl sat down, too.

"What do you think we should do then, Rabbit Boy?" she asked.

Totchli sighed. "Fact is, I don't think we *can* do anything much about it. We might as well just let it all go to ruin."

"Like Meztli?"

"No, Meztli was trying to change *us*. Thought—well, I still don't know exactly what he thought. But he thought we needed to become something different, something that could live with the mice." Totchli's voice was bitter. "Let the damn mice have the planet if they want it so much. Serpent knows I don't."

Above them, the sun was going down, great long streaks of red across the sky to the West. He could hear warriors coming back from their daily assignments, talking loudly, evening and night watch patrols gearing up. More distantly, the hissing and clanking noise of a kitchen beginning to prepare dinner, and a faint smell of chilli and beans drifted up on the wind. A set of cheerful shrieks somewhere in the vicinity of the living quarters, that ended in faintly lascivious laughter. He felt very far away from it all.

"Look at that." Coyotl pointed to the stalks of maize.

Totchli, following her finger, saw little flickers of movement within the field. Looked closer. Mice. Pink, hairless mice, like up North.

Coyotl chuckled. "Little beggars have made it this far south," she said, almost affectionately. "They'll be colonising *our* territory soon."

"They'll kill us off," Totchli said.

Coyotl shrugged. "If they do, it'll be because we failed to adapt," she said. "But they've adapted. Reckon if they can, so can we. Meztli be damned."

---

After dinner, Totchli repaired to the common area. The room was spare and chilly like the rest of the Bunker, but with more than a few attempts at decoration courtesy of the warriors. There were blankets, cushions hand-sewn out of whatever materials happened to be at hand (mostly, it seemed, old sacks and worn-out shirts), slightly battered musical instruments, data boxes where you could download stories or videos for your scroll, collective film-viewing equipment, and a selection of pictures and cheap figurines, most, naturally enough, skirting the boundaries of good taste. Totchli, who might have found them vulgar before his trip North, now found them strangely reassuring. After nodding in what he hoped was a not-unfriendly but none-theless curiosity-discouraging way to the few warriors who were variously occupied about the place, he sat down on a hard instagrowth bench in front of the radio link, under a dog-eared picture of an implausibly dressed woman looking pleasantly surprised at the sight of a priapic giant squirrel, touched his scroll to the radio-receiver, activated the visual and checked the messages in his pigeonhole. He'd been disinclined to do so since returning, but decided he should make a start. After sifting through a few uninteresting work messages and skimming one from his mother, he paused on one from Ocelotl.

*...I've taken the liberty of contacting the labour office and requesting you remain with the colonisation project,* it read after the usual greetings and assurances. *Rest assured, we won't have you pursuing any more lunatics! It's just that some of the vision-quest technicians here in Axoxoctic have been crunching the numbers, and we've got an interesting new project we think you might like to get involved with. On a purely voluntary basis, of course; you can opt out if you don't like the terms, but I do hope you'll at least give it a chance. Mazatl's on board already, she's one of the leading researchers...*

Mazatl? Oh, yes, Mazatl. *That* Mazatl. Totchli blew out his breath in a discreet snort, raised his eyebrows. Ocelotl's message was so cautiously phrased, it seemed fairly obvious that this was another strange, and probably dangerous, project. Part of Totchli revolted at the thought, resolved to have nothing more to do with the Temple and Ocelotl's ideas. Another part of him, the part that had said yes the first time round, was intrigued. What could vision-quest technicians have to do with a colonisation project?

Well, he supposed he could lose nothing by paying Ocelotl an exploratory visit, before reporting to the labour bureau for corvee redeployment. He had to stop at the Temple anyway for them to sign him off the project officially, so it wasn't as if he was doing anything unexpected or unusual. Ocelotl was right that he could refuse to continue with the project if he didn't want to. It was corvee, not slavery. And at least he should find out what was going on...

*That way lies madness,* the more sensible part of him

warned. *That sort of thinking leads to ruined campsites and sentient mice.*

It was right, of course, but he knew he'd do it anyway.

Whatever it was, it would at least be more interesting than building bridges. He could decide for himself later, if "interesting" was what he wanted.

# CHAPTER FIFTEEN: WATERSHIP DOWN

"TENOCHTITLAN," Ken said.

"Gesundheit," Al replied.

Ken smiled. "Seriously. It was one of the major cities of the Aztec empire, according to the fieldpad."

"I thought you said we were in Mexico City?"

"We are, or will be. It was built over Tenochtitlan, or rather, expanded out from it. It's supposed to be around here somewhere, a couple of klicks ahead. The ruins of it, I mean. We might be able to see them still."

"Great, more ruins," Al said. "Let's hope the lost civilisation we find *this* time's got a few humans in it."

"Careful what you wish for, private," Manders said.

———

After leaving Disney Land, they had found the predicted marina, on the coast. Found a couple of boats which could be cleaned and fixed; spent a few days doing so, complicated by the fact that none of the motors worked and none of them knew very much about sailing. Eventually they focused on one of the sailboats as the least worst option, and, cobbling together the remains of some sails they found in a ruined boathouse, supplemented with oars from the holds of other boats, managed to rig up something which more or less worked, powered by a combination of wind and paddles.

As per their agreement, they headed South, along the coast, fishing and gathering to sustain themselves, and looking for a sign. The jungles here seemed to be as deserted as the ones further North—if not more so, since Ken had yet to see any evidence of abandoned marinas, houses or Theme Parks—but from their position, it was difficult to tell.

The jungle composition was changing. Fewer fruit trees, more plants that Ken failed to recognise, or even conclusively identify using the increasingly irrelevant information on his fieldpad.

The absence of people was puzzling in another way. For decades, there had been first reports, then rumours, of a movement of people determined to change, or perhaps restore, civilisation. Like the Inuit in Nunavut, they wanted to move away from European influence, develop a new North American way of living. They spoke a lingua-franca version of Nahuatl, were re-establishing farms and towns based on the old Aztec system. There were rumours that there were scientists, trying to work out a way of surviving the changes in climate.

Ken hadn't expected to find any thriving cities, but he was surprised not to encounter, at the very least, communities along the lines of Thule. Then again, perhaps it was Thule which had started the rumours... *All I can do is observe and report*, Ken had written on his fieldpad. *It's for other people to make sense of it all.*

A couple of days into the journey, Ken had sighted it again.

It stood on a small beach, in front of the jungle, in plain sight. Bony, bucktoothed, skinny and ragged. Its arms were raised and out, making a flag of its body. Ken almost felt relieved to see it. A familiar sight in a strange wilderness, which, after so long, felt like an old friend.

Ken pointed. "Over there," he said. The other two sighted the Bunny Girl, turned the boat to shore.

"The homing signal?" Al suggested.

"Makes sense," Ken said.

By the time they had pulled into the beach, it was gone.

"We'll have to leave the boat here, then," Al said.

"Cover it and make it as secure as we can," Manders said. "Try and mark our trail so we can come back to it. Doesn't look like there are many boat thieves in the area, and, once we're done here, it'll be a faster way to Westcoast than walking."

"Safer, too," Al said. Sighing, he dug around in his rucksack for his machete. "More jungles," he said. "More stupid fucking jungles."

---

They had continued inland, following the occasional sightings of the Bunny Girl—or Girls, Ken reflected—until reaching the current set of ruins, apparently the outskirts of a city. Probably Mexico City, Ken deduced. The jungle was lower, denser, than the Northern one. It seemed, perhaps surprisingly, to have been uninhabited for longer, though they did still occasionally find the odd overgrown dwelling, restaurant, even, once, the stub of an office building, now a weird square shape covered in vines. Ken found himself morbidly imagining the same fate happening to the cities further North.

He was heartened, though, by the fact that the trail was indeed pointing to central Mexico. He had been right all along, there was something important to the biotech-makers in the area.

Al had been particularly keen to develop theories about the situation. Lost cities of Nahuatl-speaking biotechnicians, deliberately isolating themselves from the world. People disappearing through folds in the space-time continuum, fleeing this world for a better universe somewhere else. Or magic. Ken had been polite, ruling out nothing and writing down some of the better ideas. Manders had been openly scornful, though knowing both Manders and Al, Ken reflected that he was probably trying to encourage Al.

Now Al pointed above the trees. "Usagi," he said, "look."

Ken looked.

Visible above the jungle was the largest black pyramid the three of them had seen. The surface seemed to glow and breathe softly in the light of the sun. Like the ghost, Ken reflected, of the ancient Aztec city which once stood there.

"It's bigger than the one in the mountains," Ken said. "And that one was pretty big."

"We've got to check it out," Al said. Manders nodded.

---

There were other, smaller black plastic structures on the way to the pyramid. The size of sheds, or cars, or cottages. A couple looked uncomfortably like the geodesic domes from

Thule, and Ken wondered if the people in the pyramid up
North had somehow been able to send the image to this one,
or if it was just a coincidence. He remembered something
about geodesic domes being an ideal structural form, an old
black-and-white video with a faded-looking man presenting
it, talking about Spaceship Earth, the planet as closed
ecosystem. A few black plastic extrusions that looked
strangely like abstract sculptures, much like the one
Coyote's daughter had made. Again, coincidence, or
evidence of communication? The jungle was clearing, too,
Ken noticed. They hadn't had to use their machetes for a
while.

"No animals," Manders remarked. "Or birds. Except
those crows."

It was true, Ken realised. He hadn't heard anything
rustling, flying, or making any sort of noise since they began
on the approach towards the building. But Manders was
right. Around the top of the pyramid, a couple of crows or
ravens circled, silently, as if looking for prey.

The three of them stood at the base of the pyramid,
looking up.

"Do you reckon we've found the source of it all?" Al
asked.

"No bears," Manders said. "Or bear-equivalents. It
doesn't think it needs to protect itself, perhaps."

"So, maybe it *is* the source," Ken said. "Whether it is or
not, it's certainly something important to it."

He thought of the word *Mictlan*, but couldn't
remember why.

The smooth front of the pyramid parted, a human-sized
entrance. Like curtains, like a Venus flytrap opening.

"I've got to go in," Ken said. "You two don't have to. If
I'm not out in a couple of hours, go back to the coast."

Manders shook his head, slid off his rucksack, unholstered his pistol. "I'm coming in, too," he said. "Might be a one-way trip, but I've been expecting to take one of those for far too long. And if it is, I'll have done something really interesting on my way out."

Ken took off his rucksack too, taking out his fieldpad and one or two other useful objects, plus the last of the biltong. *The rucksack should be safe enough*, he thought, *no one would steal it, this close to the pyramid.*

Al said nothing, but likewise doffed his rucksack and followed the other two in. Ken wondered what Al's possible motivation could be. Arrogance, perhaps, a denial of mortality?

*Ask him later. If you all get out.*

The pyramid closed. They were in a long room, or a corridor, leading in. Black-walled, no light. A beam flared; Al, finding his LED torch in a pocket somewhere.

"Everyone OK?"

"What now?" Manders, hoarse and faded. "I suppose we have to go further in?"

Ken shrugged. "Do we have a choice?" He began to follow the route, hearing the two sets of footsteps behind him, muffled by the plastic floor.

"Better, or worse, than the jungle?" Al began a few minutes later.

"Really, private," Manders responded.

"Just making conversation," Al said. "After all, one thing that's worse than the jungle here, it's boring." A pause. "At least it's not wet. Or cold."

"If you're trying to pass the time interestingly, private," Manders replied, "you're failing."

After continuing in silence for a while, they came to a room. Another black, unlit room.

"I would have expected people by now," Manders said.

"Me too," Ken said. "Even if they're ant-people, like up at the community. Where *are* they all?"

Al tucked his torch under his arm, made a megaphone of his hands. "Attention, people of the pyramid!" he shouted. "You have visitors! This is Ken Usagi, this is Captain Henry Manders, and I am Baron Samedi, Loa of the Dead and Dying."

Ken turned to look at him in shock, but Manders, from what Ken could see in the dim light from the torch, seemed unconcerned. "My purpose is madness. It's the only way you can really tell what happens," Al continued. He waited for a minute, but there was no reply from the dark silence.

Then Ken saw it, or thought he did. A flicker of rags, an impossibly small tinny footstep. A glimpse of a bony, beaky face. Then gone.

"Bunny Girl," he said. "Up ahead."

"You sure?" Manders asked.

"No, but then I'm not sure of anything, in here," Ken said. "I'm going after it. It's the first hint we've had that there's anything in here at all." He suited actions to words, and behind him, could hear the sounds of the others following.

———————————

Some time later—Ken was not sure how much later—the torch went out.

Al swore. Ken heard him fiddling with the switch, then a slight cracking noise, as if Al had thrown it onto the floor. "Time to embrace the darkness," Al said. His voice sounded hollow in the pyramid.

"You still Baron Samedi?" Ken asked, trying to be facetious.

"I'm *always* Baron Samedi," Al said, deadpan or serious.

"Put your hands on my shoulders," Ken suggested.

"What? Oh." Al understood, did as Ken said.

"Now, Manders, do the same with Al."

"Done it." Manders' voice, sounding far away.

"Then let's move forward." Ken put one hand on the wall and held the other in front of him, continued moving, slowly, blindly, shuffling along, feeling with his feet as well in case of sudden drops. He mustn't take anything for granted, he realised. He could feel Al's hands, squeezing his shoulders a little painfully, but he was almost grateful for the pain, for the reminder that he wasn't alone in here.

"I've realised something," Manders said, after a long while.

"What's that?" Ken asked.

"I've realised..." Manders, incredibly, laughed. "I've realised I don't actually exist. Not outside of books." His tone was strange, light and clipped, like when he'd talked about his past back at the Circus of Form's encampment.

"The *hell*?" Ken exclaimed.

Manders went on, in the same light tone. "A figment of someone's imagination, then picked up to be the figment of several someones. Carried on, through the decades. No wonder I've lived for so long, seen so many wars. No wonder I'm tired."

"Are you crazy?" Ken said.

"No, really. I'm an actual, literary figure. I shouldn't exist. Can't exist. But I do. I live in the hearts and minds of my countrymen, like Sherlock Holmes. It's absurd." Manders laughed again. "Exist. Shouldn't exist. Can't exist." Then, serious and grim, "Don't exist."

The laugh stopped.

"He's gone," Al said.

"Manders?" Ken called. Then, "Captain?" Nothing. Feeling simultaneously terrified and silly, he tried, "Um, Henry?" Still nothing.

"I'm telling you, he's gone. Vanished," Al said.

"Let go a minute," Ken said. Keeping his hand on the wall, he walked back, and forth, then back again. Couldn't feel anything other than the walls. No sudden drop-offs, nothing to indicate how a man could just disappear.

"Gone crazy, then vanished," he said. "How the hell does that happen?" Groping blindly, he found Al, held on to him for a minute.

"Going on?" Al asked.

"Have to," Ken said.

---

They continued as before, Ken leading, Al with his hands on his shoulders. The corridor was silent except for their tense, anxious breathing and the shuffling sound of their feet.

Then, after how long Ken couldn't tell, he felt the hands vanish off his shoulders.

He called out, "Al?"

No reply.

As before, he went back along the wall, then forwards. He couldn't hear any breathing, any footsteps. He was alone.

"Al? Benjamin?" He tried to remember other names. "Mumbotu? Alistair? Little man from another place?"

A faint reply. "...*Baron Samedi, Loa of the Dead and Dying...*"

"Baron Samedi, then!" Ken shouted, relieved and panicked at the same time. "Whatever you like! Just—where the hell are you?"

No reply.

"Have you found a way out?"

Another faint echo. "...*Dead, and dying...*"

Ken sank down, wrapped his arms around his knees, sobbed. There was no Al, just the echo. And after a while, there wasn't even that.

There were no more voices.

———————

After a while, Ken thought, *I'd better go back.*

He wasn't sure if he *could* go back, or if he'd be able to get out if he did. But having lost two men, he wasn't about to be the third. He turned around, one hundred and eighty degrees, put his hand on the wall, started to move.

Then he saw it.

A flare of light behind him.

He turned, looked.

Further down the corridor, another brief flare of light. Silhouetted in it, the Bunny Girl, apparently bursting ptarmigan-like into the world. Ken stood, stared, then rushed towards it, almost crying. The cyborg creatures had guided him thus far. Surely they wouldn't abandon him now? *One raven driving the rabbit on, the other hopping in front...* He moved faster, following the flares of light, following the sound of it, the rustling of the rags that he'd never noticed before, in the pyramid, but now he did. Following, as he'd followed it all along, since New York, since Nunavut even. He knew he could find the answers, if he followed it. Knew it must be taking him someplace where he had to be. *Show me the truth*, he thought. *Get me out of here, but first, show me the truth.*

---

And then, the Bunny Girl vanished.

Ken continued for a while, hoping to see another flare, hear its footsteps and ragged fluttering. But nothing came.

His legs grew weary, the corridor endless.

It occurred to him that he was never going to see the Bunny Girl again. He was lost, deep in the pyramid, with no idea where to go, no friends, and no guide. He slowed, stopped.

Ken realised there was no way out. He said this to himself, over and over, and gradually began to realise it was true.

A meaning came back to him. *Mictlan*, he remembered. The Aztec afterlife, a faded memory from Native Cultures class. Faded images of skull-faced creatures, flayed people, weird brown-and-green animals painted on rocks or skins. He almost laughed, or cried. This place *was* the afterlife, or at least the gateway to it.

He sat down, leaned back, pressed his spine against the wall-substance. He could feel it, warm like skin. Thought of his parents, of his friends—his enemies, even. They would never know how he died. No one would know. After a while, when they failed to report in, Iqaluit Online News would declare him missing, eventually acknowledge his death. He'd never be able to say goodbye.

He found himself, for no good reason, remembering a cafe. Just a little greasy-spoon fast-food place, set up in a prefab building near his old high school. He used to go there a lot after class, still liked to go back when he was visiting his parents.

He'd never see it again.

That lukewarm cup of coffee had been the last he'd ever drink there.

What about afterwards? He'd never given it much thought. His mother, with the slightly distracted agnosticism of the Ontario Scots, had told him about heaven and hell, but had admitted that, probably, it was all just a myth. He'd read about near-death experiences, *a bright light moving towards you, a spirit guide*, but dismissed it as superficial foolishness. Learned about traditional Inuit beliefs in school, but the Inuit kids made it plain they didn't welcome converts, especially not swamp-boys. He'd flirted a little with a New Age group in university, but found the idea of reincarnation as difficult to believe as the idea of an afterlife. His grandmother, and later his father, had taught him about the family *butsudan*, the ancestor shrine, and about using it to remember the dead.

Another pang.

He would never be someone's ancestor.

His own ancestors would fade away, forgotten.

That line of thought made him remember one of the nights back at Thule, a warm summer night with the sun sinking lazily back over the mountains, insects buzzing away in the fields, dinner finished and those people not on kitchen duty carrying on the conversation. Coyote had started it, by asking if Ken believed in reincarnation. Ken had politely explained he didn't, and Mustang had jumped in with a mocking comment about credulous Texan New Age fools.

Coyote rounded on him. "So what do *you* think?" he

demanded indignantly. "That we're all going to Heaven, like some Red-State Jesus-Freak?"

Mustang scoffed. "I think we're all animals, and when we die, we go back to the soil. That's all. Isn't that enough?"

Lioness, who had been listening for a while, now spoke. "I'm not sure organised religion has it right either," she said. "But I think we're part of something bigger, part of a wider purpose. A greater being, if you like."

Frog nodded. "We're remembered," he said. "We touch other people, they remember us, it all becomes part of the human collective."

Lioness smiled. "Or perhaps something else," she said enigmatically, though Ken knew, even then, that she was talking about the pyramids, the castles, the system.

Now, he thought, I'm in that system, I've found the heart of it. And I have no more answers. And my death is going to be just as absurd, as pointless, as anything else in the world.

"I'm sorry, Lioness," he said aloud. Why not? There was no one to hear, but there was no one to take exception. "I'm sorry, Frog, Coyote, Mouse, Mustang, Swift, Ibex, all of you. I'm sorry, Tina, Lee, Chris, Lacey, Trish. I'm sorry, Patel, General, Hackney. I let you all down."

Suddenly he flashed back again, to those interminable moments crouched in the dilapidated and sodden shed, waiting for the bears to pass, Red and Seaboard distinctions forgotten in a moment of shared animal fear. "I'm sorry, Woolf," he said. "And Rennert, and Bayer. I really am. And I'm especially sorry, Manders and Al. I didn't want it to be like this."

He shut his eyes, tried to think of nice things. Tried not to think that he was going to starve to death, or suffocate, or dehydrate. Tried not to think about what that would be like. *A frightened little animal, alone and abandoned in the dark.*

Tried to remember how pleasant it had felt, to be there and part of a community, on that warm night in the mountains, in the summer. But all he could think of was how soon it had all ended, and *how* it had ended: the pyramid with the ant-people, the horrible pursuit, Manders shooting Swift and Al crying out. Tried to think further back, to the Circus of Form, remembered only the scoured-flat saltpan where the camp had been, the traumatised soldier, Wang, sobbing out his memories of the prophet Elisha and the bears. Remembered the United Prairies, and Louanne's bar at the raucous crossroads of the tiny town, but again could only see Josh's blank face as he rejected his own father. The days and nights with Patel, Al, and latterly Manders, out by the growing castle, taking pictures, correlating reports, again ending in the explosions, the general's angry face against the flames as the wind whipped up the dust. *It never ends well*, he thought. *I go out hoping to find answers, to help people, but people only end up dying, and no one ever gets any answers, never at all.*

He remembered the stuffed rabbit, falling, falling, *never mind, Kennie, you're a big boy now.* Falling into the dark water, distorted, vanishing forever. Gone.

He was falling into the dark water, his self dissipating, distorting, vanishing forever, like the rabbit, all the love it meant to him, vanishing forever.

---

And then, in the distance, he saw a faint light. Dim, and misty, but definite. The Bunny Girl again, glowing like before to show him the way? He thought he saw a shape in

it, lumpy and animal. Not the Bunny Girl, but the Kermode
bear, coming to give him safe passage, as before? Al or
Manders, coming back for him from wherever they'd gone?
*A way out?* At least a way to somewhere. Ken scrambled to
his feet, called out in case the others could still hear him.

"Al? Manders?"

He saw the bear clearly now, white, but glowing, haloed
in light. A spirit bear. Good luck. The phrase *walk towards
the light* entered his mind, and he laughed. The bear would
guide him out. He would follow it. He would keep going.
Going, going to safety.

Into the darkness, his self dissipating, distorting,
vanishing forever between the calm, dark waves.

Gone.

---

Ken opened his eyes, focused on the bright, shining opal
mist in front of him. After death, he thought. A bright light.
*Walk towards the light.* You come to a shining place, where
you are met by a spirit guide; a friend or an ancestor, or your
totem animal. Follow your guide, and you will come safely
to the next life.

The opal mist dissipated, and a human figure moved
into view. Small, golden-skinned, compact. A face thin,
triangular and remote, but kind. "Don't try to move just
yet," a female voice said in a language Ken didn't know, but
understood. She was doing something to one of his arms,
but he couldn't see, couldn't tell what. "Wait until you're
fully disconnected from the unit."

"Where is this?" Ken asked.

"Sorry?" the woman said, moving to his other arm.

"He's speaking English," another voice, male, out of

view, said. The word he used wasn't "English", but Ken knew what it meant. "It'll take him a few minutes to regain his identity. He's been under for almost a week, remember? It takes time."

"A week!" Surely the journey had taken months, maybe even a year? Ken stared straight above him. He could see what looked like the curved hood of a car, but in translucent smoky-quartz plastic, raised above him. It looked, he thought, like the beak of a raven, wide at the base and tapering to a point. Above that, a pale blue ceiling, soft embedded lights of a kind he'd never seen before, and yet at the same time had seen all his life.

"There, you're disconnected," the woman said. "Take deep breaths. Move when you feel ready, but don't try to rush things."

Ken regained control of his neck, was able to look around. He was floating in a kind of thick, translucent opal fluid, with a faintly spicy smell, in a tank of the same smoky-quartz plastic. Presumably, he realised, the thing he'd seen over his head was the lid, raised. Fully closed, the device must look a bit like an egg and a bit like a coffin. Around him, wires and tubes and pipes were gently retreating into the walls of the tank.

Beyond that tank, he could see two others. One closed, its human inhabitant curled in the foetal position inside, blurred by the dark walls. The other stood open, drained. Lights were positioned over both, and monitors stood around, flickering occasionally with data. The room around them was brightly lit with something that looked like big LEDs—though Ken's reference points were starting to become blurry, uncertain and dreamlike—embedded high in the walls. The floor was some kind of polished stone, or stonelike material, and the walls were painted a pale, sterile sky blue. He could see scientific workbenches ranged along the walls, what looked like sinks, containers for medical equipment, bottles of fluids he couldn't identify. There were no decorations, apart from some kind of small hand-written charts pinned to one wall. On one side of the bench, glowing red words floated in the air in a neat rectangle above a stout silver rod, too small to read at this distance.

"Ah, feeling better?" The owner of the second voice came forward, as Ken struggled to sit up. "Here, take my arms—that's right, slowly now. You're all right. Relax your shoulders, try to remember who you are."

"I'm Ken—" Ken stopped. "I'm not Ken."

The man smiled. Like the woman, he was small, but muscular, with dark, smooth hair, golden skin and high cheekbones. Otherwise, though, there was no resemblance, so, the man who had once been Ken concluded, they were members of the same ethnic group, nothing closer. The man was clad in a short, plain, green robe-like garment that went into complicated folds below the waist, and what looked like some kind of moulded athletic sandals. He wore no jewelry apart from two discreet gold rings in his ears. Part of Ken thought it looked ridiculous, like something from one of the cheaper European historical dramas he'd largely ignored at school. Part of Ken thought it looked normal, perhaps a little over fashionable but nothing more. The man—the word *berdache* came into Ken's mind, though he didn't know why —looked about forty, wore his black hair short around his ears and neck, had strong teeth, unstained and even.

"No, you're not."

"You," the man who had been Ken began, "you are..." It clicked. "You're Ocelotl. The vision-quest technician. And that's Mazatl. The doctor."

"You remember." The woman rolled her eyes. She had a

sarcastic edge to her voice, but the corners of her mouth quirked, indicating there was humour behind it. She wore a simple blue medical coverall, and the man who had been Ken realised belatedly that he wasn't actually wearing anything.

"It's OK, I've seen it before," Mazatl teased, but she did turn her back politely to let him climb out of the tank and dry off with a piece of cloth. Flimsier and smaller than the towels he had known as Ken, but more effective. Ocelotl handed him a white cotton robe, which he spent a few minutes remembering how to arrange, but then found he could do so automatically. *Just let your muscle memory take over*, he thought.

"Do you remember who you are yet?" Ocelotl asked.

The man who had been Ken nodded. "I'm Totchli," he surprised himself by saying. "Junior biotechnician, formerly at the Biotechnical Temple in Calixtlahuaca, taking leave to fulfill my corvee obligations, temporarily seconded to the Great Biotechnical Temple of Axoxoctic." He thought a bit more. "I've been on a spirit journey. A worldquest. And before that—"

A sudden flash of trauma, nightmare images of *bears in black plastic helmets, a tall bald man in ragged clothes, a short woman with one arm and terrifying eyes...*

Totchli felt people helping him up, realised he'd fallen to the floor. Might have screamed. Probably had, from the way Mazatl was looking at him. He felt hugely embarrassed. "I'm sorry," he said.

"You don't actually remember...?" Ocelotl touched Totchli's face with a concerned, but professional gesture; he looked hard at Totchli's eyes. "No, you don't. Hm. Yes, that's unusual but not entirely unknown, particularly when someone worldquests after a traumatic event."

"What happened then?" Totchli demanded. There were things at the edge of his mind that he couldn't quite see, that shifted when he tried to think about them. Another image, *a huge waterspout but in the sky, a black building, a woman*—the name *Zorrah* came back to him, and with it, a set of impressions, mixed with memories of the general from the Detroit Front.

Ocelotl shook his head, cutting off the stream of consciousness. "It'll return in time. But it would be dangerous to try and force it, and in the meantime, we need to get down your impressions of the worldquest. I think we'd better get you to one of the recovery rooms before you tell us all about it in any detail."

Ocelotl joined Totchli on the terrace outside the refectory the next morning. The day was bright, sunny and warm, smelling of dust and flowers, and the terrace had a good view of the garden and outbuildings.

"Did you sleep well?" Ocelotl said. He sat down, chose a piece of mango from the brown institutionware bowl at the centre of the rattan table with surprising delicacy.

"Yes, and I ate well, and exercised," Totchli replied with a smile. "I found the gymnasium, and, obviously, the refectory, without trouble." He'd actually found that experience slightly disturbing. He still couldn't consciously remember much of his life as Totchli, and so it had felt rather as if his legs, walking easily around the various parts of the temple complex, knew something that his head didn't. The exercise equipment had been unfamiliar as well, but again his body had taken over.

Still, some other instinct, or perhaps another buried

memory, warned him against being too emotionally open with Ocelotl, so he didn't go into detail. "The Temple staff found my scroll for me, so I've been reading the news, and my messages, and feeling much better adjusted, thank you."

He'd also (though again something warned him against admitting it) spent a long time looking in the mirror. The face was Ken's; the hair was long and dark like Ken's, the eyes green like Ken's, the body was recognizably Ken's, albeit stronger and better muscled despite the time spent in the tank. Ken had, of course, lacked the benefits of a good diet, plenty of sun, and regular, leisured exercise. The face was a little broader and the skin more golden, and yet still, on the streets of Iqaluit or Deecee, most people would easily take him for Ken. But it was all Totchli. Ken was the fiction, the avatar.

He hadn't answered any of the messages, not even the one from Coyotl, who, he got the impression, was someone he owed some kind of explanation. Her message was full of long-winded, roughly phrased anecdotes about the courier placement she had been sent to work around Texcocociti, and urging him to write to Itch and Tot (vague memories of thin young men, nervous and eager like deer) on their new assignment at the Bunker (vague memories of a low, black building surrounded by squat outbuildings and sunlit fields). And, between the lines, unspoken concerns for his health and mental stability.

The rest of the previous day had been spent, once Totchli had recovered physically enough to do so, in strange, tense interviews, where Totchli spoke into recorders, wrote and drew on scrolls, trying to put down everything he could remember from the worldquest. Everything, from tiny details about Ken's childhood (the playground legends, *watch out or the frogmen will get you*) to floor plans of the farmhouse at Thule. Reported conversations, descriptions of the Red soldiers on patrol and the bears in the woods, the incident with Weena the mouse.

Ocelotl had not conducted the proceedings, as Totchli had expected, but instead had left it to another technician, a thin, hook-nosed man whom Totchli did not recognise and whose manner generally indicated that they had not met before, who introduced himself as Colotl. He had not been hostile or unkind, but had urged Totchli on to continue to the absolute limit. "It's essential that we get down as much of this as we can while it's still fresh," he said. "Over the next few days, of course, you'll be remembering more things about the journey and about your avatar's life, and having interviews with experts who'll want to ask questions about specific aspects of your quest. But it really is important that we get preliminary notes down now."

Finally, when Totchli was almost unable to speak from exhaustion, was contradicting himself and confusing different events in his mind, Colotl called a halt to proceedings, and had one of the temple assistants take Totchli to his room in the guest quarters. It was sparsely furnished but spacious, with pleasing soft colours and soothing blue rugs, a bed which Totchli judged to be big enough to sleep a family of four, a desk with what he now recognised as a radio-unit to use with his scroll, and a wide balcony with a beautiful view of the pyramid at the Temple of the Gods in the distance. The sort of thing that wealthy merchants and politicians paid huge sums to experience, but Totchli could not feel much pleasure in having it for free, collapsing unfeeling into the bed and having troubled dreams in which he was being chased through the woods by the bald-headed man and a cohort of white bears.

He'd been able to piece together some of his activities

before the quest, using what he could find on his scroll (again, his body seemed to remember how to use it much better than his mind had), and with that had come the return of some of his memories. Working in the village; the boat ride to the Bunker; some of his conversations with Ocelotl, Coyotl and Zorrah. There were unexpected gaps in memory and logic, though, and some words which didn't make sense to him yet. He supposed that would return in time, too.

"You'll be finding things strange for the next couple of weeks," Ocelotl said. "This is your first one apart from your namequest, isn't it?"

"Yes," Totchli said. "It's a bit harder at twenty-four than at fourteen." There were other differences, of course. The state-of-the-art facility here in Axoxoctic was rather better than the carefully maintained one in his local municipal temple, and he'd only been under for a couple of hours, looking for his spirit animal and his ritual name. The local priest had been a jolly, sports-obsessed type, and his cheery insouciance had somehow made what Totchli had expected would be a solemn occasion into something more like an end-of-term contest prizegiving. *So, my boy, tell us what you've won!* Even the namequest itself had seemed anticlimactic, just a journey down a strange road, led by two ravens, then the rabbit, driving the ravens away.

The priest had cheerily interpreted the symbol as meaning that Totchli had a curious nature, an interest in science, a sociable, cooperative spirit, but a tendency to rest-lessness and withdrawal, something that pretty much anyone at the academy could have told him. He failed to provide satisfying answers on what the ending of the quest had meant. And he had, of course, had to spend the next ten years laughing off jokes about seeing four hundred rabbits on your namequest.

"Every one's different," Ocelotl said. "I've done a few, of course, and you can never tell how easy or hard it will be till you're in it. There was one where I didn't regain my proper identity fully for months—don't worry, that was an extreme case, and you do seem to be recovering nicely."

Totchli nodded. "You do seem to keep talking me into things." Memories of Ocelotl, and a jar of palm-wine in the gardens of the Temple, telling him how absolutely well suited he was for the task at hand, how much of a contribution he could make, then how this might help lay to rest the demons of the nightmare journey up North to the colony. How it could help them, help him, make sense of the encounter there, maybe explain the secret of the mice.

He remembered, unbidden, Ken in the labs at the community in the mountains, lost in Thule, dreaming of making scientific history with his observations. Another thing he had in common with his avatar, he supposed. A desire to explore and make history, but, in the end, finding nothing that everyone else hadn't figured out before him.

Ocelotl looked a little rueful. "I hope that's not a complaint."

Totchli smiled again. "No. You were right about one thing, it was certainly more exciting than splicing genes back in Calixtlahuaca, or building bridges, or slinging sandbags. I miss it in a way." He remembered the Red soldiers' corpses, Woolf's astonished face, the sound Bayer made as he died. "Some parts of it, anyway." And, he thought, it was less dangerous than going up North in a boat. But even he, too blunt as usual, wasn't going to say that to Ocelotl.

"So, any preliminary results, then?" Ocelotl helped himself to more mango. A couple of ravens, perched in a small conifer in the garden near the terrace, had a brief quarrel about something, then fell silent.

"It was... not exactly what I expected," Totchli said. "It wasn't a fantasy world, and I didn't meet any gods."

"You're certain?" Ocelotl said.

Totchli shook his head and smiled. "Quite certain. No gods." Though a memory surfaced again, *Baron Samedi, Loa of the dead and dying*, Manders asserting confidently that he was himself a fiction. "I was in the past, or possibly in a parallel universe where the civilisations to the North of here dominated." He corrected himself. "*Had* dominated. They were in decline. Facing the same problem we are, the change of climate. But in denial over it." He thought again. "I was a journalist—that's like a writer for the scrolls, but employed by only one data-provider. There was a war, and biotechnology—again, like here, but different. And two men, who, at the end, were claiming they were fictional..." He stopped. "Ah. They were. Or might have been."

Ocelotl nodded. "That's how it is with the worldquests. Parts of them are real, and parts aren't. They all seem real, though. Like how dreams make sense, no matter how surreal they are. The questing journals are full of papers on what it all actually means."

"And you?" Ocelotl, Totchli knew, or rather had remembered, had some controversial theories about the nature of the quests and their possible role for prognostication which had given him something of a media profile.

Ocelotl smiled. "I just focus on the experience."

Totchli breathed deeply. "There were parts that seem, in hindsight, to reflect what happened up North." *Or to blend in with it, or to be part of it.*

Ocelotl nodded. "We'd expected that."

"It's why you asked me, isn't it?" Totchli said. "You

wanted more information about the colony in the North, and you'd exhausted the factual and psychological, so now you're going for the spiritual." He wondered if they'd done the same to Coyotl and her crew. "I'm your research animal. Load me up and send me into the danger zone, study my brain patterns when I get back."

Ocelotl looked a little pained. "We'd hoped it might also help you. We were fairly certain the colony had failed. We didn't know how strange it had become. And the mice... don't look at me that way, I believe you, and it's something we need to consider. That there's another sentient species, perhaps better adapted to survive and expand, and that they might be our competitors, maybe even our replacements. But we need to know how."

"Do you?"

Ocelotl spread his hands. "Do *you*?"

"I'm still trying to figure out how much of it was real," Totchli said. "I mean... was Ken? He had a whole past, opinions, experiences..." He then spoke something he'd been thinking for a while. "It was a lot like... like history. You know? What we learn in school, about the origins of modern civilisation, emerging out of the collapse of the North. People speaking Language rising up, building Axoxoctic on the ruins of Mexicociti, which was built on the ruins of Tenochtitlan. Could Ken have lived then?"

"He might have been," Ocelotl said evasively. "There was a time period like that once, there were people like him."

"But not necessarily," Totchli completed the thought.

"There are other possibilities," Ocelotl said. "Whether the quest involves inhabiting someone who exists, or creating someone new... or a bit of both, perhaps taking someone who existed and changing them... we don't know.

It's controversial." He smiled again, as if at a private joke that would take too long to explain. "That's why we call them quest-worlds. To differentiate them from pasts that may or may not already exist."

"You're making my head hurt." Totchli helped himself to more water. *Pasts? In the plural? That may or may not exist?* "When I came out of the quest, I thought he died. Did he die?"

Ocelotl shrugged. "Many report similar experiences, but we've no real way of knowing. Maybe he did. Maybe it was just the connection between you being severed." He changed the subject. "So who were the fictional men?"

"One was... Bunny Manders." Ocelotl looked blank. Totchli realised that he wouldn't have heard of him. "From the Raffles stories. The Amateur Cracksman?" More blankness. Totchli sighed inwardly. The problem with having a hobby like classical literature was, you spent so much time with your fellow enthusiasts that you forgot the rest of the world didn't have the same reference points. "Ancient literature, portions of it have survived. You can get it on the scrolls. Stories about a leisured, privileged man who wanted adventure, and"—he couldn't help sounding a little accusing —"died looking for it."

Ocelotl nodded, satisfied. "Yes, one reason why you were selected as a candidate for the colony mission was because you had the right balance of arts and sciences in your personal profile. The interest in classics probably influenced what you encountered on the worldquest as well. So, who was this Bunny? More importantly, what did he represent here?"

Totchli thought. "I'm not entirely sure," he said. "Manders in the stories was a weak man, in thrall to a more powerful man, who he loved, and who ruined his life. This

Manders was older, he had regained face, but as to what he represented..." He thought some more.

"Tell me about the other one," Ocelotl said.

"He was many characters. He changed, depending on the occasion," Totchli said. "Kept giving himself different names. References to *Castle Keep*, David Lynch, Sven Hassell." Ocelotl plainly did not recognize any of the words, but nodded as if to encourage Totchli to go on. He realised. "The Trickster. They said I might encounter the Trickster, when they were preparing me for the quest. I expect that was him."

"So, you did encounter gods. Two of them," Ocelotl said, satisfied. "That's good. I've never yet seen a quest where the gods didn't figure, even if the quester's an atheist. A trickster and a god of wisdom, or of war. Or both. That's not unexpected, given the nature of the problem. I'm asking you all this," he added suddenly, "because, you do remember, I'm going to have to make a report, too. As are you, and Colotl, and Mazatl, and the others, before it all goes into our final presentation."

Totchli nodded. "I know. On the failure of the colony project. I'm still not sure I was the right one for them to choose."

Ocelotl, with a gesture, suggested they walk down to the garden. Totchli followed, still a little unsteady from lack of muscle use. The ravens made alarmed noises, flew away. "I think you were, and so does Cahuayoh."

Totchli stopped, leaned on the nearest plant for balance. It turned out to be a barrel cactus, and he steadied himself abruptly, shaking his hand. "*The* Cahuayoh?"

Ocelotl nodded. "Same one."

Totchli shook his head. "I suppose I should have

known," he said. "This whole thing, the colony, the worldquest, it's all down to the Survival Committee."

"You sound as if that's a bad thing," Ocelotl said.

"Isn't it?" Totchli was bitter. "The government doesn't want to admit we're doomed, that the climate has changed too much. So they set up a committee of technicians. Futile. Like trying to dam up the river."

Ocelotl raised an eyebrow. "Isn't that exactly what *you* were doing, when we requisitioned you?"

"That was different," Totchli protested. "We can't just let people drown."

"So," Ocelotl said, as if that settled it. "The Committee's a lot more diverse than you might think, in any case. You know about Cahuayoh's theories about the climate. Believe it or not, he's been very interested in your reports—both on the colony and on the worldquest."

Totchli shrugged as he walked carefully beside Ocelotl, along careful gravel paths between the cacti, the scrubby and dusty dwarf palms, their tall, precarious cousins, some curiously shaped and dense conifers, fat and glossy succulents like abstract soapstone statues, a stand of bushes heavy with blossoms and thorns. Along the paths, little streams bubbled, seemingly natural but actually part of a complex irrigation system. Totchli vaguely remembered reading about how it worked. "Cahuayoh's an idealist," he told Ocelotl. "I saw enough of the primitive in the quest. It's bloody, and brutal. The idea of abandoning cities and going back to some kind of tribal life, like in Cahuayoh's texts, is not something I'm happy supporting. If Cahuayoh thinks I'm the right man for his cause, he's deluded."

"The selection process was quite rigorous," Ocelotl said. "It wasn't entirely down to your expedition to the colony. We took the views of everyone on the Committee, did polls, soundings, qualitative tests. We identified people from all of civilisation who had the right personality and profile for a quest that could give us the sort of information we could use, then narrowed it down progressively."

"And I was the winner, out of how many million candidates? The only one who can have the right worldquest?" Totchli did not bother to disguise his scepticism. "Nothing to do with me coming back from the North, talking about mice and madmen?"

"We've done other quests with different personality types, too, so as to triangulate results," Ocelotl said. "One, but only one, of the others on the expedition. I'm not telling you who, that might affect you. A couple of the survivors. Other people with the right personality and profile, who know absolutely nothing about what happened up North. All of it will go into the decision-making process."

"Could I read the reports?" Totchli said, interested.

"Later," Ocelotl said. Meaning, *never*. "You need to contextualise your own experience first. Let's say you're not abnormal, though, from all you've said."

"The man in the other tank, when I woke up," Totchli went on, "was he one of the others?"

Ocelotl frowned, not understanding, then remembered. "Oh, *him*! No, he was recommended a worldquest by his therapist. He was in a glider crash a half-year ago, keeps having nightmares, delusions. There's three main reasons to do a quest, in adulthood"—he began ticking them off on his fingers—"prognostication, that's you, therapy, that's him, and artistic insight—"

Totchli stopped walking, exclaimed in shock.

Ocelotl glanced where he was looking. "Sorry, are they bothering you?"

"Bunny Girls," Totchli said uneasily. A trio of them

were marching through the garden, the weird, tottering, puppet-like gait as they passed between rows of spiky cacti. The masks and armature were gleaming, the skull-like, beaky faces unbattered, unworn. The cloth was whole, not ragged. But they were unmistakable.

"Cyborgs," Ocelotl said, as if to a child. "You've forgotten, of course, but they're very common. You've even worked with them yourself. Basic biotech, used in military and civilian projects. Scout-units, seeder-units. Nothing special. The Temple cyberneticists are just testing some new mobility modules—" Ocelotl fully registered Totchli's alarm and distress. "Sorry, did they trigger a bad memory? We can go somewhere else if they're bothering you."

"But I saw some of them, in the worldquest." Bits of his experiences began coming back again, but different when Ken's memory was matched with Totchli's, contextualising things, providing a new perspective. Other memories, too, of the colony, of the Bunker, of the scouts and animals and what had happened to them. Ideas, objects, were coming back. Alpacas, with biotech—no, not biotech implants, but *helms*, ordinary guidance systems for animals, and the strange black castles and pyramids—just ordinary instabuild —and then, a memory of helms on *humans*, and the chilling realisation of what that meant. The colony, and what had happened to it.

"The Bunny Girls—the scouts, on the worldquest. Guiding me. Not just those, either." He remembered more names. "Control centres, habitation modules. Helms. Instabuild. Modern technology. In the past"—and another connection fell into place—"and in the North. In the past."

"Well, as I said, that's a matter of some academic debate —" Ocelotl began, but Totchli cut him off.

"In the past, in the North. *That's* not right."

"Ah. Yes. Well. You wouldn't know about *that* part of the project yet." Ocelotl suddenly looked a little ashamed.

"Go on," Totchli said, danger in his voice.

Ocelotl thought for a while. "It was Cuetlachtli's idea, but it's Zorrah who's really pushing it now."

"Zorrah!" Totchli said. Remembered her leaning back, looking like she was going to say something, then changing her mind. It made a certain amount of sense.

"There's been some experimental work pending, into sending material into the quest-worlds. We've been taking the opportunity to test if it's really possible."

"What, into the *past*?"

"We don't know for sure it's the past," Ocelotl said quickly. "I told you. No alterations to known history have been noticed, and as I told you, there are schools of thought that the quest-worlds are alternate universes, spiritual experiences, psychological states..." He saw the look on Totchli's face and interrupted himself. "Anyway, the idea would be that we could abandon this world, recreate our civilisation in a quest-world. Even better, if we could find a quest-world that was very close to ours. Maybe the one you..." Ocelotl seemed to realize he was babbling and caught himself.

"So, the quest-worlds do have reality, then," Totchli said. "They're not just visions—or not all the time, anyway." He frowned. "Wait, how is it they've got *gods* in them, then?"

"We're not entirely certain," Ocelotl said. "There are some people over at the Physical and Mechanical Temples who have theories. It's all very complicated, something about the nature of reality and how it's determined by observation. I can introduce you to them if you like..."

"So, while I was off in a quest-world—or inventing a quest-world, or discovering it—you were experimenting on it?" Totchli was torn between laughter and anger. "Sending things to that world? Changing it?"

"We needed a quest-world with a good strong connection into it," Ocelotl said. "It might not have been you. Indeed, some of us didn't think it should be, given the trauma you'd been through in the North. But when we saw how strong the connection was, well, it was an opportunity not to be missed. We sent a small number of seeder-units through into key areas, let them do what they're supposed to. I could go into the technical details..."

"You don't need to," Totchli said. "That's appalling! Taking somebody else's world away from them? Colonising them!" One of Ken's memories surfaced unexpectedly. History teachers, back in Nunavut, talking soberly about the country's tragic birth through invasion, deception, appropriation. Ken had resented it, since even the friend-liest teachers always brought it back to the fact that the colonists had been Southerners like him, and it gave the Inuit children more insults to hurl at the swampies in the playground. But now, Totchli was appalled. "We'd be no better than the Seaboarders and Reds. Worse than them, even. They're just trying to survive."

Ocelotl spread his hands. "We're all human, if it comes to that. We all need to live, and our situation is becoming more and more precarious. I know you're going to ask why we don't just try again to colonize the North," Ocelotl continued, before Totchli could interrupt, "but we need to explore other avenues. We're not sure how far North the habitable area goes, or even if it's habitable at all. If the mice are sentient, then at best we'd be committing genocide, and at worst, we'd be bringing genocide on ourselves."

"You think?"

"They destroyed two control centres, by your own

account, and I'm not entirely sure they didn't have a hand in exacerbating Meztli's mental state," Ocelotl said reasonably. "In any case. On the Committee, the argument in favour of continuing North is now a minority opinion. The primary division has now come down to Zorrah's faction, who support more research into this kind of colonisation—hear me out, hear me out—and Cahuayoh's, who support, as he puts it, just letting nature take its course."

"You mean giving up," Totchli said. "Letting the weather become worse, the food crops scarcer, and children rarer, until we get down to Cahuayoh's magical sustainable levels. Or going North and killing off the mice, destroying something perhaps better suited to the planet than we are, only, perhaps, to die in turn. Or stealing someone else's world, enslaving them or starving them out." He remembered the bears, the ant-people in the pyramids. Lioness was right, he thought, it *is* an alien invasion. By humans.

"There are other factions," Ocelotl said. "Some favour more intervention, some less. Some favour seeing if the mice can be reasoned with. But the experimental extrusions in your particular quest-world mean that your report is going to be very important. No, crucial. It could decide what path we take."

"Hang on," Totchli said, putting together several things and not liking the result. "A good strong connection—you used *me*, didn't you? My mind. To build the connection. To send those things into the quest-world."

Ocelotl looked guarded. "Well, that's not exactly how it works, but it's part of it," he began. "I said I could explain the technical details..."

More things were falling into place. "And that's the real reason why you sent me to the colony," Totchli accused. "I *thought* it seemed peculiar to choose some know-nothing biotechnician two years out of his studies for a warriors' scouting operation. Pick someone with the right psychological profile, cue them up with a trip up North, then put them in the tank and see what sort of world they generate?"

Ocelotl now looked slightly offended. "We *did* need someone to investigate what had happened to the colony. Admittedly, it didn't have to be you, but it did all work out rather well, I think you'll agree..."

"I think I want to go back to the Temple," Totchli interrupted, suiting actions to words.

---

Totchli avoided the gardens after that, and to some extent avoided Ocelotl, seeing him only when he had to as part of his recovery programme or report-making. When not in conversation with experts, he spent a lot of time with his scroll. Not answering his messages, his friends still seemed strange, fictional to him now, and he certainly didn't want to watch any of what had once been his favourite videos. Instead he spent, or possibly wasted, hours paging through news, opinion, fanatical raving, religious lunatics. Trying to make sense of the issues, the decisions he had to make. Decide what to say to the Committee.

He spent time at the Temple's gymnasium, trying to relax. Took out some of the books he usually read in a crisis, *Castle Keep*, *Lost Horizon*, but found he couldn't enjoy them anymore. Kept thinking of Ken's world, remembering Manders and Al. He thought he saw them, in the scrolling words, the gods or fictional men, and then the loss became hard to bear. He tried reading some contemporary literature, but found it irritatingly postmodern and clever, smugly wrapped up in itself. A message came through about a dig to the East of Mexicociti, and he threw it away angrily, not wanting to see ancient/familiar objects or speculate about whether there had been a real Ken, who, somewhere else, in a world with no pyramids, had maybe gone to Mexicociti, met Totchli's own ancestors. *Damn you, Ocelotl, you just ruin everything you touch.*

There was an eclipse of the moon coming up, and he declined a few invitations to ceremonies and to post-ceremony parties, not feeling ready to handle large groups just yet. He'd made an experimental foray or two out onto the streets, and the light and sound overwhelmed him. In Ken's world, the cities and towns had been so sparsely populated and sprawling. The only thing to compare to Axoxoctic in Ken's experience was Deecee, and even that was spread out and thin compared to Axoxoctic's vigorous concentration of people, nine million in nine square miles. The renewed memories of the expedition didn't help. He'd see something out of the corner of his eye, get a flash of one of the survivors, or the animals, or the pyramid, and have to go sit down somewhere while the panic subsided. Moreover, he was afraid that, if he met some of his friends or colleagues in his present state of mind (or absence of mind, as it were), he would somehow make a ridiculous faux pas and wind up ruining the evening, if not the entire relationship.

The night of the eclipse, Mazatl joined him in his room, dressed in red, bringing a bottle of cactus wine and trying to distract him with funny stories about the Temple's medical research team. They sat out on the balcony, wrapped in a blanket and gazing up at the sky. She was trying to be friendly, even flirtatious. Totchli couldn't remember if they'd been lovers, and the evidence didn't provide him with an answer one way or another. He was feeling too embarrassed by this to ask.

He could hear the distant cheers from the pyramid at the Temple of the Gods, where the sacrifices were being held, voices rising as the paper-straw-and-rag human and animal effigies were thrown into the bonfires. Later, when the eclipse finished, there would be fireworks and hot chocolate, music and dancing, families carrying sleepy children wrapped in blankets home. Closer to him, there was warmth and noise and the clink of ceramic ware from the direction of the refectory.

Totchli felt alone, isolated, standing apart from the warm and cheerful crowds enjoying the holiday.

As the red stain spread across the full moon, Mazatl took his arm. "Look," she said, "the rabbit."

Totchli smiled. "He's there, isn't he? Some of the people in the quest-world didn't see a rabbit, you know, they saw a man."

"How?" Mazatl asked.

Totchli showed her.

"Oh, I see. Huh, I'll never stop seeing it now. Thanks for that."

"The rabbit in the moon," Totchli said. "Or the man. The rabbit is the man, and the man is the rabbit. You can't divide them, but you can only see one of them at a time."

"Isn't everybody like that?" Mazatl said, wickedly. "Have some more wine, it's a good cure for philosophy."

———

Later that night, Totchli woke. He left Mazatl sleeping. She had eventually got tired of his reluctance and broached the subject; Totchli had done his best, but she seemed slightly pensive afterwards in a way that left him wondering if she was disappointed. He went onto the balcony, looked up at the now-clear moon, with its man-rabbit. The light shone out over the gardens, with the trees and bushes casting sharp shadow onto the gravel.

Something moved, down below. He followed it, saw a couple of rabbits, hopping swiftly among the verges of the paths, sniffing and nibbling at the smaller plants. He smiled despite himself. His name-animal; *totchli*, the rabbit. A couple more, sensing that it was safe, joined them, until he could see five or six little brown forms scurrying about the greenery. Not four hundred, but not one alone either.

He remembered the rabbit in the Arctic snow, the two ravens surrounding it. One driving it forward, one leading, pushing the rabbit on to some mysterious purpose.

But there were no ravens in the garden.

As Totchli watched, two of the rabbits turned on each other. They posed, arched, kicked out with their hind feet, spasms of combat, squealing, scratching, biting. The loser turned and fled swiftly; the winner returned to browsing.

Totchli remembered his namequest. The way it ended, which the priest had refused to interpret for him; the rabbit leading him further on, the ravens waiting at the end of the path, Totchli crying out in fear, and the gentle, hopping rabbit had turned, lashed out, slashing the ravens with its feet and teeth until the birds rose, disappearing with an agonised, human cry. Then the part he'd never told the priest, where the spirit rabbit had turned, looked at Totchli with human eyes, saying, *that was a lesson, child, remember it*. He'd seen that many times since, the way peaceful, timid rabbits turn on their rivals, turn on predators if they have to, fight. *The ravens*, Totchli thought, *don't always get the better of the rabbits*.

Totchli stood on the terrace outside the Temple refectory again. The sun was climbing, the sky cloudless. The temperature, expressed in terms Ken would know, was forty-eight degrees. Ken would not survive it, but Totchli felt it as a mildly warm spring day, due to get hotter, the gentle heat of the sun on his UV-resistant skin. He blinked, let the membrane cover his eyes.

"The disaster that threatened Ken's civilisation," he said. "They didn't survive it, of course."

Ocelotl nodded. They were speaking again, thanks to Mazatl's quiet persistence, but cautiously, delicately, avoiding the question of how Ken's world had been colonised by the biotech, and especially of who had authorised, who had done, the terrible thing. And avoiding the subject of Meztli and the colony entirely. "The decline and fall of the Americans. Whether it was the past, or a parallel universe, or a world you created, or a dream, that's clearly what you experienced. Now, those parts of the far North are mostly uninhabited. Mostly uninhabit*able*, perhaps. Deserts, dust bowls. Radiation. Perhaps, in the future, a playground for historians, for classicists—for archaeologists," he added with a smile.

"But humans survived as a species. Adapted to the new climate, smaller numbers in smaller spaces, hotter conditions," Totchli mused. "Here, and in the states to the South. The places that eventually became civilisation. Perhaps in other places, too. Europe, Asia. Deliberate engineering? Natural selection?" He spoke the taboo words, broached the forbidden subject. "Our intervention—the pyramids and pods? Did we create our own world by interfering in theirs?"

Ocelotl shrugged. "We're still trying to find out. The people to the far North didn't exactly keep good records towards the end, and they also made the mistake of having a lot of important cities along what used to be the coastline. Civilisation, also, didn't keep detailed records at the start. Most of the art and literature we have predates the climate change period, comes from more stable times, so it tells us nothing about how the end came. There's a DNA-sequencing project, though, that's looking promising, up at the Temple in Texcocociti. Might explain whether the changes were natural selection or something more, shall we say, direct."

"Then the same is true for us," Totchli said. "Either we'll survive the changes this time, or we won't. But we have to find our own solution, do it our own way. Retreating into the past, or traveling to another world, is a guide, a point for comparison. It's not an answer."

*Better to be eaten by bears than nibbled away by rabbits?* he wondered. *But rabbits kick, and bite.* He thought carefully about what he was going to say next, a decision that had been a long time coming. Something he'd wanted to do since the colony, but the direction hadn't crystallised till after the worldquest. He'd talked it over with Mazatl, who had seen the logic, rehearsed many times with her what to say about it. "Ocelotl, I'm going to change my name."

Ocelotl nodded. "Lots do, after a quest, especially an important one."

"I'll be Usagi," Totchli said. "It means the same thing as Totchli, just in Japanese, and it will remind me of what it was to be Ken." *Remind others that I went on the quest, that I was changed by it; that we were all changed by it, and what the cost of it all was.*

"Usagi, then," Ocelotl said.

Usagi sat on a bench outside the palace. Like most official buildings in the city, it was a rough, stepped pyramid; this one of black instabuild. Usagi tried not to see that as an omen, or anything connected to Ken's strange non-death as he left the quest-world. Tried not to think of narrow corridors bustling with ant-people.

Crowds of humanity bustled past him, with legal or political business on their minds, or just on their way to the marketplace. A prominent stateswoman drifted through— he recognised her vaguely but couldn't recall her name— followed by a comet's tail of reporters all holding up their scrolls to capture and transmit her words. A mother with two whining children, a lidded cup of hot chocolate in her hand, the tension around her face and arms betraying that the children were bringing her close to the edge. A flying wedge of emergency medics carrying equipment rucksacks, people getting out of the way for them. Shops across the street opening, the owners talking to each other, complaining about weather and prices and taxes. An advertisement for an acrobat show, a quintet of smiling identical tumblers in matching loincloths, again making Usagi think of his quest, of Polymorphia, the Circus of Form. Too many tiny little dramas intersecting.

Usagi was feeling better about the crowds, but he was still no longer comfortable. He wasn't sure he ever would be, again. Perhaps, he thought, he would seek out a rural Biotechnical Temple when all this was over, spend some time in pastoral near-solitude, splicing genes and growing embryos for the increasing numbers of the infertile. Perhaps he could find some of the peace he'd known in Thule, without the shock and horror of the ending.

Or perhaps he should give it all up, retrain as an archaeologist, or just go to work as a hired labourer on excavations.

He thought ruefully that his family would take some persuading that a departure like that wasn't some form of career suicide. They had pushed him into biotech, encouraged him to apply for his job in Calixtlahuaca, after all. His last message from his father, dated just before he went on the quest, had been proud of the honour of being chosen for such an assignment, but at the same time a little bit scandalised. It was the tradition in his family to work hard, do well, but not do anything too unusual or exciting.

Again, the question of what was real and what wasn't. He saw echoes of his own parents—his pale, anxious mother and blunt, pragmatic father—in Ken's own, saw similarities between his own teachers and schoolmates and Ken's, even down to Steve Tulugaq. Wondered how much of Ken's early memories came from his own, his parents' move to Tochtepec when he was a child, fleeing earthquakes rather than rising water—though even the flooding of Ken's childhood home could come from memories of corvee labour. Saw parallels in the technology—pads and scrolls, different forms of biotech. He was pretty sure he recognised Zorrah, and Cahuayoh, or people very like them, in Ken's world.

But then, he reminded himself sternly of the differences. He had a sister (remembered her, flamboyant and fiery with a mane of wild hair), had cousins and aunts and uncles and no less than three living grandparents. He knew more, ironically, about ancient Northern literature than Ken did. Had no interest in warfare, or in getting anywhere near war. Liked rock-climbing, and archaeology, and basketball. Lacked Ken's appetite for the strange, too. He thought that Ken would have dealt with the events of the colony far better than he had. Perhaps, Ken wasn't an avatar of himself, but a real, historical person, that he had been drawn to him because of their similarities.

*If that's true, Ken, then I hope you made it out of Mexico.*

Or perhaps, it was down to the similarity of human existence. Usagi had never been to anything like the Circus of Form, but the poster showed they had their analogues here. Presumably they had their following, their leaders, their arguments over whether to stay in the capital or to move somewhere more artistically stimulating. He thought of some of the videos Ken had liked, the one about the house that was white and red like the farmhouse in the mountains, the cold, blonde lady saying to the perplexed man, *I died here.*

He reflected that he would have liked them, too, wondered if he could find any of them, if they still existed.

Usagi paged through the notes on his scroll distractedly, went over the arguments for the Committee in his own mind. *What the quest-world taught me,* he thought. *What I learned from Manders and from Al, or Alistair or Alfred or Benjamin—the little man from another place. We have to find our own solution to the climate crisis. We can look to other worlds, but we can't start using them. Our problem, our solution.*

"And a solution," he said aloud, "has to exist. Here, in this world. Even if that solution is the end of us." A teenage girl in a school uniform—late, or absent without leave—glanced at him, curious. He smiled, to persuade her he was harmless, not a lunatic. *Just a scientist who had a very strange dream and hasn't quite woken up.*

He felt strangely calm.

"There you are." Ocelotl bustled up, in a short, black, formal gown and jaguar headdress. "Are you all right?"

"I'd say so," Usagi said. He himself was in formalwear, appropriate for serious political and legal business. *Dressed,* he thought, *for battle*. Well, he might not have been a warrior himself, but he'd learned a few tactics.

*Rabbits fight*, he thought. *They fight well, and win.*

"Are you ready to make your report?" Ocelotl said.

Usagi nodded. "Let's go in."

Just in case Ken was real, and could hear him, he tried to direct a thought into the quest-world, the past or the alternate universe or whatever it had been. *Goodbye, Ken. I'll miss you. Live your life. Do good.*

---

Ken came to in the jungle, face down in the leaf cover. He rolled over onto his back with a moan, looked up at the blue sky, the gleaming black pyramid looming behind him.

What the hell had he just dreamed? he wondered. Or, perhaps, what the hell had just happened? Fragments. The parallel world, the strange avatar of ancient Tenochtitlan, but with heat-resistant people, afraid of a takeover by sentient mice. Which Usagi had dreamed which?

*All part of the Red King's dream*, came the thought, and he tried to remember where he'd heard the expression. Something he'd read in Thule, perhaps, or something Lioness used to say.

He sat up, looked around. Saw his own pack, but not Al's or Manders'. There was no other sign of the two soldiers. Somehow this disturbed him less than it should have.

He wondered detachedly if they'd ever been there at all.

"Got to get back North," he said, out loud, to no one in particular. He heard a startled caw as a crow or raven took flight in a burst of wings. "Got to tell them," he went on, in the direction of the raven. His voice was harsh, as if he hadn't used it in a while. "Can't fight it. *Can* work with it. Work with it, then survive. Some of us survive, anyway. Biotech, or evolution, but we'll change to fit the new world. Hear me, you stupid bird?"

Then he laughed at himself.

He stood up. Legs still working. He hoisted his pack, found the trail back to the coast, set out along it. Time to find out if the boat was an illusion, too.

But one way or another, time to go home.

# ACKNOWLEDGEMENTS

I would like to thank my agent, John Jarrold, and the whole team at Epic, for helping this book finally see the light of day.

I would like to thank Hayden Trenholm, Edward James, and Ian Whates, all of whom provided helpful editorial comments on all or part of the manuscript; Lawrence Miles and Daniel O'Mahony for the initial inspiration; Alan Stevens for introducing me to E.W. Hornung, William Eastlake and Sven Hassel, as well as the story about the ravens and the rabbit; and the anonymous audience member who contributed the book's epigram.

I wish I could individually acknowledge all the sources on Northern and Mesoamerican native cultures and languages that went into this book, but I'll just have to express my indebtedness more generally.

# ABOUT THE AUTHOR

**Fiona Moore** is a BSFA Award and World Fantasy Award finalist, writer and academic whose work has appeared in *Clarkesworld, Asimov's, Interzone,* and five consecutive editions of *The Best of British SF*. Her publications include one novel; numerous articles in journals such as Foundation; guidebooks to *Blake's Seven, The Prisoner, Battlestar Galactica* and *Doctor Who*; three stage plays, four audio plays and the textbook *Management Lessons from Game of Thrones*. When not writing, she is a Professor of Business Anthropology at Royal Holloway, University of London. She lives in Southwest England with a tortoise-shell cat which is bent on world domination. More details, and free content, can be found at www.fiona-moore.com, and she is @drfionamoore on all social media.

# EXCERPT FROM THE MIRRORS BY WHICH I END THE WORLD

### BY KIRA BLACKWOOD

Michael Sanders's life could be contained in a fourteen by eighteen-inch suitcase, and all proof of his existence could be stowed away in a Chinese food take-out carton. This was just as well because Michael Sanders did not exist. The fact that he did not exist did not stop him from being an ordinary looking man in his mid-twenties who hadn't held a stable job for more than a few months at a time, just as it did not stop his eyes from opening when he heard three car doors shut below his motel room window.

His heart pumped a wave of cortisol and adrenaline through his bloodstream. It was a situation he had become all too used to. He always slept fully clothed, with the exception of his socks and shoes, which were wearing thin.

Through the broken metal slats of his window, he saw the same details he always saw: a black car with tinted windows and no plates driven by men wearing dark, long-sleeved shirts and matching pants, as if dressed in shadow. The street beyond was desolate, the parking lot empty, the sky blank. Neither man nor God would protect him.

He skipped socks, shoving his feet into sneakers, then

snagged his toiletry kit from the bathroom sink. He shoved it into the constantly packed suitcase he had left at the foot of his bed. He made sure it stayed packed, ready to grab at a moment's notice, whether to keep him organized for a hasty escape or to use as a blunt weapon if they got the drop on him. The man crouched low, listening to where his would-be abductors were.

The sound of splintering wood came from somewhere nearby as somebody kicked in a door. Damn it, they're close. Another slam, this time from the room next door. They're learning. They split up this time.

Michael crouched behind the corner of the bed, pressing himself flat against a floor stained by countless former tenants. The doorknob rattled shortly before the door itself exploded inward in a shower of splinters, dust, and rusted hinges. His eyes, which had adjusted to the darkness, focused on the looming silhouette of his latest stalker. A hand wreathed in darkness snaked through the air to the nearby light switch, temporarily blinding him.

Mentally spouting off a string of obscenities, he listened as the soon to be assailant trudged into the bathroom, flicking a switch in there as well. He would only have one moment, one chance to get out of there, but there would be no way of leaving undetected if he didn't make the first move. Michael counted to five and darted from his cover, flicking the lights off.

He heard the alarmed grunt of someone who both was and was not expecting this to happen. He crouched low again as the individual stepped back into the dark room. His attacker would need a moment to adjust from the lights outside to the darkness in Michael's room. That moment of transition was more than enough.

Michael sprang, curling a hand around the man's jaw

while using the other to remove the attacker's dark sunglasses. Such affectations, though seemingly pointless at night, were part of The Order's uniform, as they prevented him from using his powers. The man behind the lenses was thick and balding, probably about forty years of age. His skin was sunburned and there was a slight tinge of jaundice in his eyes.

There was no doubt that the attacker had been instructed extensively on why he should never look into the eyes of the man who called himself Michael Sanders, but few who knew of his ability could resist the temptation to see it in action. This curiosity got the better of him.

Connected only by their gaze, the attacker found himself transfixed, trapped in a bluish-black tunnel that seemed to surround them, each staring down the other through a luminescent tunnel. Memories poured from the man, Elijah Johnson, who had a severe drinking problem and had been promised salvation from the emotional struggles that drove him time and time again into the bottle. He was nothing but a lowly acolyte, someone who had been sent along as backup, a disposable bruiser who happened to find their target before the higher-ranked members. Elijah had been assured things would turn out all right in the end; he was an animal that had been brought along as a distraction. Michael couldn't bear the thought of inflicting pain on an individual so lost.

It was easy to grant him the relief The Order emptily promised. Michael felt a familiar sensation flow through him, a tension where there had been nothing before, like steam filling a sealed container, pressure rising, yet not ready to blow. Elijah's face softened, the pain attached to his memories ebbing away like driftwood being brought out to sea. The alcoholic's past became Michael's. Elijah remembered the history, but not the sorrow.

"Now you know they weren't lying." Michael's voice shook as he fought the sadness of a life that wasn't his own. "Get out of here and stay away from The Order." Elijah could only nod as Michael grabbed his suitcase and left. He vaulted over the railing, landing hard, though the cultists were making too much noise to hear his comparably quiet landing.

He reached his car when heavy footsteps came from behind. One set. Male. Moderate size, aggressive. A man Michael had been waiting for. Each abduction regiment had a leader, and tonight, this was the unfortunate soul tasked with taking him in.

Michael spun and delivered a devastating right jab to the bridge of the group leader's nose, smashing cartilage and the plastic frame of another set of sunglasses. The leader found himself slammed into the side of the '98 Volvo Michael had been given a few months earlier. Michael pried the leader's eyelids open, locking their gazes. He unleashed the two decades of alcoholism and emptiness he'd collected from Elijah upon the man, apparently named Herschel; Elijah's pain now resided in this attacker's heart. It would kill him, as it had been slowly killing its original owner. Michael thought nothing of dooming a man who'd condemned so many others.

When Michael looked away, he heard a thud, followed by Herschel sobbing hysterically on the ground. He rolled his shoulders and smiled.

"Thanks. I needed to get that off my chest."

He slid his key into the ignition, the engine kicked over, and Michael barreled down the interstate, heading north along the east coast. A few hours passed with nothing but the dark windows of nearby buildings and long-past-blooming foliage to keep him company. As the sun crested over the horizon, Michael found himself pulling over, parking in a small lot by a beach in Maryland. There were a few other cars there, some with surfboards still strapped to the top. They were unimportant, their owners easily avoided.

Getting out, he retrieved his wallet and other pieces of ID from his suitcase, then got a Chinese food take-out carton from his trunk. A splash of kerosene would ensure it burned up in a minute, tops. He brought his satchel with him.

Crossing the sands to a nearby jetty, its rocky outcropping thrusting back at the relentless crash of the ocean, he sat cross-legged atop the rocks and sighed. That one exhalation was all the mourning he'd allow. He didn't have time to grieve the death of Michael Sanders. Since he was a boy, he'd led a series of short lives punctuated by a sudden burst of flame. He was no phoenix, though. There was no rising from the ashes. He was an arsonist at a masquerade ball, setting fire to his own costumes.

Flipping through alternative identities, he eventually decided on David "Dave" Helmholtz. He then made a few calls: one to Jill Palls, to let her know Michael was returning to California after a death in the family; one to Louis Jorgen, a short order cook at the local diner, to say that he had to leave for Europe due to work; and one to Phillis Glabbern, the motel proprietor, saying that someone had broken into Michael's room, he didn't feel safe and would be heading to Florida.

After this, he snapped the burner phone in two, cheap little flip-phone that it was, and threw it in the Atlantic. After sealing his cut-up driver's license and registration for the Volvo in a take-out container, he shut the lid, tucked the box in between a few boulders, and lit a match. Michael Sanders perished in that flame, trapped inside a tiny cardboard tomb that smelled of soy sauce.

Glancing at a man and woman who were dressed to surf (though they seemed busy tearing each other's wet suits off), he made sure no one else was around. His privacy secured, Dave pulled out a new vehicle registration card and changed the plates, bending the old set in half as a reminder that they could no longer be used. He heard splashing from the waves and knew that the two beachgoers were either awful surfers or great at having sex in the ocean. Dave spray-painted his gray Volvo a pale blue and, with a swift kick, dented the rear side paneling, to ensure people wouldn't recognize his car.

Moments later, he drove away, the giant red sun and burning sky seeming to reflect the endless process of transition in which he'd been caught. An endless road yawning out before him, hours ticking by until, eventually, he found himself in White Plains, a town of roughly seventy-five thousand people along the south-eastern edge of Pennsylvania.

Dave found an affordable apartment building—twelve hundred a month for one bedroom—and dragged his one suitcase to his room. He surveyed the flaking paint, meager fixings, and cracked bathroom sink. This was the nicest place he'd been in two years.

"Yeah...this could work," he mumbled aloud, as if striking a business deal. He took one glance out the window to appreciate the town around him, another into the mirror to take in his bloodshot eyes, and stumbled into the bedroom, letting his eyes shut as fatigue dragged him into the void, where he didn't have to be anyone at all.

Get your copy of *The Mirrors by Which I End the World* wherever books are sold.

Visit the Epic Publishing website (www.epic-publishing.com) for a direct link to your favorite retailer, and be sure to sign up for the Epic News List to keep up with all of our new releases and promotions.